Chapter One

As the train pulled into the Gare du Nord, Frederick Rowlands was already on his feet, reaching for his stick and valise, both of which he'd stowed in the overhead rack. Moments after the engine slowed to a halt, with a grinding of brakes and a final burst of steam, he was descending from the first-class carriage in which he'd travelled from Dieppe, onto the platform of the great Parisian terminus. All around him was bustle and excitement: the slamming of carriage doors; the shouts of porters pushing trolleys; the joyful cries of people meeting their loved ones for what might be the first time in six years . . .

'O! Maman, Maman . . . Est-ce vraiment toi?'

These, combined with that unmistakable smell of French cigarettes and the delicious aroma of roasting coffee beans emanating from a nearby kiosk, told him he was once more on foreign soil. He was still getting his bearings – surely someone would have come to meet him? – when he felt a touch on his arm. 'Hello, Frederick.'

'Miss Barnes. I wasn't expecting . . .'

'I insisted on meeting you myself. It's the least I could do, since you've come all this way. How *was* the journey?'

'Fine.'

'Good. I'll take your arm, shall I? It's this way.' She began piloting him through the slowly moving crowd, whose voices intermingled, in that vaulted space, in a kind of symphony:

'*Mon Dieu! Cela fait si longtemps que nous ne nous sommes pas recontrés . . .*'

Interwoven with these heartfelt utterances were those of the more phlegmatic English: 'I say, old chap. Fancy a spot of lunch?'

'Rather. Shall we see if we can get a table at Maxim's?'

American voices, too, rose above the rest.

'Gee, ain't it swell to be back in gay Paree?'

'Sure is. Last time I was here was on the back of an army truck . . .'

By contrast with all this ebullience, Rowlands and his companion exchanged only the blandest remarks about the weather – fine – and the crossing – smooth – until they were seated in the car Iris Barnes had waiting. It was not until the big Citroën moved out from the side street in which it had been parked and into the Rue La Fayette, that she broached the subject of what had brought him to Paris. 'You must know,' she said in a low voice, although the glass panel between them and the driver was shut, 'that your coming here at such short notice has been much appreciated in official circles.'

'I wanted to come,' he said. 'Although I'm not sure how much use I can be.'

MURDER IN PARIS

By Christina Koning

MURDER IN PARIS

CHRISTINA KONING

Allison & Busby Limited
11 Wardour Mews
London W1F 8AN
allisonandbusby.com

First published in Great Britain by Allison & Busby in 2025.

A CIP catalogue record for this book is available from
the British Library.

First Edition

ISBN 978-0-7490-3246-3

Typeset in 11/16 pt Sabon LT Pro by Allison & Busby Ltd

By choosing this product, you help take care of the world's forests.
Learn more: www.fsc.org

FSC
www.fsc.org
MIX
Paper | Supporting
responsible forestry
FSC® C018072

Printed and bound in Great Britain by Clays Ltd. Elcograf S.p.A

EU GPSR Authorised Representative
LOGOS EUROPE, 9 rue Nicolas Poussin, 17000, LA ROCHELLE, France
E-mail: Contact@logoseurope.eu

For Maia and Cecilia

Paris, April 1945

'We've cabled her brother, of course,' said Miss Barnes. 'But his ship's in Simonstown. No chance of his getting here for another few weeks – always supposing that the Navy give him leave.'

'Well, I'll do my best,' he said, as the car moved out into what he guessed, from the increased speed at which they were travelling, to be one of the *grands boulevards*. He wondered if it all still looked the same as it had when he'd last set foot here.

'Do you remember Paris before the war?' asked his companion, perhaps guessing his thoughts. He realised as she spoke that she meant the war that had just ended, and not the Great War, which was the defining one for him.

He said that his memories were distinctly hazy, since he'd only visited a couple of times on leave, soon after his division was posted to France. The streets had been full of soldiers – both French and English – and there had been a hectic, hedonistic mood across the city, as if everyone was doing their best to forget what was happening not many miles away.

'What I do remember of the city was its beauty,' he went on. 'Notre-Dame and the Pont Neuf, and all those tall stone houses with the shutters.' And that steel-blue light over everything, he thought, but did not say. Yes, he remembered the light . . .

'*My* first visit was a school trip with our French assistant, when I was fifteen,' she said. 'Mam'selle did her best to impress on her charges – horrid little girls that we were – the superiority of French culture, while trying to stop us running after the local youth . . . not always successfully,' she added. 'In fact, I can date my interest in subterfuge to that very time. Then there was the couple of years I spent at the Sorbonne, after my father was posted to Paris . . . Ah, here's the Place de l'Étoile. I expect you remember that?'

He said that he did.

'It was here, just eight months ago, that the General had his great triumph,' she said. 'Over a million people turned out to cheer him. They were hanging out of windows and climbing on lamp posts to get a glimpse of him. It was quite a spectacle. Seeing him marching along the Champs-Élysées, with his head held high, as if he and he alone were responsible for beating the Nazis . . . Oh, he was revelling in it, all right! France's great liberator.'

The last words were said with a certain irony. 'It's just a pity that when he made his speech to the cheering crowd he forgot to mention the men and women – not all of them French – who'd made that liberation possible. Those who'd fought the Germans on various fronts, and who'd carried out acts of resistance. I don't,' she went on, still in the same dry tone, 'make any particular claim for my own outfit. We did what we could – which was never enough. But a word of thanks would have been nice. *Arrêtez ici,*' she called to the driver as the car, having traversed the great space, with its radiating avenues, passed down one of these and turned at last into a side street.

This, said Miss Barnes, was the Rue Saint-Didier, where the Hôtel Cécil – present headquarters of her 'outfit'– was to be found. 'It's seen better days, of course,' she said. 'What remains is a rather faded version of its *Belle Époque* glory . . . Not that anything here is as it was,' she added cryptically. 'Some might think Paris was lucky to escape the bombing London endured – but in a way, what's happened here is worse. It's as if the heart has been torn out of the place, leaving an empty shell . . . albeit a beautiful one.'

Entering the hotel, whose marble-floored foyer had the echo of a more spacious *fin-de-siècle* era, they climbed the stairs (the lift was out of order, said Miss Barnes) to what Rowlands surmised, after counting five flights, to be an attic floor. Here, the MI6 officer opened a door, saying apologetically, 'I hope this is all right? We're rather full up here, at present.' Rowlands murmured that he was sure it would be fine. The room, although evidently small, was airy, with windows opening onto a tiny balcony. 'I wouldn't advise going out there,' said Miss Barnes, after a glance. 'Looks decidedly rickety. Lovely view, though . . .'

If she realised the irrelevance of this remark as far as he was concerned, she didn't allude to it. 'If you leave your bag here it should be quite safe. We'll go and find some lunch. We'll need it for what we've got to do later.'

Descending the four flights up which they had just come, she halted at the first floor. 'We'll step into my office for a minute. There's someone you ought to meet.'

As they walked in, the rattle of typewriter keys greeted them; the sound stopped abruptly. 'I wasn't expecting you back so soon, madame,' said the typist.

She spoke in English, but Rowlands detected the trace of an accent – French, he thought – a supposition confirmed when Miss Barnes said, 'Don't let us interrupt you, Louise. I just wanted to introduce Frederick Rowlands, a friend from England. He'll be staying with us for the next few days. This is Mrs Collins, Frederick. My right-hand woman. There's nothing that happens in this office she doesn't know about.'

'Good to meet you,' said Rowlands, holding out his hand. From the brief contact that followed – scarcely prolonged enough to count as a handshake – he gained an impression of a slight, rather nervous woman, whose hand, despite the mildness of the weather, felt cold in his.

'Have you got those lists for me?' Iris Barnes went on, evidently deciding that the social niceties had gone on long enough.

'They are nearly done, madame. I was just finishing them,' replied the secretary.

'Then we'll leave you to get on,' said Miss Barnes, after shuffling through a few papers on her desk. 'We're on our way to Fresnes. I take it they're expecting us?'

'Yes, madame. I rang the directress first thing this morning.'

'Good. Lunch first, I think, Frederick, don't you?' Then to Mrs Collins, now busily typing, 'I'll be out for the rest of the day. You needn't stay beyond your usual time, Louise.'

'Madame.'

'She's the best secretary I've had since I came to this place,' Miss Barnes confided in a low voice, as she and Rowlands descended the last flight of stairs. 'Keeps everything running like clockwork. That's one advantage of employing an older woman – they've more sense of responsibility than some of the flighty young things you get nowadays.'

'She can't be all that old,' said Rowlands, to whom the voice, and the nervously clammy hand, had suggested someone not long out of her teens.

'Oh, she's probably not more than twenty-five,' said the MI6 officer carelessly. 'War ages people, I suppose.

Louise Collins is a widow. Husband was in the Resistance. He was British – or rather, Irish. Captured and shot, after being tortured by the Gestapo. That was two years ago. I don't think Louise has ever got over it.'

As they crossed the lobby they encountered two men, deep in conversation, who'd just come in. 'Ah, Rosalind, so you're back, are you?' said one of them, addressing Rowlands's companion. 'I take it this is the witness of whom you spoke?'

'Yes, sir. We'll be on our way to Fresnes within the hour.'

'Good show, good show. Well, keep me informed of any developments, won't you?'

'Sir.'

Then the two men, neither of whom were introduced to Rowlands, continued on their way upstairs, still talking in low voices. 'You must see,' said the man who had asked to be kept abreast of developments, 'that it's a question of the balance of power . . .'

'"Rosalind"?' enquired Rowlands, when they had exited the building.

'A *nom de guerre*,' replied Miss Barnes. 'It needn't concern you. We'll go this way.' Taking his arm, so that any onlooker might have supposed that he was the one escorting her and not the other way around, she drew him along the street until they reached an intersection with what appeared to him, from the increased volume of traffic, to be a large thoroughfare. 'There'll be somewhere we can get a bit to eat along Avenue Kléber,' she said, confirming this. 'If we can find a place that hasn't run out of food.'

A few minutes' walk brought them to one such establishment, where, after some consultation with the proprietor as to what was good that day, she ordered plates of rabbit stew and a bottle of wine. 'Not the best,' she said after a mouthful of this. 'But it's all one can expect, these days. There's still rationing here – although you can get most foods at a price.'

'It's the same in London.'

'I suppose it must be. I've spent very little time there during the past two years. Well,' said Iris Barnes, chinking her glass against his. 'Here's to the success of our venture.'

'I still don't know,' said Rowlands, 'what you hope to achieve from our "venture", as you call it. I'm hardly the best witness you could have chosen – given that I've never actually set eyes on the girl.'

'And I've already told you – our other witness can't get here for another few weeks. Besides which, he was a child when he last saw her. You're our best hope, Frederick.'

'Best hope for what?'

'Why, for preventing an injustice.'

'What do you mean?'

She lowered her voice, although they were speaking in English and, as far as Rowlands could tell, those sitting at the tables on either side of theirs were French. But he knew enough of what living in a city riven with fear and suspicion was like from his time in Berlin in 1933. 'There's a strong possibility,' said Miss Barnes, 'that this girl isn't who she says she is. She might be a genuine deportee, returned from the camps, or she might not.'

'But why on earth . . . ?' he began; but she answered his question before he had finished putting it.

'Do you have any idea of the treatment meted out to collaborators here – especially if they happen to be women?'

'I *have* heard something,' he replied. 'They've put some people on trial.'

'Yes, and hanged them – with good reason, in most cases,' she said, with the chilling matter-of-factness he recalled from previous encounters. 'But there are other ways one can destroy a person – not always by killing them. Women, as I said, have paid a high price during this war, and after it. Hardly surprising if our young woman – whoever she might be – prefers to avoid having her head shaved, or being spat at for the crime of being too free with her favours . . . even though in most cases she will have had little choice in the matter. It may be, of course, that she has committed worse crimes – informing being one – for which the punishment would be more severe. Yes, she – our mystery woman – has every reason to fear exposure, if she has betrayed others to their deaths.'

It was just on four o'clock when their car pulled up outside the gates of Fresnes prison. Iris Barnes gave a little shudder. 'I never see this place without thinking what *it* must have seen,' she said, as they got out. 'They held a number of our people here, as well as members of the French Resistance. Treated them with appalling brutality. Quite a few died – from torture, typhus and general ill-treatment, even before they could be transferred to one of the camps. Now, the position's been somewhat reversed, in that most of those housed here have been *returned* from the camps. It's a sort of holding pen, so to speak.'

'I see. Then these people – of which she's one – aren't prisoners, as such?'

'That's right.' She laughed. A mirthless sound. 'Although

exactly *what* they are isn't always clear. That's to say . . . *nothing* is. One thing you learn, when you've been in Paris for a while, is that all the distinctions have become blurred. Who's a victim of oppression and who's an oppressor . . . a Resistance fighter or a collaborator . . . Sometimes they're the same thing.'

They had by this time entered the gaol by a wicket gate to one side of the main portal. After a cursory glance at the documents proffered by the MI6 officer, an official waved them through. 'They know me here,' said Miss Barnes; although he had worked that out for himself. 'This way. You'd better stick close to me. It wouldn't do for you to get lost in this place – it's a labyrinth.' This, too, he hadn't needed to be told. The prison had the smell of all such places: a combination of strong carbolic, barely masking the stench of urine; institutional food (cabbage seemed to be the main ingredient) and something else he was inclined to characterise as the smell of fear. As if the horrors this place had seen had seeped into its very walls.

They crossed an echoing entrance hall and came to an iron staircase. 'We go up here.' Having climbed the stairs, which clanged beneath their feet, they went along a mezzanine whose floor was an iron grid. Ahead of them marched the wardress (they were in the women's section of the gaol) to whom Miss Barnes had stated their business on arrival.

'I needn't tell you that you'll probably find her changed,' murmured the latter. 'Physically, I mean.'

Before he could remind her that he, of all people, was hardly likely to notice this – given that he'd only the vaguest idea of what Clara Metzner looked like – they

16

reached a door, the wardress unlocked it with a jangle of keys and they went in. If Rowlands was surprised that Miss Barnes should have chosen to interview the girl in her cell, rather than in the more convenient surroundings of an interrogation room, the thought was immediately swept aside by the physical sensations of finding himself in that cramped space, with its heavy, almost tangible atmosphere of pain and disgrace.

As he stood there, awaiting the moment when either the woman who had brought him here or the one he had come to see would break the silence, he felt the sweat spring out on his forehead. A foul metallic taste was on his tongue.

'Well, Clara,' said Iris Barnes at last. It came as a shock that she spoke in German. 'I have brought you a visitor, you see.' *Ich habe Ihnen einen Besucher mitgebracht, sehen Sie.*

'*Ja, gnädige Frau . . .*' The girl hesitated, then spoke again. '*Mais je préfère parler français, s'il vous plait.*'

'And English? You speak that too, don't you?'

'Yes. A little. My English . . . it is not good. But I will try.' She must have held out her hand then, for she said, addressing Rowlands, 'How do you do, sir?'

He took the hand in his, and was appalled to feel how thin it was – no more than a little bundle of bones. She was standing closer to him now – he could smell her sour breath – and he estimated her height at a little over five foot. Perhaps five foot two or three. How tall had Clara Metzner been? He couldn't now recall. Only that the impression he'd had, all those years ago, in Berlin, was of a lively, energetic girl, full of charm and mischievous humour. Not a bit like this spiritless, emaciated creature.

She was speaking again, in the same careful English – as if, thought Rowlands, she was weighing every word she uttered. 'I know you . . . do I not? There was an English man . . .'

'Yes . . .' began Rowlands eagerly; Iris Barnes put a warning hand on his arm.

'Don't prompt her.'

But the girl said nothing more to the purpose – except to murmur brokenly, 'It was so long ago. I do not remember. Only that there was an Englishman.'

'Well, we will leave that for the present,' said Miss Barnes. 'Tell us what you do remember. Your name, please.'

'Clara Metzner.'

'Age?'

'Twenty-nine years.'

'Address?'

There was a faint note of mocking humour in the young woman's reply that recalled the Clara Metzner that Rowlands had once known. 'Do you mean apart from Ravensbrück camp?'

'I mean your address in Berlin.'

'There were so many,' sighed the girl. 'But I think you are referring to 36 Marienburgerstrasse, where I lived with my mother and brothers. All dead, now,' she said flatly. Rowlands found that he was holding his breath. Surely she knew that, out of all her family, at least one had escaped? She must have sensed his unease – or perhaps his expression had given away more that he imagined – for she added, 'As far as I know.'

'All right.' The MI6 officer wasted no time offering condolences. 'Father's name?'

'Jakob. He died when I was a small child – of wounds received in the First War.' This, at least, was accurate, thought Rowlands.

'Mother's name?'

'Sara. She died in the camp. Of typhus.' At this, Rowlands felt a pang. He had been very fond of Sara Metzner.

'Other family members?' went on this relentless catechism.

'Two brothers. Joachim – the elder – and Walter. I have not seen either of them for many years. Both left Berlin when I was still at school.'

'And what was your job, after you left school?

'My job? I was an elementary school teacher, until I think, 1935 or 1936 . . . when all Jews were proscribed from teaching. By that time, my mother and I had moved away from Marienburgerstrasse. Or rather, we *were* moved. Do you want to know the addresses where we lived after that?'

'No, that will do.' Miss Barnes now turned to Rowlands. 'Do you have any questions for this woman?'

He thought about it. 'One or two. What floor did your family live on, in Marienburgerstrasse?'

She barely hesitated. 'The third.'

'And what was the name of your school – the one you attended as a pupil, I mean, not the one you taught at.'

'It was Heinrich-Heine-Oberschule, on Driesener-strasse.'

These were things she might easily have been told by someone else. Uncomfortably aware that he was trying to trip her up, he said, 'One last question. Can you tell me what your brother Walter liked reading about most, when you saw him last?'

There was a pause, which lasted so long that Rowlands began to fear that it would end only with the girl breaking down and admitting that she was a liar and a fraud, and not whom she pretended to be. But all she said at last, in the same expressionless tone that bore no resemblance to that of the girl he had known, was, 'I do not remember. It was all so long ago.'

'There were two girls,' said Iris Barnes, in the car going back to Paris. 'One German, one French. Both Jewish. They met in the camp, of course. The German was the girl we have just been to see – Clara Metzner, or so she claims. The other was called Amélie Mendl. A seamstress by trade. Quite a highly paid one, too. She worked for Gaby Bonheur, before the war.' She paused, as if to allow him to comment. 'You will have heard of *her*, I imagine?'

'The dressmaker.'

'She would say "couturier". They take dressmaking very seriously here. But it amounts to the same thing.'

'What happened to her – Amélie Mendl, I mean?'

'She's dead, or so the other girl says – the one calling herself Clara. *Is* it her, do you think, Frederick?'

He hesitated. 'It's difficult to say for certain. There were moments when I was almost sure . . . and others when she sounded like a completely different person from the one I knew. It *was* twelve years ago.'

'I realise that. But were there any similarities – of voice, for example?'

Again he reflected. 'I think so. Given that she's now a

young woman, not a girl of seventeen, and considering . . . well, all that's happened since.' He meant the camp, and the privations – physical and mental – Clara Metzner must have endured.

'Understood,' said Miss Barnes. 'Go on.'

'There was a moment when she spoke of her mother. I thought the emotion sounded genuine.'

'She isn't the only one to have lost a mother,' was the rejoinder. 'Anything else?'

'She knew the names of her parents and siblings – and that Jakob Metzner had been wounded in the last war. The fact that she couldn't answer my question about Walter is hardly surprising.'

'No. But it is suggestive. If she's lying about who she is, then she'd only have known about her brother's interest in cinema . . . or actresses, or whatever it was . . . if she'd been there at the time. She could have picked up the family's names and the other details she mentioned from talking to the real Clara. If this girl's impersonating her, then there's no one alive who can prove it. Except you,' she added slyly.

He was silent, thinking about the conversation that had taken place in the prison. The sound of the young woman's voice – listless, indifferent – as if she were only half alive. If this was Clara Metzner, then she had changed immeasurably in the dozen years since he had been in Berlin. 'What did she do, this Amélie Mendl, that would make her want to hide who she really is? Did she betray somebody?'

'It's not so much what she's done, as what she *might* do,' was Miss Barnes's typically evasive reply. 'If she's who we think she is, then she's in possession of some information that might be very useful to us.'

'What kind of information?'

But on this, Iris Barnes would not be drawn. 'Suffice it to say that it will help us identify some *real* traitors,' she said. 'It's why I asked you to come to Paris.'

'I thought that was because you wanted to prevent an injustice,' said Rowlands. 'Only it seems as if it's more about setting a trap.'

Chapter Two

After what had been an exhausting few hours, Rowlands was looking forward to a bath – to wash the prison smell from his hair and skin – followed by a leisurely stroll before dinner. But they had no sooner arrived back at the Hôtel Cécil, than Miss Barnes announced that they would be going out again within the hour. 'There's a party we should go to. Oh, don't worry!' – seeing his dismayed expression – 'You needn't dress. It'll be quite informal.'

And so there was no time for more than a hasty wash and shave, and a change of shirt, before Rowlands was on his way again. He remembered this about Iris Barnes – she never wasted time, if she could help it. Social occasions were, for her, mere opportunities for the gathering of information, which was her stock-in-trade. Even her moments of relaxation were no more than the necessary pause before action – like an athlete's momentary immobility before launching himself into a run; or a tiger gathering itself to pounce.

Once more, they traversed the city, bowling smoothly along its great wide boulevards in the official car. 'No, no, not that route,' she said to the driver, in her rapid French. 'Take the Avenue Victor Hugo, then Boulevard de Courcelles as far as the Parc Monceau. Then Rue de Moscou to the Boulevard de Clichy . . .' She offered no further details of where they were going until they were almost at their destination. 'Montmartre,' she said, as the car began the climb up the steep streets. 'Favourite haunt of artists, *flâneurs* and revolutionaries. And this' – as the vehicle came to a halt, a few minutes later – 'is 49 Rue Gabrielle, where you will find examples of all three.'

After Miss Barnes had given the driver orders to take himself off for an hour or two ('But stay close, mind? I might need you . . .'), they got out. 'Ah,' said his companion. 'It would appear that things have already started.' This Rowlands had worked out for himself, from the raucous strains of 'hot' jazz that drifted out into the evening air.

At the MI6 officer's bidding, they entered the building by the street door, which stood open, and climbed a flight of stairs, already thronged with partygoers, to a room on the third floor. This, Rowlands gathered, from the strong smell of oil paint, linseed oil and turpentine that even the powerful reek of French cigarettes could not disguise, was an atelier of some kind. That the studio – evidently a large one, occupying the whole width of the building – was crammed with people was evident from the deafening racket that greeted them as they went in.

By dint of pushing and shoving they got themselves into the room, while shouted conversations went on all around them. That these were mostly in French came as no surprise to Rowlands; nor that the subject of most of these exchanges (as far as he could gather) was art.

'*A-tu vu l'exposition?*'

'*Malheureusement, oui. Mon Dieu! Quelles affreuses peintures!*'

'*Oui, bien sûr. Mais elles sont très populaires, tu sais . . .*'

From this cacophony of voices others arose, speaking in more familiar accents:

'Good God! What the hell's it supposed to be?'

'*I* think it's rather good . . . once you get used to the fact that the eyes are both on the same side of the nose. I rather like the green hair.'

'You would. Personally, I think all this Cubist stuff is a fad that won't last . . .'

One of these two voices was familiar to Rowlands, but as he began to move (not without difficulty) towards the speaker – of course, he *would* be at a gathering like this – a drink was thrust into his hand. 'Best I could do, I'm afraid,' said Iris Barnes. 'But it won't poison you. Come on. There's someone I'd like you to meet.'

She drew him towards the centre of the room, where a man was holding forth – also in English – although his accent suggested he was a native of a city other than Paris. Somewhere further south, Rowlands guessed. Madrid or Barcelona. 'I am a simple artist,' he was saying. 'I know nothing of politics.'

'B-but surely, Señor Ruiz . . .' stammered the young man to whom he had addressed these remarks. 'Surely your work has often dealt with political themes . . . I mean . . . the war in Spain for example . . .'

'That was a long time ago,' was the sharp rejoinder. 'I was a young man. Young men like to express their political views. Since then, I have become wiser . . . Ah!' At once, he switched his attention from his young acolyte to Rowlands's companion. 'Mademoiselle Rosaline, is it not? I did not expect to see you in my humble studio.'

'You know I never miss one of your shows, Diego,' she replied. 'This is Mr Rowlands, who is also an admirer.'

Rowlands held out his hand, and felt it firmly gripped. From the muscular strength of this, and the height from which the other man's voice came, he envisaged a short, powerfully built individual – and one with a penetrating gaze, as evinced from his next remark: 'I fail to see how he can admire my paintings, since he cannot see them.'

This, thought Rowlands, was a very shrewd character. 'What my friend means, Señor Ruiz,' he said, 'is that your fame precedes you. Even in England, we have heard of your work.'

'Ah yes,' replied the other, with some complacency. 'The English appreciate good art – having so little of their own,' he added with a laugh.

'Oh, I don't know,' said Rowlands. 'Turner. Gainsborough. Constable. I'd say they were all pretty fine painters. It's true that I haven't had the good fortune to see *your* work, Señor Ruiz – but I wonder, will it stand the test of time as well as these artists have?'

There was an awful silence. Ruiz was evidently not a man used to being contradicted. Then, from somewhere near at hand came a burst of laughter. 'He's got you there, Diego! Admit it. You Frenchies can't have it all your own way where painting's concerned.'

'I am Spanish,' said Diego Ruiz in a withering tone. 'As you well know, Loveless. And what you say is true, Mr Rowlands. There have indeed been *some* English painters – the ones you mention and a few others – whose work I would deem passable. But nobody worth mentioning in modern times.'

'As you've pointed out, I'm not in a position to judge,' said Rowlands mildly. 'But I'm told Mr Loveless here is a good painter. And what of Isaac Goldberg?'

'Ah, Goldberg is another matter,' said Ruiz. 'But then he is a German Jew. I will allow you Goldberg.'

'Big of you,' muttered Percy Loveless; then to Rowlands, 'It's good to see you, dear old spy. It must be ten years since we last met. I wonder what brings you here, to this newly liberated city? Or shouldn't I ask?'

'You may certainly ask,' interjected Iris Barnes. 'Whether Mr Rowlands here would be well advised to answer is another matter.'

'Ah, the lovely Miss . . . whatever your name is,' replied Loveless. 'Looking just the same as when you sat for me a dozen . . . or was it fifteen . . . years ago? Good to see you're still following your *artistic* bent.'

'Oh yes,' she said drily. 'I've never lost interest in the arts.'

'Of course, our friend Diego Ruiz is very much the centre of the Paris art scene,' said Loveless innocently. 'Oh yes, he knows *everybody* – don't you, Diego?'

But Ruiz was no longer paying attention, caught up as he was in what sounded like a friendly dispute on the relative merits of Titian and Caravaggio. 'For me, there is no contest,' he was saying flatly. 'The one was a master of colour and light – whereas the other was a mere showman, performing his tricks for the crowd.'

'Come *on!*' protested the other. An American, Rowlands surmised. Paris seemed to be full of them. 'You can't deny his mastery of chiaroscuro . . .'

'Like I said – trickery,' replied the artist. 'Besides which, he was a murderer. And I dislike murderers.'

The American laughed, as if Ruiz had made a very good joke. 'Sure you do,' he said.

Only Ruiz wasn't laughing. 'When are you going to pay me for that painting I did for you?' he demanded. 'We artists have to eat, you know, Harrington.'

Of course, thought Rowlands, Boyd Harrington *would* be here. The industrialist had done very well out of the war, it was said – his factories in the USA supplying aeroplanes and guns to Allied forces across the globe. Some of the wealth he'd acquired by these means was evidently being spent on enlarging his renowned art collection. 'You'll get your money, don't worry!' he said cheerfully. 'Just as soon as the Foundation takes delivery of the work. You promised it six months ago.'

'Six months ago we had barely got rid of the Boche,' replied the artist coldly.

'Oh, sure,' said the American, still in the same bantering tone he had used throughout their exchange. 'I guess it must have taken a while for you to straighten out your affairs in that respect.'

There was a charged silence. 'What exactly do you mean by that?' Ruiz spoke quietly, but there was an underlying menace in the words.

'Just what I said, old sport,' the other replied. 'You

weren't the only Paris resident to get tangled up with the Nazi overlords. I mean, they kinda *ran* the show for more'n five years, didn't they? Hardly surprising if people got drawn in. Don't suppose any of you had much choice . . .'

'If you're suggesting I had anything to do with those bastards, you'd better take it back right now.' Ruiz's tone was ugly.

Boyd Harrington seemed to realise he'd gone too far, for he said quickly, 'Easy, old sport. I didn't mean anything by it. Only I really would like that painting. I paid for it, you know . . .'

'You'll get your painting,' said Ruiz. 'Now get out of my studio.'

'Hey!' said the American, his tone still affable. 'No need to take that attitude, old sport.'

'I said get out.'

'Boys, boys!' said another voice: a woman's, also American. 'What's all the ruckus? We could hear you on the stairs, couldn't we, Avis?'

The woman's companion murmured something that Rowlands didn't catch – her voice being drowned out by the resonant tones of the first speaker, who now addressed her countryman. 'Hello, Boyd! Knew I'd see you here. Picking out some nice pieces for your collection, I guess?'

'Hello, Gerda. Guess you're here for the same reason, now you're back from Switzerland, or wherever it was you were hiding out . . .'

'Savoy, actually. Avis and I never left France.'

'You were lucky, then. Some people had no choice *but* to leave . . . But maybe you had friends in high places, like our friend Ruiz?'

'Are you still here?' demanded the artist rudely. 'Gerda, I want a word with you about that new piece. How much are you prepared to give me for it?'

'How good to know that, after the turmoil and bloodshed of the past six years, the art world has returned to what it does best – talking about money,' murmured Loveless in Rowlands's ear.

'Did it ever stop?' said Iris Barnes. 'It's good to see you, Loveless. How was Canada?'

'Cold. My wife liked it, though. But then she's German. They know about cold winters. How was your war, Rowlands, old man? I must say, you're looking remarkably fit.'

Rowlands was still reeling from the news that Loveless had a wife – although come to think of it, hadn't he once said he was married? It had sometimes been difficult to know whether Loveless was joking or not. 'I got through the war all right, as you can see,' he said.

'And your charming spouse?'

'She's well, too.'

'Good to . . . hear—' The remark was lost in a fit of coughing. 'Sorry . . . sorry,' Loveless gasped, when he could speak again. 'Wretched bronchitis. Don't seem to be able to throw it off.'

The studio, which had been full to capacity, now showed signs of emptying out, as people downed last drinks and made plans to go on elsewhere for dinner. Loveless, too, muttered something about needing to see a man about a painting, and drifted off. 'Let's meet up before you leave Paris,' he said to Rowlands. 'I'm at the Hôtel d'Angleterre. You can find me there or at the dear old Select any day of the week. Do say you'll come! One has so few friends left one can really *talk* to the way I can talk to you, dear old spy.'

Rowlands was struck by how much his friend had changed in the years since they had last met. Gone was the loud, bombastic individual he recalled. This man was quieter, almost subdued in manner. When he shook Loveless's hand, agreeing that they must try to meet again before his return to England, he got the impression that the artist had lost height, and bulk. Illness, perhaps, had done that.

'Poor old Loveless. He's not looking at all well,' said Iris Barnes, once the artist had left. 'His eyesight's not getting any better either – judging by the thick lenses in those glasses he was wearing.'

Rowlands was sorry to hear it. For a man like Loveless, whose life had been devoted to the visual arts, the realisation that he could no longer see clearly must have seemed like a catastrophe. As he was musing on this, and on the unfairness of life in general, Rowlands felt a tug on his sleeve. 'Now that the crowd's thinned out in here, we can take a closer look at what's on the walls,' said Miss Barnes. He guessed she had a reason for this, apart from a simple interest in Diego Ruiz's paintings. Iris Barnes, he had come to know, had a reason for everything she did.

'Some interesting work,' she said, as they paused for her to examine the paintings displayed on the far wall. 'All portraits, of course. That's Diego's favourite subject, the human face. Even though one might be forgiven for thinking that some of these resemble the faces of animals – or monsters – rather than anything human.'

Rowlands, who vaguely remembered the beginning of the Cubist experiment before the Great War, murmured that he supposed it was the fashion. 'Indeed,' was the reply. 'Although Diego would say he was the one who started the fashion. And he does it superbly well, one has to admit. Take this one, for example – *Seated Man*. You can tell it's a man from the fact that he's wearing a suit and tie. But the face is that of a creature from a nightmare – as if the features have been broken apart and reassembled. The effect is rather disturbing.'

Her companion, who had seen faces broken apart and reassembled – not by an artist's hand, but by the action of a rifle bullet or a hand grenade – made no reply. 'Ah, now *this* is a much more attractive image,' Iris Barnes went on. 'It's a portrait of a young woman – pretty, too. Diego always did have an eye for a pretty girl. Funny, this face looks familiar. It's one of his earlier, more naturalistic series – before he started distorting the features and shifting them around . . . Yes, it's her all right.'

'Who do you mean?' Although he already had a suspicion.

'Why, the very girl we've been talking to . . . or someone very like her. As I said, he likes pretty women, both as subjects and . . . well, in all the obvious ways.'

'Are you saying this is a portrait of Clara Metzner?'

'It might be her, or it might not,' was the reply. 'The title of the piece is suggestive, however. *The Little Seamstress*,' she added. 'That would indicate that it's not Clara, but the other one. Amélie Mendl. But who, now, can tell them apart – except you, Mr Rowlands?'

* * *

They had dinner in a restaurant in Place du Tertre – a homely place, to judge by the rustic wooden tables and chairs, the former covered with the coarse cotton tablecloths Rowlands recalled from similar establishments visited when he'd been in Paris during the last war; his companion confirmed this. 'Oh, places like La Mère Catherine haven't changed in fifty years . . . or a hundred years, come to that. Same red-and-white checked tablecloths, same rough red wine – made from grapes grown in the local vineyard, not three hundred yards away, it might amuse you to know. Same reliable dishes. I hope you like chicken, by the way, since that's all they've got?'

Rowlands said that sounded good – and indeed, the smells wafting towards him from the kitchen at the back of the place were making his mouth water. 'Funny to think that only six months ago this restaurant was overrun with Germans,' said Iris Barnes. 'It was popular with all ranks of the Wehrmacht – although of course the top brass preferred the smarter places on the Right Bank.'

Rowlands didn't ask her how it was she knew this, given that she could hardly have been in Paris during the hostilities, unless it had been under a different identity . . . which was probably the case, he thought. 'It must have been a strange time,' was all he said. 'Living under occupation, I mean.'

'Oh, it was,' she replied off-handedly. 'But then I've found people can accommodate themselves to almost anything.' She broke off, took a swig of her wine, then said, without further preamble, 'Well? What did you think of him?'

'You mean your artist fellow?'

'Of course. Is he a traitor, do you think? Or merely a clever man who knows on which side his bread's buttered?'

Rowlands laughed. 'How on earth should I know? I've only just met the man.'

'You have an instinct for these things. But no matter. There'll be time for you to make up your mind over the next few days. In the meantime, there are a few other people I want you to meet.'

'Iris . . .' He couldn't help feeling that he'd been inveigled into something more complicated than he'd first supposed. 'I came here – at no small inconvenience, I might say – for one reason and one reason only . . . which was to try and identify Clara Metzner. So far it seems I've failed miserably. As for these "other people" you mention, I fail to see . . .'

'But they're all connected. You saw that painting . . . or rather,' she corrected herself impatiently, 'you didn't *see* it, but you heard it described by me. Don't you think it's suggestive?'

'Of what exactly?'

'Why, at the very least, of complicity,' she said. 'Ruiz knew Clara Metzner – or Amélie Mendl, if that's what she was calling herself . . . Ah, here we are!' Their food had arrived and conversation, except of the more general kind, ceased. Only when they'd disposed of the – surprisingly good – *poule au pot*, and Miss Barnes had called for the bill, did she say softly, 'It's important that you see the bigger picture, Frederick. To do that, you'll need to stay at least until the end of the week. Tomorrow we'll visit the girl again, and see if you can't get some more out of her. In the afternoon, we've another engagement . . .'

'Oh?'

'When was the last time,' she said, 'that you attended a fashion show?'

Chapter Three

They set off for Fresnes prison soon after breakfast – a modest repast of coffee and brioche that left Rowlands (who liked his bacon and eggs) feeling unsatisfied. Although it was something more than hunger which had left him with this uneasy feeling in the pit of his stomach . . . As the Citroën slowed to a halt in front of the prison gates, he did his best to shake off the sensation, which was perhaps no more than the effect of a disturbed night, and the unsettling thoughts arising from the day which had preceded it.

Once more, they passed through the wicket, and were nodded through by the porter. Once more, they found themselves in the echoing entrance hall of the great fortress, with its smells of carbolic masking fouler odours; its atmosphere of fear and suspicion. But as they began to make their way in the direction of the iron staircase that led to the upper floor, a door along the corridor opened and someone put her head out. 'Mam'selle Rosaline!'

'Madame Bodin. How very kind of you to meet us! But

I assure you, it wasn't necessary. Mr Rowlands and I are quite capable of finding our way around.'

'But Mam'selle . . .'

'This is Mr Rowlands, by the way. He is helping me with the investigation into the Metzner girl. Frederick, this is Madame Bodin, the directress of the women's prison. It's she who's responsible for the welfare of the women here – including Clara. Speaking of whom, we really should be on our way. She'll be expecting us.'

'Then you do not know?' said the directress, cutting across this. 'You did not receive my telephone message?'

'I'm afraid not.'

'Ah! A thousand pities. I had hoped to prepare you—'

'Prepare me for what?' said Iris Barnes sharply.

'Why . . . that is . . . I . . .' The directress seemed momentarily lost for words. 'You had better come with me,' she said at last. With which she turned and, heels clicking, set off in the direction of the staircase. This they climbed, in a silence heavy with apprehension. Again they walked, footsteps echoing hollowly along the metal floor of the mezzanine, and came to a halt outside Clara Metzner's cell. 'In here,' said Madame Bodin, simultaneously thumping the door with the flat of her hand. The door opened, and the directress ushered them in. 'You see how it is,' she said. 'She was already dead when we found her.'

'Yes.' Iris Barnes was silent a moment. For Rowlands, the slight gasp – swiftly checked – she had given, on seeing what he guessed must be Clara Metzner's body, told him all he needed to know. That, and the smell of death that filled the room. 'What time was this?'

'Two hours ago – that is, a little after seven. I called the doctor and telephoned your office soon after.'

'Who found her?'

'The maid cleaning the rooms could not get a reply when she knocked. When she unlocked the door, she saw how it was, and summoned Wardress Charbon.'

'Was it you who cut her down?' said Iris Barnes to the wardress – evidently the one who had let them in.

'Yes, madame.'

'And where was she when you found her?'

'Hanging from the window bars. Saw she was dead, straight away. Quite cold, she was. And blue in the face.'

'A dressing-gown cord,' said the directress. 'It should have been taken from her, but . . .' Rowlands could envisage the shrug which accompanied her next words. 'We cannot supervise them twenty-four hours a day.'

'No, but you might have known she was a risk to herself,' said Miss Barnes. 'These women have endured a great deal. It takes very little to tip them over the edge.'

'She seemed no worse than any of the others,' was Madame Bodin's reply. 'But if you think there is cause for complaint . . .'

'No matter.' The MI6 officer sounded as if the subject bored her. 'What time did it happen, as far as you know?'

'The doctor thought she'd been dead between four to six hours.'

'So . . .' Miss Barnes made a calculation. 'She died between three and five this morning. I assume,' she said, with the cold detachment Rowlands still found unnerving, 'that the cells are locked during these hours?'

The directress said that they were. 'Reveille is at six. But some of the women sleep in if they don't feel like breakfast.' To hear her speak, they might have been pampered starlets, sleeping off a night's excesses, instead of poor, broken-down survivors of a terrible war.

'And so she – Clara – wasn't found until an hour later?' persisted Iris Barnes.

Again the other must have shrugged; it was in her voice. 'As I have said, it was the maid sweeping out the rooms who found her.'

'I'll need to speak to the maid.'

'That will not be possible, mam'selle. She was distressed, you understand. I sent her home.'

'Even so she will have to be interviewed. Have the police been called?'

For the first time, the directress sounded faintly embarrassed. 'I thought, mam'selle, that I should wait until *you* had seen her.'

'Well, I've seen her. You'd better get her to the mortuary now. I'll want a copy of the doctor's report. And I'll talk to the police.'

'Yes, Mam'selle Rosaline.'

'Wait,' said Rowlands, as the two women turned to go, leaving the wardress in charge of the body. 'Has she been formally identified? I mean . . . do we *know* it's actually Clara Metzner?'

'We have to assume so,' said Iris Barnes drily. 'Since we have no way of proving otherwise.'

In the car on the way back to Paris, Rowlands said what had been on his mind ever since they'd been taken to view the body in Clara Metzner's cell. 'Was it my visit yesterday that drove her to do what she did?'

His companion reflected a moment. 'We can't know that. People kill themselves for all sorts of reasons not necessarily obvious to the outsider. But yes, I'd say the timing was not coincidental.'

'I feel responsible.'

'Don't. We don't even know for certain that . . .' She broke off. 'Let's just say there are too many unanswered questions.'

'Such as?'

'Such as who was the last person to visit her in her cell? We left at just after five, yesterday afternoon. Another twelve hours passed before she died. Plenty of time for . . .' Again, she broke off.

'What are you saying?'

'I'm saying that we don't yet know the full story of what happened to the girl. There's still the post-mortem report to come. And I want to talk to that maid . . . the one who found her.' She consulted the slip of paper on which she'd written the name and address. 'Claire Hubert. 5 Rue du Chemin-Vert. We can call in on our way.'

'Where are we going?'

'Didn't I say? To Rue Cambon. It's where Gaby Bonheur has her atelier,' said Iris Barnes.

Rue du Chemin-Vert was a side street off Boulevard Richard-Lenoir, and not far from Place de la Bastille. In the middle of this, a tall column, topped by the winged figure of Liberty, commemorated an earlier period of turbulence in the city's history, Rowlands recalled. 'Not the most select area,' remarked Miss Barnes as, having left the driver to park his vehicle on the broader street, they walked the hundred yards or so to the gateway of Number 5. 'Artisans' dwellings, mainly. But respectable enough.'

Passing through the tall wooden gates, they entered a courtyard, and after enquiring at the concierge's lobby, were directed to a ground-floor flat. In this tiny, one-room apartment, they found Claire Hubert, her mother and two younger siblings. The young woman was engaged in washing some clothes, and was at first reluctant to speak to them. 'I told Madame what I saw,' she said in a truculent monotone. 'Don't see as I have to say it all again.'

'Perhaps,' said Miss Barnes pleasantly, 'you'd prefer to accompany me to the nearest police station? There's one a few minutes' walk from here, I believe.'

'You're not the police,' retorted the girl.

'No, I'm something a good deal worse – as you'll find out, if you keep up this attitude,' was the reply.

This must have had its effect, for Claire Hubert said sullenly, 'What do you want to know?'

'My daughter's done nothing wrong. She was just doing her job, like—'

'Indeed she was, madame.' All three women were speaking French – Claire and her mother with an accent Rowlands found harder to follow than Miss Barnes's crisp pronunciation. 'She is also a witness to a crime. That is why I wish to question her. Is there somewhere we can speak privately?'

Until now, the conversation had taken place in the courtyard – attracting the interest of those in the surrounding apartments, some of whom had come out onto doorsteps and balconies to pass comment on the

41

proceedings. 'We can go inside,' said Claire Hubert. 'Mother, take Jean and Joseph to Mrs Genet's, will you? It's hard to hear myself think with their racket going on.'

In the tiny apartment, she sat down at an oilcloth-covered table, and invited Miss Barnes and Rowlands to do the same. 'What's all this about a crime,' she demanded. 'She hung herself didn't she? Horrible it was, too.' She shuddered.

'Suicide's a crime,' said the MI6 officer. 'And I want to know exactly what you saw.'

'I've already said—'

'And you'll say it again – from the moment you first noticed something was wrong.'

'All right. Well, I'd nearly finished that corridor. Her cell was the last. I like to finish the whole block by nine, so I can get off for my lunch. There was two more corridors to go – forty cells in all – and I didn't want *hers* to hold me up, so I . . .'

'A moment. What time did you start?'

The girl seemed puzzled by the question. 'You mean what time did I start doing corridor C, or what time did I start work?'

'The latter. What time did you get to the prison?'

'A quarter to five. I like to have a cup of coffee before I get going . . . that's usually at five . . . sometimes ten past, if the train's late.'

'Very well. So you were at work by 5 a.m.?'

'About that. I did corridors A and B first, then moved on to C, like I said.'

'What time was that?'

'Seven, or thereabouts. I knocked, as I always do –

42

because some of 'em are washing or getting dressed when I do my rounds . . . Sometimes they're using the bucket, too,' she added with a snigger. 'Don't fancy walking in on *that*! When she didn't answer, I got my keys and unlocked the door. Thought she must be sleeping. She did sleep a lot,' she said, as if this had just struck her. 'Anyway. Saw she was hanging from the window bars. So I went to call for Marie to get her down.'

'You didn't check first to see if she was still alive?'

'She looked dead enough to me. Just hanging there, like a sack of potatoes . . .' Again, she shuddered. 'Do I *have* to say all this again?'

'Just a few more questions. So you summoned Marie – that's Wardress Charbon, I take it? – and the two of you cut the body down . . .'

'Marie did it by herself. She's a big girl, is Marie. You have to be pretty strong to do her job. And the other was skin and bone – nothing *to* her, poor devil. Afterwards, she put her on the bed – Marie, I mean – and I made her as decent as I could, although it wasn't easy . . . My God, she stank! Happens, doesn't it, when . . .'

'All right, we get the picture. So what happened then?'

'Marie said we should tell Madame what had happened, so we locked the cell, and—'

'You're talking about Madame Bodin, I take it?'

'Yes. We went to report it, and Madame said Marie was to stay there, until the doctor came. I could finish my rounds, she said, and then I could go home. So that's what I did. Honest. I don't know nothing.'

'Hmph.' The MI6 officer sounded as if she didn't believe a word of it.

'Are we done yet? I need to finish that washing . . .'

'All right,' said Miss Barnes. 'You can go, I suppose, since you've nothing more to tell us.'

'One more question, if I may,' interjected Rowlands. 'After you started work at five, did you notice anyone else around, in that part of the building?'

The girl thought about it for a moment. 'Well, there was Béatrice – she's the other maid. She does the offices and ground-floor rooms. I said hello to her, and—'

'I meant, anyone you *didn't* recognise – anyone who shouldn't have been there?'

'I . . .' Again, she hesitated; then said slowly, 'No. No one at all.'

'You're sure?'

'*Oui, m'sieur.*'

Iris Barnes got to her feet. 'That's all for now,' she said. 'But if you think of anything . . . anything at all . . . that struck you as unusual, or out of place, I'd like you to telephone this number. Or you can come to the Hôtel Cécil, in Rue Saint-Didier. You'll need to get the metro, because it's all the way across town, near Étoile. Have you got that?'

The girl said she understood. Her manner, it seemed to Rowlands, was now decidedly subdued. Outside in the street, as the heavy gates closed behind them, he said, 'I think she saw somebody.'

'So do I. The question is,' said Iris Barnes, 'whether she realises how much danger withholding that information puts her in.'

Arriving at 21 Rue Cambon, they entered a marble-floored entrance hall, and climbed a broad flight of stairs, at the top of which a young woman waited. She must have consulted a list, for she said, 'Names?'

'Iris Barnes and guest. English *Vogue*,' was the reply – which seemed to satisfy the girl, for she said, 'But of course, madame. Your seats are reserved.'

They entered what Rowlands guessed – from the sheer number of people gathered there – to be a large reception room. This impression was confirmed by his companion, who murmured as she took his arm, 'Watch out for the chairs. It's easy enough to fall over them, even when one can see.'

Her warning proved all too prescient, for a moment later, Rowlands stumbled into one such item of furniture (fortunately unoccupied) at the end of a row. It was flimsy, probably gilt, and (he surmised) no doubt replicated many times around the room. 'I said to take care, didn't I?' said Miss Barnes, steering him along the row, past a succession of knees belonging (he gathered) to women clad in furs and silk dresses. 'Here we are,' she said, sitting herself down on one of two vacant chairs in the centre of a row. 'We'll get a good view from here.'

'But what have we come to see?' he asked, using the verb in more than its literal sense. He knew it was his powers of observation (limited as they were) that were required here – but was at a loss as to how to employ them in this company of scented and befurred women (he had not yet detected a male voice), all intent on what was surely a wholly female concern. Fashion. Of course he knew the value of a well-cut suit as well as the next man, but the seasonal variations of hats and frocks, and all the other sartorial details with which women occupied themselves, were a closed book to him. 'Can you at least give me an idea of what we'll be looking at?'

'Shh. It's starting,' she said. 'Don't worry. It's what happens *after* the show that might prove interesting.' Her words were drowned out by a murmur of appreciation, followed by a ripple of applause, as the first of the mannequins walked in. 'Very nice,' said Miss Barnes, in his ear. 'A tailored costume. One of her "signature" styles. If only,' she added cryptically, 'she'd stuck to designing clothes, we wouldn't be here now.'

Further examples of the couturier's art followed – each greeted, as the first had been, by polite applause, as the young women modelling the clothes walked slowly along the aisle between the rows of chairs. 'Evening wear,' said Iris Barnes, for Rowlands's benefit. 'Quite a daring look, with those trousers. The nightclub crowd will love it, of course . . .' More trousers, this time in the form of beach pyjamas ('Perfect for Saint-Tropez'), were followed by variations on the coat and skirt combination so beloved of 'Madame's' clientele: 'She's perfected the art of dressing well with the least possible fuss,' said Rowlands's companion. 'One has to admire the achievement.'

There came a parade of what Rowlands was informed were evening gowns, each more extravagant than the last. More delighted gasps ensued. 'The wedding dress next,' said Iris Barnes. 'Then we'll see what we shall see . . .' Quite what they would 'see' she didn't say; but he got the distinct impression that it had nothing to do with clothes. 'Oh, very chic!' she exclaimed, as the mannequin bride swept past. 'Chantilly lace. Makes a change from parachute silk. They'll be clamouring for that in the smarter arrondissements.' She got up while the applause was still going on. 'Come on. Let's get a glass of champagne to celebrate Gaby's return, shall we?'

But as they began to push their way back along the row of chairs (to the muttered annoyance of those still seated upon them), there came another murmur of approbation, followed by an outburst of applause, louder than before. 'Well, well,' said Iris Barnes. 'So she's dared to show her face, after all . . .'

'I assume you're referring to the woman who's behind all this?' he said, in an undertone.

'Indeed I am,' was the reply. 'Imagine, if you will, a Black Widow spider, clad in a jersey suit and pearls – always pearls – and you will have a good idea of the creature that is Gabrielle Bonheur. I must say,' said Iris Barnes, softly, 'four years of living it up at the Ritz with her Nazi lover, on a champagne and cocaine diet, hasn't done her any favours.'

'Are you going to introduce me? Because if so, I should tell you I know nothing about women's fashions.'

'Oh, we won't get near her at the moment,' said Iris Barnes. 'Madame is surrounded by her acolytes and hangers-on, all gasping to tell her how marvellous she is . . .' And indeed, the excited buzz of voices seemed to confirm this.

'O! C'était merveilleux. Merveilleux!'

'Vous êtes une génie, Madame . . .'

'There's Pamela Whitstable,' said Miss Barnes in Rowlands's ear. 'She never misses the new collections. And Genevieve Le Clos – the actress, you know. Madame designed the wardrobe for her last Hollywood film. The

47

word is she gets her clothes for nothing. Good advertising, you see . . .' She took his arm. 'I think we'll forgo that glass of champagne,' she said, still in the same quiet tone. 'Time for a look behind the scenes . . . or, in this case, *above* them.'

Chapter Four

They left the big drawing room where Gaby Bonheur and her admirers were assembled, the latter's cries of approbation following them up the stairs like the shrill twittering of exotic birds. Rowlands knew better than to ask where his companion was leading him. Miss Barnes always had her reasons. As they reached the second floor, a door flew open and a young woman darted out. '*Madame! Attendez! Vous ne pouvez pas . . .*'

But Iris Barnes paid no attention to this, continuing to ascend the stairs, pursued by the girl's despairing cries. '*Madame! Descendez, s'il vous plait. C'est interdit!*'

They reached the third floor – or perhaps it was the fourth, counting from the ground floor, thought Rowlands, never quite sure how these matters were organised on the Continent. Whatever floor it was, it proved to be an attic, with a volume of space overhead that suggested the atelier. 'Workrooms,' said Miss Barnes, confirming this impression. 'This is where it all happens.' That it was a workplace was indeed evident from the quiet hum of sewing machines, and the no less subdued murmur of women's voices. *Seamstresses.*

Of course, thought Rowlands. 'Is this where she worked?' he said. 'Amélie Mendl, I mean.'

But before Miss Barnes could reply, an incautious step in the wrong direction brought Rowlands into contact with the edge of a table – one of a number arranged in rows across the room, he was to discover. 'Careful!' said his companion, putting out a hand to steady him. 'You almost made one of the cutters drop her scissors. One wrong snip, and the toile she's making would have been ruined.'

Rowlands was stammering an apology to the woman when their presence in that sacred domain was noticed by another of the seamstresses – this one more senior than the other, to judge by her air of authority. 'Excuse me, madame,' she said, addressing Iris Barnes in French – in which language the other also replied. 'This part of the house is closed to members of the public . . . unless one is here for a dress-fitting. But I do not think that is so with you.'

'You are right,' was the reply. 'I am here for another reason. I have some questions that need answering. Madame Bonheur is occupied with her guests, and so it is you I must ask, Madame Fournier.'

'Questions? What kind of questions?'

Rowlands didn't think he'd imagined the guardedness in the woman's voice. 'Amélie Mendl,' said Miss Barnes. 'I believe she worked for you?'

'What if she did? That was five years ago.'

'And you have not seen her since?'

The other woman hesitated. 'We had to let them all go – the seamstresses, the cutters – when the war started. Some came back. Some did not.' It was not quite an answer to the question.

'When did you last see her?' Iris Barnes persisted. 'It was more recently than five years ago, was it not?'

'Perhaps,' replied the other. 'I could not say. Girls come and go.'

'But you remember her, do you not? Five years is not such a long time.'

Madame Fournier made a sound – uniquely Gallic in Rowlands's experience – disparaging the previous remark. '*Bof*' might have expressed it phonetically. 'Yes, I remember Amélie Mendl. She was a good worker. Quiet. Clean. I was sorry to let her go. But I had no choice in the matter.'

'Surely there was no need for the business to close when it did? Many others kept going throughout the war.'

Again, that faintly contemptuous, plosive sound. 'It was Madame's wish. She did not think that selling dresses was patriotic in wartime . . .'

'And yet she continued to sell her perfume,' said Iris Barnes drily. 'No matter. I should like to talk to these women,' she went on. 'Maybe some of *them* will remember when they last saw Amélie Mendl.'

'They do not have time,' said Madame Fournier. 'They must hurry to finish a large order.'

'I thought Bonheur Modes only worked with individual clients?' said Miss Barnes. 'That is what makes your clothes so special. Their unique quality. Their attention to cut, stitching and detail. My questions will not take long,' she added. 'The less we delay now, the sooner your seamstresses can go back to doing what they do best.'

The other considered this. 'Very well,' she said. 'Ask your questions.' Although it seemed to Rowlands that the seamstresses of Bonheur Modes were unlikely to be very forthcoming with their supervisor standing there.

Miss Barnes seemed determined to make the best of a bad job, however. 'All right,' she said. 'Which of you knew Amélie Mendl?'

There was a silence; then one of the young women spoke up, her hesitant tone indicating how very little she relished having to do so. 'I did. It was not for very long, you understand. I started work a few months before she left.'

'When was that?'

'I . . . I do not remember exactly. It must have been the summer of 1939 . . . after the Boche came—'

'It was,' interjected Madame Fournier. 'We closed in the autumn of '39. Madame's orders.'

'Thank you. And during those months that you worked together,' went on the MI6 officer, in a tone of friendly interest, 'what impression did you form of Amélie?'

'I . . . . We did not know each other well,' said the girl uneasily.

'So you said, Miss . . . what is your name?'

'Sylvie. Sylvie Dubois.' It was said in a terrified whisper. Hardly surprising, thought Rowlands, after years of living in the shadow of the Gestapo.

'Thank you, Sylvie. You were about to tell me your impressions of Miss Mendl.'

'I . . .'

'For instance, was she talkative or reserved?'

'Rather reserved, I think. We . . . we are not supposed to talk, except during breaks . . .'

'They are supposed to get on with their work,' said Madame Fournier.

'Did she talk about her family?' asked Miss Barnes, ignoring this interruption.

'A little. She . . .'

But before Sylvie Dubois could say anything more, there came the sound of women's voices, funnelling up the staircase towards them. Of the two – both speaking in English – one had a pronounced French accent. The other . . . but Rowlands wondered if his ears deceived him. For the other speaker was familiar to him. There was no mistaking those languorous, honeyed tones; nor the delicious scent that wafted from the woman's clothes as she came in, mingling roses, jasmine and the muskier smell of Turkish cigarettes.

'Lady Celia,' he said, turning towards her. He felt as he had all those years ago, at their very first meeting: unsettled; thrown off-balance; shaken to the core.

Nor was he the only one to suffer a reaction to the arrival of these two – although he guessed, from the nervous whispers that ran around the room, that it was the presence of the other woman, Gaby Bonheur, which had occasioned this. '*Alors*, Madame Fournier . . .' she began, in her curiously hoarse tone – that of the heavy smoker, Rowlands thought.

She broke off, seeing that there were others in the room whose presence required an explanation. 'Who are these people?' she demanded of her subordinate, reverting to her native tongue. 'I have not given permission for anyone to visit the workrooms . . . apart from dear Lady Celia,' she added, in English. '*She* has my special permission to be here.'

The latter, ignoring this blatant piece of flattery, focused her attention on the unauthorised visitors. 'How nice to see you again, after all this time, Frederick! How long has it been since you were in Ireland?'

'It must be six years.'

'I suppose it must be. I hope you and your charming family are well?'

He said that they were.

'We've met too,' Celia Swift went on, turning to Rowlands's companion. 'In London, wasn't it, some years ago?'

'It was,' replied Iris Barnes. 'I was a guest at one of your parties, before the war.'

'Ah yes.' Lady Celia was thoughtful a moment. 'There were a lot of parties, in those days . . .'

'But these are your friends, Lady Celia! Why did you not say?' cried Gaby Bonheur, in the heavily accented English she had been employing as the two women ascended the stairs. 'I *adore* the English! Why, the only man I ever truly loved was an English milord.' When there was no response to this – or none Rowlands was aware of – she said, 'But will you not introduce me, dear Lady Celia?'

'Of course. This is Frederick Rowlands, an old friend, and this—'

'Rosalind Barry,' said Iris Barnes, without missing a beat. 'Delighted to meet you, madame. I very much enjoyed the show.'

'You are too kind.' Gaby Bonheur gave what might have passed as a self-deprecating laugh. 'I try, with my little efforts, to raise the . . . how do you say it? . . . the *morale* of my poor countrymen and women. And of course,' she added, with the same show of modesty, 'what you English call "fashion" and we French call "*la couture*" contributes *something* – I do not say how much – towards our national economy. Although I know little of such things, being only a humble dress designer.'

'Oh, I'd say you were rather more than that,' said Iris Barnes.

'You are *très gentille*,' was the gratified reply. Then, as if switching once more to French had reminded her of the purpose for which she and her client had come, she addressed Madame Fournier. 'But where is the gown for Lady Celia? I was assured you would have it ready. Quick! I have no time to waste. There are important people waiting to see me. The ambassador's wife. Miss Whitstable – so charming, that one! And Lady Brixton. Although she is at least a hundred years old,' she added with a malicious chuckle. 'Let her wait. *Alors*, the gown . . .'

'It is ready, madame. If you would come with me . . .'

'This way, Lady Celia,' said Madame Bonheur, in unctuous tones. Without another word to her ladyship's friends, she swept away.

'Goodbye, Frederick,' said Lady Celia. 'Lovely to meet you again, Miss Barry. I wish I could stay and chat, but I'm being summoned for my dress-fitting, as you see. Gaby's time is money, and so . . .'

'It was good to see you,' he said.

'I'm at the Crillon. Come and see me there, won't you?'

She touched his hand. 'We've a lot to talk about.'

Still slightly dazed by the encounter, he murmured that he would.

'Come on,' said Iris Barnes, when the other woman had walked away. 'We're finished here, for the time being. No sense in expecting any of these girls to tell us anything useful while the Black Widow's within earshot.'

They descended the stairs in silence. As they passed the open doors of the big salon on the first floor, the shrill sound of women's voices could be heard, as the society ladies, fuelled by copious amounts of champagne, discussed topics dear to their hearts – such as the advisability or otherwise of retrieving one's furs from cold storage, and the difficulties of finding a reliable maid in these hard times.

Glasses clinked and the air was filled with the smell of cigarette smoke, mingled with that of the perfume Bonheur Modes had made famous. Rowlands realised with a pang that it was this that he had smelt on Celia Swift's clothes and hair. He had thought her scent unique to her, but now saw that it was just another saleable commodity.

Distracted by these thoughts, and by the revival of feelings he had believed extinct, he wasn't paying attention to what his companion was saying, as they exited the building and made their way towards the waiting car. 'A pity the Black Widow arrived when she did,' Miss Barnes was saying. 'I'm convinced that girl had something to tell us.'

'What? Oh yes,' he said. 'I expect you're right.'

His companion laughed. 'I've heard of the effect Celia Swift has on men. But this is the first time I've seen it at close range.'

He was silent.

'Now I've made you angry,' she said as they reached the car. Again, he made no reply. The chauffeur had by now got out, and was holding the door open for his passengers to get in. 'No, I've had a better idea,' she said. She gave an instruction, and – having closed the door, and returned to the driving seat – the man started up the car, and drove away. 'He'll meet us on the quayside,' said Iris Barnes. 'I thought we'd walk through the gardens, as it's a fine day.' She touched his arm to direct him along the street that lay in front of them. 'To tell you the truth,' she went on, as if he had spoken, 'it's a relief to get out of that place and find somewhere one can breathe.'

At the end of the street, they came to an intersection – it was the Rue Saint-Honoré, she said. They crossed, and continued walking for another five minutes. It was, as she had said, a beautiful spring afternoon. Where better to spend it, said Rowlands's companion, than in the Jardin des Tuileries? Even here, amid the sharp smell of the clipped box hedges that edged the formal flower-beds, and the rustle of new leaves on the trees lining the geometrically perfect gravel paths, they had not left the war behind. 'This was the site of one of the last battles of 1944,' said Miss Barnes, as they began walking slowly towards the ornamental lake in the centre of the park. 'There were French and German tanks lined up on opposite sides of the gardens.'

He said he could picture it. Reaching the row of wrought-iron chairs that formed a circle around the lake, they chose two, side by side, and sat down. Here, in happier times, people would gather to enjoy the balmy air of a summer's evening, and to admire the magnificent view of the Louvre in one direction and the Jeu de Paume in the other. Now, they were the only ones there – of this, at least, Rowlands was sure. She would not have chosen the spot if there had been any risk of their being overheard.

'I realise,' said Iris Barnes after an interval, 'that I have not been entirely straight with you.' A flock of seagulls flew up, quarrelling, from the lake. 'During the war,' she went on, 'I was . . . that is, my *organisation* was . . . quite involved with the Special Operations Executive. Specifically, those operatives who were deployed in France. I was not myself a member of the SOE, you understand. My responsibilities were more of an organisational kind . . .'

As they had been since he'd known her, he thought. There'd been that time in Berlin – now over ten years ago – and that time in Barcelona, during the civil war. Not to mention the last time they'd had dealings with one another, in Oxford. Then, as before, she'd been in charge of running things. He made a sound in his throat, indicating that he understood the point she was making.

'My . . . ah . . . activities in Paris during the same period – that is, from the spring of 1942 until the present time – have been of this kind. I don't carry out operations, I just arrange them . . . and, where necessary, clean up after them.'

'Yes,' he said, remembering certain instances of what 'cleaning up' had meant.

'So while it's perfectly true that the reason I've asked you here is . . . or rather was . . . to identify the Metzner girl, I haven't yet given you the full picture.'

'No,' he said. This, too, wasn't news to him. Iris Barnes

seldom revealed her hand, unless she was forced to.

Now she seemed reluctant to go on with what she had to say. 'Cigarette?' she said.

'I'll smoke my own, thanks.' Hers would be that filthy-tasting French brand. Both lit up and for a moment, neither spoke.

'I don't need to go into too much detail about our networks in Paris. Suffice it to say that one of the most important of them was compromised sometime during the summer of '43. The Gestapo rounded up over a hundred and fifty of our agents. Some were shot, trying to escape, others deported. Some disappeared without trace. We think this was a deliberate policy on the part of the Nazi authorities. They called it *"Nacht und Nebel"*, which means—'

'Night and fog,' he said.

'Exactly. The idea was that no one would ever find out what had happened to these people – or if they were alive or dead. A cruel twist, to an already cruel fate . . .' She was silent a moment, exhaling a cloud of pungent smoke. 'Amongst these "disappeared" were eight women, all of whom worked for us in some capacity. Since the Liberation, I and my colleagues have made it our business to discover what happened to each of these women. Suffice it to say,' she added softly, 'we now have a pretty good idea of where and what was done, and when, and to whom.'

Rowlands said nothing. He already knew that what he was about to hear would be nothing good. There would not be tales of miraculous survival, or death-defying escape. This was about bearing witness, merely; about apportioning blame, if those deserving of blame could be discerned through the miasma of night and fog.

'There were eight women, as I said. Four of them died in Dachau – shot in the back of the neck.' Her voice was cold and emotionless. 'Some reports say that they were together when they died; others that they were alone in their cells. There is evidence that at least one of them was tortured before she was shot.' Iris Barnes took a deep drag of her cigarette. 'Of the other four women – all of whom had been connected, in one way or another, with the Paris network I mentioned just now – there is less information. What information there is, is confusing.'

Night and fog, he thought.

'We know, for example, that following their arrests, the women were first taken to Ravensbrück. From there, it is thought that they were taken to Natzweiler-Struthof, a camp in the Vosges region. After that, there has been no more word of them. It is to be assumed that they are dead.' She was silent a moment. 'What I want is justice,' she went on, still in the same cold, level voice in which she had recounted the preceding facts. 'And that means that I cannot rest until I find out who betrayed them.'

'So you think that Clara Metzner might have been involved in all this?'

'I think she knew something about it, yes,' was the reply. 'That is why she was killed. For which I blame myself,' she added, lighting another Gitanes. 'I thought she would be safe enough in protective custody at Fresnes – but it seems I was wrong.'

Rowlands, too, had felt himself to blame for the girl's death. 'Would it have made a difference to where she was kept, if I'd been able to positively identify her?' he asked. 'I mean – would she have been any safer?'

'I doubt it. These people – whoever they are – are ruthless. If a prison couldn't keep them out, then nowhere would have been safe. Come on,' she said getting to her feet. 'Let's go and find a drink – and something stronger than champagne.'

Chapter Five

The Café de Flore was already full to capacity, even though it was still early; people were crammed seven or eight to a table designed to seat four, and those that couldn't find places within spilt out onto the pavement, where numerous smaller tables were clustered beneath the awnings of the famous establishment. As Rowlands and his companion pushed their way through the throng that was gathered around the entrance to the café, they were met by the deafening roar of competing conversations, as those on one side of the room harangued those on the other:

'*Mais non, mais non! C'est impossible . . .*'

'*Tu ne sais pas de quoi tu parles . . .*'

'*Ecoute, espéce d'imbecile . . .*'

Interspersed with these passionate outbursts were shouts for more drinks to be brought, as waiters scurried back and forth between the tables. 'What a madhouse,' observed Iris Barnes. She had evidently spotted a couple of chairs which had become vacant at that moment at a nearby table, for she piloted Rowlands towards one, before taking the other for herself. '*Deux cognacs*,' she demanded of a passing waiter. 'It's always like this when *la famille* Schweitzer is in residence,' she said.

And indeed from the centre of the room came the rumble of a deep and sonorous voice – the voice of a man used to holding forth on all manner of subjects, and to having his opinions deferred to.

'But my dear fellow! It's no more surprising to me to find that men are base, unjust and selfish than it surprises me that apes are mischievous, wolves savage or vultures ravenous . . .'

It struck Rowlands that it was not the first time that this remark – pronounced of course in the speaker's native French – had been delivered. In spite, or perhaps because of this, it was met with appreciative chuckles from the group surrounding the speaker. So this was the celebrated philosopher, Jacques Schweitzer, he thought. How Anne, his middle daughter, would have relished this encounter! Having spent her sixteenth birthday in Paris, the year before the war, Anne had never lost her romantic view of the city. For her, the café society of the Left Bank epitomised all that was most admirable in cultural and intellectual life – and Schweitzer, its de facto leader, was to her a kind of hero.

'When you speak of men as no better than wild beasts, you of course exclude *women* from your generalisation?' said another voice – a woman's – in sarcastic tones. At which interruption there was more laughter, as well as a few whistles and slow handclaps.

'Sandrine never misses a chance to bang the feminist drum,' murmured Iris Barnes in Rowlands's ear. He nodded; but in truth he felt completely out of his depth. Weren't these people renowned members of the Resistance? This was surely the last place one would expect to find Nazi sympathisers. 'We think she came here – the girl – on a number of occasions . . . before her arrest,' said the MI6 officer, as if guessing his thought. 'It's also possible that she was denounced as a *"mouche"* – their word for an informer – by one of the regulars at the Flore. It was around that time – two years ago – that she disappeared from view.'

'I see.' Rowlands sipped his cognac and wondered if he'd ever understand what was going on in this most divided of cities. 'Do you think she *was* an informer, then?'

'I think it's likely she knew who the informer was, and was therefore a danger to that person . . . Oh, don't look so surprised! Every gathering of this kind had its quota of snitches . . . and its quota of spies. We ourselves,' she added, meaning her organisation, he supposed, 'like to keep an eye on the goings-on at the Café de Flore, and other similar establishments. It's the only way to keep track of what our friends – as well as our enemies – are up to . . . Ah, here's Arthur Chabrol . . . or rather, "Beauregard",' she went on, as someone else joined the group in the centre of the room. 'He and Schweitzer have a sort of friendly rivalry going on, so we might hear something to the purpose.

'Beauregard's his *nom de plume*, of course,' Iris Barnes went on, in an undertone. 'It's how he signs his columns in *Attaque*, the radical paper he writes for. Some of his ideas are quite interesting – a cut above the usual revolutionary rants,' she added, as the new arrival took his seat, with friendly greetings to those in his immediate circle.

'Hello, old man!' he said to Schweitzer. 'So you're still here, are you?'

'Where else would I be,' grunted the other, 'if not here?'

'And Sandrine, too, of course! Where one is to be found, the other is never far away . . .'

'Who else would remind him when to get up in the morning – and when to go to bed at night?' was the truculent reply. Rowlands got the distinct impression that there was little love lost between the affable Chabrol and the acerbic Madame Bertrand. 'Tell me,' the latter now said, in the same ironical tone, 'what have *you* been up to in these past few days? I do not think I have seen you in your usual haunts.'

'Wherever those are,' Chabrol amended cheerfully. 'No, I have been away from Paris. I had things to see to. People to see.'

'Well, that is nothing new,' rumbled Schweitzer. 'You are a busy fellow, my dear Chabrol.' Again, Rowlands had the feeling that there was a veiled animosity beneath the civil words.

'Of course, their rivalry extends beyond the political sphere,' said Iris Barnes – still sotto voce, although it seemed to Rowlands that with the noise level in the Café de Flore being what it was, there was little danger of their being overheard. 'Schweitzer had always had a reputation as a womaniser – much to La Bertrand's discomfiture. Although, as the younger and decidedly better-looking of the two men, Chabrol might be said to have the advantage. To add insult to injury, he's regarded as the better writer by at least some of the Left Bank crowd – even if Schweitzer's books sell better. Rumour has it,' she added, 'that *la belle* Sandrine writes the best bits of them . . . Hello, Julien! I was hoping you'd turn up.' This last remark was to a man who'd come in with Chabrol, and who now sat down next to her. 'It's been a while since we last met.'

'Yes,' he replied. 'It was at the Brasillach trial, in January. A shocking affair, was it not?'

'You were one of those who signed the petition in favour of clemency.'

'I was. Not that it made a difference. They still shot him.'

'They had to make an example, I suppose,' said Iris Barnes. 'And he *was* an avowed fascist who supported that cause in print. Another brandy?' she said to Rowlands; then to the newcomer, 'Will you join us?'

He accepted; then Miss Barnes said, 'But I haven't introduced you gentlemen. Frederick Rowlands. Julien Corbeau. Julien is a writer and an artist . . .'

'I make films, too,' said the other; adding, without a trace of false modesty, 'Some say these are my best work.'

'I only wish I were able to appreciate them,' smiled Rowlands.

'Ah, *you* are English, too!' cried the other, ignoring the implication of Rowlands's remark. Perhaps he was one of those who could only focus on one thing at a time, Rowlands thought. But then Corbeau said, 'Blindness. That is an interesting concept for a filmmaker. How to convey the thoughts and sensations of a blind man, when the face is so less expressive. One would have to rely a good deal on sound, of course – both as regards dialogue and otherwise.'

'Yes,' agreed Rowlands. 'One would.'

The brandies arrived. Corbeau took a swig of his,

then addressed the MI6 officer once more. 'So tell me, what are you doing here – apart from paying court to the emperor and his concubine?' He meant Schweitzer and Madame Bertrand, Rowlands supposed, gathering from the satirical tone in which the remark was made that Corbeau felt little inclination to 'pay court' himself. '*He* did not sign,' he went on, without waiting for an answer. 'His type believe that the punishment should fit the crime.' Again, the words had a sarcastic ring.

'No,' said Miss Barnes thoughtfully. 'He did not sign. The affair has split the literary world,' she explained to Rowlands. 'Those that signed accused the others of callousness towards a fellow writer, and those that didn't said that the signatories were giving comfort to the enemy . . . Since you ask,' she added, turning once more to Corbeau, 'I am here for a reason. I'm looking for a missing person. Do you remember the little Jewish girl who used to hang around with the Schweitzer crowd, a year or two ago? Dark hair. *Gamine*. Rather pretty. I believe you used her in one of your films.'

'Did I? I can't say that I recall.' It was said too quickly. Rowlands was left with the impression that, despite his disavowal, the filmmaker knew exactly who it was that Iris Barnes had referred to.

'There were rumours that she was an informer,' Miss Barnes persisted. 'It was after that that she disappeared. I've been trying to track her down . . .'

'Another candidate for the firing squad?' said Corbeau with distaste.

'On the contrary. I think *she* might have been the one betrayed.'

'Then I'm sorry for her – if she's still alive, that is.' Corbeau finished his drink, and set down the glass with emphasis. 'I must go. Things to see to. People to see.' It was almost exactly what Arthur Chabrol had said on being asked about his movements by Sandrine Bertrand. Iris Barnes, too, seemed to have caught the echo, for she said, 'I suppose you and "Beauregard" have some scheme afoot?'

'Perhaps. *He*, at least, put his principles before his politics,' said Corbeau. He got up. 'It was good to see you again, Rosaline. I hope you find your little girl.'

He crossed the room to where the Schweitzer 'family' and Chabrol were sitting. They heard him exchange a few words with the latter. 'Arthur Chabrol was another of those who signed the petition,' said Miss Barnes softly. 'His abhorrence of the death penalty outweighed his abhorrence of fascism – although I believe it was a close-run thing. On the whole,' she said, 'one feels more sympathy with the vacillations of the liberal conscience than with the inflexibility displayed by some sections of the Left. But there are times when one must set one's finer feelings aside.' Her voice, as she pronounced these words, was cold. It occurred to Rowlands that this was the nearest thing to a credo he had heard the MI6 officer express.

As they were leaving the Café de Flore, someone else was coming in. 'Why,' said Iris Barnes, in a gratified tone, 'if it isn't my old friend, Marcel! I wondered if I might see you here.'

'Madame, you are mistaken,' the man replied. 'That is not my name.'

'Not now, perhaps,' she said. 'But when you were a member of the Palace network that was the name you were known by, was it not?'

'I . . .' Cornered, the man prevaricated. 'I do not like to talk about that time,' he said, adding piously, 'I lost too many friends.'

'So did we all,' said Iris Barnes. 'It is good to see you again, Marcel – or whatever you call yourself now. This is Frederick Rowlands, a friend of mine from England. Have a drink with us, won't you?'

'I . . . I cannot stay long,' said 'Marcel' unhappily. 'I only looked in for a minute . . .'

'You have time for a drink with an old comrade, surely?' She had, by this time, steered the three of them towards a table under the awning, where she sat down, then signalled to a passing waiter. 'What'll you have?'

Reluctantly, the man accepted a cognac.

Wondering what his companion was up to now, Rowlands refused another of the same, saying he'd rather have a cup of coffee. 'I'll join you,' said the MI6 officer. '*Deux cafés et un cognac,*' she said to the hovering waiter. 'Now then, Marcel . . . I'm afraid I can't seem to get out of the habit! What have you been doing since Paris was liberated? You used to run a bookshop, as I recall.'

'I still do, madame,' was the reply. 'Although business has been bad for some time. Very bad . . .'

'The shop was used as a dead letter drop,' said Miss Barnes to Rowlands. 'Any messages that had to be sent to other members of the network went through there. It was a valuable service.'

'I did what I could,' said 'Marcel' complacently, taking

a sip of his cognac. 'Those were dangerous times.'

'For some more than others,' replied Miss Barnes. She sipped her coffee meditatively. 'You remember Celestine?'

'I am not sure. There were so many . . .'

'Oh, come! Tall, red-haired girl. Worked as a courier. She was always in and out of your shop.'

'I believe I do remember her, now you mention it.'

'Yes, she was one of the first to be picked up by the Gestapo. She was arrested with some of the messages on her, unfortunately for her . . .'

'Messages?'

'The ones that had been concealed in the books. You remember. A clever ruse – was it you who thought of it?'

'Not I, madame,' said the other. 'I merely ran the shop. What use was made of it I preferred not to know . . . as you will doubtless understand.'

'Of course,' said Iris Barnes. 'In those days, it was better not to know too much.'

'I never trusted that man,' said the MI6 officer, as having left the Café de Flore behind, they walked along the Boulevard Saint-Germain in the direction of Saint-Germain-des-Prés. 'He was the sort that would rat on his grandmother if he thought there was some advantage to himself in doing so.'

'Do you think he might have been the one who betrayed them – the women?'

'Unfortunately not. We've already investigated him pretty thoroughly, and his story adds up. He was away from Paris at the time the network collapsed. He had nothing to do with it.'

'Mightn't he have had a collaborator?' said Rowlands. 'I mean, someone to whom he passed on the information that brought about the collapse?'

'If so, we haven't been able to find one,' said Miss Barnes wearily. 'I'm afraid he's out of the picture. Come on, let's see if we can pick up something to eat in one of the local brasseries.'

Earlier she'd dismissed the driver – 'no sense in having him hang around all evening' – saying that they could find themselves a cab along the way. Now she seemed abstracted, scarcely aware of Rowlands's presence, it seemed to him, as they threaded their way between sauntering crowds of off-duty American soldiers and their girls. Perhaps, he thought, she was recalling her student days at the Sorbonne, when the Left Bank and the adjacent Latin Quarter would have been her stamping ground . . .

Just then there came a shout from the terrace of Les Deux Magots, which they happened to be passing at that moment. 'I say! Over here! My dear old spy! I thought it must be you.' It was Percy Loveless. 'This *is* a bit of luck,' he said, as they accordingly joined him – Rowlands sensed this was with some reluctance on his companion's part. 'Believe it or not, I was just thinking about you, old man . . . and the charming Miss Iris, too – or whatever you're calling yourself these days, dear lady. Beers all round, I think, don't you? *Garçon! Trois bières, s'il vous plait.*'

The stream of nervous chatter continued as the beers were brought. 'What are we celebrating? We must have something to celebrate . . . The end of this blasted war, for a start! I remember when the last one ended . . . as I expect you do too, old spy. We thought it was the end of all war. How wrong we were. Well, here's luck,' said Loveless, chinking his glass against Rowlands's before taking a deep draught.

'Here's luck,' echoed Rowlands, feeling a stab of pity for his old friend – once so noisily combative, now reduced to a muttering shadow of his former self. 'What have you been up to since we last met? Been to any more private views?'

'Oh, a few, you know – Paris being Paris. One can't *move* without falling over some fellow practitioner of the arts . . .' Loveless took another swig of beer. 'Saw that dreadful old poseur Edgar Hathaway the other day,' he went on, referring to a well-known American writer of truculent disposition. 'Masquerading as a war correspondent. Oh, he's very *in* with that *Time* crowd. Suppose he thinks it makes him look like a "he-man".' The artist guffawed.

This was more like it, thought Rowlands. Loveless was never more himself than when he was being rude about a 'fellow practitioner', as he put it. 'And yet, you know,' Loveless added, in a more conciliatory tone, 'underneath all that swagger, he's the mildest of men. Not a bad writer, either – although he wouldn't thank me for saying it. I thought his book about the war was actually quite good. Surprisingly sensitive, for someone who likes to present himself as a man of action . . . Speaking of which,' the artist went on, 'I take it you've been at the Café de Flore, fraternising with our celebrated heroes of the *Résistance*? Heroines, too – if one includes the formidable Madame

Bertrand. I must admit, that woman terrifies me. I should think she'd be quite capable of taking out a collabo or two with a single basilisk glare . . . Was Chabrol there?'

'He was,' said Iris Barnes.

'Rather a dashing fellow, with those leading-man looks and that Bogart trench coat he affects. I must say, of the two, I prefer him to Schweitzer. That public intellectual pose of old Jacques's is a bit of a bore, don't you agree?'

Miss Barnes neither agreed nor disagreed with this assessment, but lit a cigarette, without offering one to Rowlands – who in any case would have refused it. He'd always found the French brands too strong for his taste. 'So what's brought *you* to Paris, Percy?'

'Please!' The artist gave a theatrical shudder. 'I never use my Christian name, if I can help it. And I'm here because I managed to get a passage from Halifax to Le Havre three weeks ago . . . I've always liked Paris,' he added inconsequentially. 'Spent a good deal of time here, in my younger days. Before the war – the last war, I mean – and after it. That was a glorious time. You could stroll along the Boulevard Saint-Germain and find artists of every stripe occupying all the bistros and cafés. Cubists in one establishment, Surrealists in another. You could rent a studio in Montmartre for next to nothing. Now, thanks to the likes of Diego Ruiz, the rents in once-affordable areas have gone sky-high . . . and the Left Bank has been given over to communist fellow-travellers like Schweitzer and his gang.'

'Jacques Schweitzer's not a communist,' said Iris Barnes.

'You think not? Then he's certainly got some odd friends,' replied Loveless. He yawned – perhaps a way of signalling that the subject wasn't worth pursuing. 'Shall we have another beer?'

'All right.' Miss Barnes must have signalled to the waiter, for the beers arrived in short order. Knowing that his old friend was often in an impecunious state, Rowlands guessed that it would not be Loveless who'd be paying for them.

'Well,' said the latter, taking an appreciative draught of his beer. 'Here we are again, old spy. We don't see one another for ten years, and then we meet twice in as many days. But that's Paris for you. One minute you're standing about, quaffing champagne and admiring that charming portrait of *The Little Seamstress* – or whatever it's called – the next, you're mingling with the reddest of the "Red" intelligentsia.'

'What did you say?' demanded Miss Barnes sharply.

'Just my little joke, old thing. I was referring to our friends at the Café de Flore.'

'Before that. You mentioned the "Seamstress" portrait.'

'So I did. One of Diego's better efforts, in my humble opinion. And I wasn't the only one at the private view who thought so . . .'

'Explain.'

'Nothing much *to* explain. It was something that American chap, Harrington, said. He and Ruiz were having a bit of a row, as you may recall . . . in fact, dear old Diego – such a volatile fellow – was on the point of throwing Harrington out. It was then that he – the American – pointed to the portrait of the girl . . . the one you're so interested in . . . and said, "Tell you what, old sport, I'm prepared to take *that* picture instead of the other one." To which Diego replied that it – *The Little Seamstress* – wasn't for sale.'

'He said that, did he?' said Iris Barnes.

'Far as I can recall. Why, is it important?'

'It might be.' Again, she hesitated. Then appeared to make up her mind. 'Did the name Amélie Mendl come up, during this row you mention?'

'Not that I recall. Who is she?'

'That's what Mr Rowlands and I have been trying to find out,' said Iris Barnes. 'What do you know about the Palace network?'

'That's easy. Nothing at all. You forget that I've been stuck in Canada for the past six years, my dear girl. All this cloak-and-dagger stuff in which you've obviously been caught up has passed me by. I take it this Mendl girl had some involvement with the network you refer to?'

'Possibly. Or she might have been the one to betray it,' said the MI6 officer. 'So you can see, Loveless, that any mention of her name – or her code name, "Seamstress" – might be highly significant. I'd be grateful if you'd keep your ears open for any further such mentions . . . or indeed if you hear talk of a girl called Celestine . . . or Paulette . . . Jacqueline . . . or Yvette.'

'And who might they be?'

'They *were* my agents. All dead, now. They were part of the Palace network, working out of Paris. It's not even a year since they died. There'll be people who remember them. People who know what happened to them. It's my job to find out who those people are.'

Chapter Six

Since it was getting on for dinner time, and none of them had eaten, they crossed the street to the Brasserie Lipp, which was just starting to fill up at that hour. Here, in an atmosphere rich with the smells of the Alsatian cuisine for which the establishment was famous, they ordered the house speciality – *choucroute garnie* – with another round of beers. This – on top of the beers he'd already had and the brandies consumed in the Café de Flore – was making Rowlands feel a trifle fuddled. Fortunately, the food when it came was sufficiently hearty and filling to counteract the effects of the alcohol.

'Delicious,' said Loveless, attacking his plate of sauerkraut, sausages and potatoes with gusto. 'I adore German cooking. Glad to find this place – a haunt of my youth – is still going. Wish I could say the same for the clientele. What a disreputable-looking bunch! Down-at-heel poets and out-of-work actors, by the look of them, with the odd professional agitator like your friend Schweitzer thrown in . . . I say, isn't that old Hathaway over there, with that rather handsome woman? Whatever you do, don't catch his eye. Last time I saw him, he threatened to toss me into the street . . . Oh hello, Edgar, old fruit! Long time no see, as you Yanks like to say.'

The answer to this remark, from the man who'd just come over to their table, was a deep bass growl. 'Not long enough, far as I'm concerned, *old fruit*.' He gave the last words a heavily ironic emphasis. 'Might've known I'd run across *you* the minute I get to Paris.'

'Oh, come now, old friend,' said Loveless, sounding in high good humour. 'It must be twenty years since we last met. It's certainly that long since I was in Paris. How are you? You're looking remarkably fit. Being back in the front line evidently suits you.'

'Hardly that,' growled the other. 'I just went along for the ride. *Collier's* wanted a report on the fighting in the Hürtgen Forest region and so I gave it to 'em. Not much more to it than that.'

'I heard that you played a part in liberating Paris,' said Loveless slyly. 'Doesn't sound like sitting on the sidelines to me . . .'

For some reason this seemed to annoy the other. 'Story's been blown out of all proportion,' he said testily. 'I hitched a ride on a tank going into the city, on the day the Germans left, is all.'

So this was the great Edgar Hathaway, thought Rowlands. A writer so famous on both sides of the Atlantic that his name had become a byword, as much for the reckless daring of his exploits, both on and off the battlefield, as for his literary output. A book described as 'Hathawayesque' would tend towards grimness of subject and purity of style.

'Doing much writing?' was Loveless's next sally – to which the reply was no less unforthcoming.

'A little.'

'Splendid. I did enjoy your last book, by the by. I was just saying so to my friends here . . . Forgive me, I haven't introduced you. Edgar, this is Iris Barnes . . . at least, so she's had me believe. Iris, this is Edgar Hathaway, of whom you may have heard.'

'Ma'am.' A courtly growl. 'And you are?'

'Frederick Rowlands.' Rowlands extended his hand and felt it grasped in an iron grip.

'Pleased to meet you, Mr Rowlands.'

'Rowlands here is a veteran of *our* war, Edgar – the one you wrote about so feelingly in your book. Although *you* saw action on the Italian Front, whereas Rowlands and I were in Belgium and France.'

'What was your regiment, Mr Rowlands?'

'First London. I was with the Royal Field Artillery.'

'A gunner, then? See much action?'

'A bit. We were at the Somme, in '16. Later they sent us up the line to Ypres.'

'That was a tough show.'

'It was.'

For a moment both were silent, as if in acknowledgement of the horrors of what had passed. Then a woman's voice – rather a nice voice, thought Rowlands: warm and humorous – broke into their brief colloquy. 'Hate to break up the old soldiers' reunion, but . . .'

'Sure, honey. Just catching up with old Loveless here. The painter, you know . . .'

'I do indeed. I believe I saw some of your paintings when I was last in London, Mr Loveless – at one of those little Cork Street galleries, you know?'

Loveless muttered gruffly that he did.

'And this is Frederick Rowlands. He was at the Somme.'

'A pleasure to meet you, Mrs Hathaway.'

'Oh, I go by my own name. Mildred Gelber.'

'I've seen your byline,' said Iris Barnes. 'You write for *Time*, don't you?'

'Amongst others,' was the reply.

'I saw your piece on the D-Day landings. It made one feel one was *there* – in the midst of the action.'

'Oh, my wife likes to be where the action is,' said Hathaway sourly. 'Stowed away on a hospital ship, didn't you sweetie?'

'I had no choice. *Somebody* had stolen my *Collier's* press pass.'

There seemed little doubt who that 'somebody' must have been – although Hathaway's only response was a disgusted snort. 'Well, it's lovely to have met you nice people,' Mildred Gelber said, after the uncomfortable pause that followed this exchange, 'but we'd better hustle, Eddie, if we're to make that show.'

'Anything you say, honey. We can pick up a cab on the boulevard. Be seeing you, Loveless. Pleasure to meet you, ma'am . . . and you too, Rowlands. We must swap war stories one of these days.'

'So that's the third Mrs Hathaway . . . or is it the fourth?' said Loveless, when the couple had gone. 'No doubt who wears the trousers in *that* marriage – although that's a good thing, in my opinion. Poor old Edgar was looking rather the worse for wear . . . Did you *smell* the whisky coming off him? He needs a nurse as much as a wife.'

'He got into hot water over his involvement with the Maquis, after D-Day,' said Iris Barnes. 'There was a group calling itself Hathaway's Irregulars that got up to quite a lot of tricks. Hathaway was their self-appointed leader. Technically, he was breaking the terms of the Geneva Convention by engaging in combat while operating as a war correspondent.'

'No wonder he was so cross when I mentioned his part in the liberation of Paris!' chuckled Loveless. 'I imagine that the American Army would prefer he stuck to writing books, rather than playing at soldiers.'

'Oh, he's done some brave things, all right,' said the MI6 officer. 'But he's twenty years too old for soldiering.'

'Yes, they made a point of sending the young to be slaughtered first in our day, too – didn't they, Rowlands? Some of 'em had only just left school.' He allowed a brief pause to elapse. 'Well, I must say that's the best meal I've had since I came to Paris,' he went on. 'I feel a new man – ready for whatever the evening may bring. In the old days, you know, one would have headed up to Montmartre, to look in at the Moulin Rouge . . . or perhaps pay a visit to the ladies of Pigalle.'

'I'm afraid *I* have to get back to the hotel,' said Iris Barnes. 'See if any messages have come in for me.' Because of course, thought Rowlands, the Hôtel Cécil was also her place of work. 'But if you gentlemen want to extend the evening, that's fine with me. You might keep your ears open, both of you, for any mention of the four women I told you about . . . or indeed of our young friend,

Amélie Mendl. She wasn't unknown in the Montmartre nightclubs. In fact, I believe that's where Diego first saw her.'

'I thought she was a seamstress,' said Rowlands.

'She was. Although by the time we're talking about, she'd lost her job – Madame Bonheur having decided, as you'll recall, to close the workrooms at Bonheur Modes during the Occupation, on the grounds that it wasn't patriotic to be making dresses for the rich while "the people" were starving.' There was a sarcastic emphasis to these last words, which showed what Miss Barnes thought of this so-called patriotism.

'That woman!' said Loveless. 'Holed up at the Ritz with her Nazi boyfriend . . . I'm amazed she wasn't arrested and put on trial for treason during the *épuration sauvage*.'

'It helps to have friends in high places,' said Iris Barnes. 'And now I must go.' She signalled to the waiter, who brought the bill. A muted contest ensued as to who was to settle it. Miss Barnes won. 'When you've had your fun, you can put Mr Rowlands in a taxi to the Hôtel Cécil,' she said to Loveless – no doubt having slipped him the necessary francs to cover the fare.

'Well,' said the artist, when she had gone. 'This is quite like old times, you dear old spy. Shall we have one for the road, or shall we make tracks for Montmartre?'

They reached the Moulin Rouge a little before ten o'clock, after an hour's walk that took them right across Paris, crossing the river by the Pont du Carrousel and proceeding, by way of the Rue de Rivoli and the Avenue de l'Opéra, to the foothills of Montmartre. As they walked, Loveless kept up a stream of reminiscences. 'I rented a studio near here, in 1910,' he threw out at one point. 'It was in the Rue Mansart. Rather a filthy hole, but it was cheap. Girl I was seeing at the time lived in the Rue Blanche. Used to model for me. Marie-Christine, her name was. Red hair. Lived up to it, too. Fiery little thing.'

Rowlands, whose own pre-war memories of Paris were confined to the few days' leave he'd enjoyed during his soldiering days in 1914, had no such romantic memories to share. He recollected being extremely sick in the gutter outside one of the *boîtes* frequented by British soldiers, after an ill-advised evening's drinking. As far as girls were concerned, he'd never got further than a bit of mild flirtation with some of the local *poules* – his reticence due, no doubt, to the fact that he'd got engaged to Maudie O'Sullivan the week before he'd been sent to France. Of course it hadn't lasted, but he hadn't known that, then . . .

'Here we are at last,' panted Loveless – for the last part of the walk had been up a steep hill. 'Ramshackle old place looks just the same as it did then. I gather it was popular with the German soldiery, so they doubtless made sure it remained standing.'

Having paid, which Loveless insisted on doing – 'My treat, old man' – although Rowlands suspected this largesse was only made possible by the francs with which Iris Barnes had supplied him, they entered the famous nightclub, which was still only half full, said Loveless. 'Pitch black in here, as ever,' he grunted, as they took their seats at one of the small tables set back from the stage, where a trio of musicians – piano, bass and saxophone – ran smoothly through a range of popular hits. At once a 'hostess' appeared, bringing a bottle of champagne. 'Take that muck away,' growled Loveless. 'Two beers. Unless you'd rather have a brandy, Rowlands?'

Rowlands said he'd stick to beer. 'The prices here are ridiculous,' said his companion. 'But it's worth it for the show . . . I wonder who's in tonight?' His question, it became apparent, referred to the audience for the prospective performance, rather than the performance itself, for having cast an eye around the place, he muttered, 'Nobody I know. Sightseers, for the most part, come for a glimpse of "real Paris nightlife".' The last phrase was pronounced with scorn – although it was only what they themselves were doing, thought Rowlands.

He sipped his beer. The jazz trio tinkled on. At the next table, a rather drunk young man was stumbling through a funny story. 'So this other chap says to the first chap . . . no, wait. It was the *first* chap who said to the other one . . .'

'Oh, do give it a rest, old bean,' said another voice. 'Nobody gives a damn who said what to anyone.' Rowlands guessed from the fact that both spoke in English that these must be off-duty army officers – or perhaps they were members of that floating population of diplomats, administrators and spies with which the city seemed to be infested.

'I was jus' trying to *tell* you,' said the man who'd spoken first, with the affronted dignity of the inebriated, 'what this chap *said* . . . No need to get all . . . *upstage* about it.'

At that moment the music, which had been of the louche, downbeat kind that seemed always to be sliding into formlessness, changed to something more up-tempo and structured – a 'big band' sound, in fact. Onstage, the orchestra had been assembling: ranks of trumpeters, saxophonists, tympanists, guitarists and violinists. There came a clash of cymbals. A roll of drums. 'Ah,' said Loveless, awakening from his gloomy reflections. 'Something's happening at last.'

Onto the stage had stepped the main attraction – or so Rowlands gathered, from the sudden hush that fell over the audience; even the noisy party at the next table were silent. The silence prolonged itself, until it seemed as if the whole theatre quivered with anticipation. Into this moment of heightened tension came the sound of a voice. It was a pure, surprisingly powerful voice, with a kind of catch in it, that spoke of barely suppressed emotion. It sang of love, and heartbreak; of pain and loss – the words echoed in the plangent sounds of the guitar, and the warm notes of the clarinet.

Rowlands found he was holding his breath. He sat, as if under a spell, while the music flowed around him. When the song was over, there came another silence – this time of appreciation – before the storm of applause broke out. 'Wonderful,' he murmured.

'She's still got what it takes, hasn't she?' agreed Loveless, as the clapping, whistling and stamping went on around them. 'Extraordinary to think that such a tiny little thing – she can't be more than five foot tall – could produce a sound like that.'

Another love song followed – this one addressed not to a person, but to the city in which they sat – the singer's tone as heartfelt as when she had been invoking a lost lover. 'Of course, she's having to be careful these days,' said Loveless, into the no less enthusiastic applause that greeted what had become, in recent months, a kind of unofficial national anthem. 'She put a lot of people's noses out of joint by performing for the Nazi overlords during the recent awkwardness . . .' He meant the war, Rowlands knew. 'She's tried to save face by pointing out that she also sang for prisoners of war in some of the German prison camps . . . but she was lucky, nonetheless, not to get pulled in by the authorities for collaborating with the enemy.'

This reminded Rowlands that they had not yet complied with Miss Barnes's suggestion that they should ask around about Amélie Mendl. He wondered who it would be best to approach – the club's manager, perhaps, or one of the 'hostesses' . . . Well, they'd have to wait until the first part of the performance was over – there'd be an interval, Loveless had said – before applying themselves to the task.

Although how were they to begin? All they had were a few fragmentary details – a name, a few dates, an image from a painting. Amélie Mendl had flitted through Paris like the ghost she had almost certainly become. She had spent a few months here or there – as seamstress, nightclub hostess, artist's model, political activist – before disappearing; only to reappear, at the tail-end of the war, in a German prison camp . . .

While he had been turning these elusive facts over in his mind, Gigi Gaspard's set had come to an end and, after the cheers and clapping had subsided, she withdrew from the stage. It was then that Rowlands turned to his companion. 'If we're going to make enquiries about Amélie Mendl, we'd better do it now.'

But Loveless's attention had been arrested by something, or someone, else. 'Well, bless my soul! I've always said that if you sit still for long enough in Paris, the whole world will pass by . . .'

Before Rowlands could ask him to explain, there came another voice – one he had heard only a few hours before – which made explanations unnecessary. 'Hello, Frederick. Enjoying the show? Marvellous, isn't she?'

'Good evening, Lady Celia.'

'Oh, don't get up! I only wanted to say hello – since we didn't have much time to chat at Gaby's . . . Hello, Loveless. It's a long time since *we* met . . .'

'Ten years. It was that ball at Dublin Castle. Very grand affair. God knows why they invited *me* . . .'

'But I'm being awfully rude,' said Celia Swift, ignoring this last remark. 'This is Major Cochrane. Nigel, these are some dear friends of mine. Frederick Rowlands . . .'

The two men shook hands, and murmured the usual pleasantries.

'And Percy Loveless – the artist, you know.'

'I believe I know your work,' said Cochrane. 'Didn't you paint that rather fine portrait of Miss Sitwell?'

'That *is* one of mine.' Loveless sounded gratified. 'Although I haven't done much in that line since before the war.'

'Pity. And you, Mr Rowlands – are you a painter, too?'

Rowlands smiled. 'I'm afraid painting's not within my capabilities,' he said. Of course, the lighting was subdued in here, so his blindness must not be obvious – but something told him that the affable Major Cochrane knew exactly who he was, and what he was doing there. More than that, Cochrane's voice was familiar. He racked his brains to remember when it was he had last heard it.

Ah, Rosalind – so you're back, are you? Now he had it! It had been in the lobby of the Hôtel Cécil, as he and Iris Barnes – or Rosalind, as she seemed to be known in some quarters – had been about to leave the building. They had passed two men in conversation, who'd just come in. This was one of them.

'I was saying to Rowlands here what a small place Paris is,' said Loveless. 'One can't turn around without seeing someone one knows.'

'Yes, but don't you think Paris has changed?' said Lady Celia. 'It's not the place it was before the war . . . I say, why don't you join us? Plenty of room at our table.' Rowlands had the feeling that Major Cochrane would have preferred to remain *tête-à-tête* – but he agreed with a good grace and all four took their seats at Lady Celia's table.

Polite enquiries were exchanged: Lady Celia asking after Rowlands's family – 'How is your wife? And your delightful daughters?' – while he returned the compliment, not without some trepidation, for the very fact of her being here in Paris, with a man who was not her husband, made questions as to the well-being or otherwise of the latter potentially awkward. But her response seemed untroubled: 'Ned? Oh, he's fine. When he isn't at horse fairs, bidding for hunters we can't afford, he's busy teaching our boy to ride. Wants him to go out with the hunt next season.' Which all sounded very like the Ned Swift (or Lord Castleford, to give him his proper title) Rowlands remembered from his first and only visit to Ireland six years before.

'I think we need another bottle of champagne,' said Lady Celia. 'I'm sure there's a reason to celebrate – if only meeting again, after so long.' It was as she was summoning the hostess that Rowlands decided that this would be as good an opportunity as any to ask about Amélie Mendl. So when the girl returned with the champagne and fresh glasses, he said, '*Excusez-moi, mademoiselle. Je voudrais parler au gérant.*' He hoped that was the right word.

'Rowlands,' said Loveless. 'I hardly think this is the right time . . .'

'If I know Frederick, he's got a good reason for summoning the manager,' said Lady Celia. 'Other than the fact that the champagne isn't chilled enough.'

After a brief interval, the man arrived, saying in perfect English, 'Monsieur wishes to see me?'

'That's right. I wonder if you can tell me anything about a young woman named Amélie Mendl. I believe she worked here, around two years ago.' As he'd said the name, it seemed to him that Major Cochrane, who was next to him at the round table, gave a start.

'Monsieur, I myself have only worked here for a year,' said the manager, adding, with what Rowlands guessed was a Gallic shrug, 'the girls, they come and go, you know. Sometimes they use a different name . . . for professional reasons, you understand? So she might have been here . . . she might not.'

'I see.' Rowlands felt a fool for not having thought of this possibility.

'Can monsieur describe her, this Amélie Mendl?' was the manager's next question. The manager's studied politeness stopped just short of irony – for after all, why would a middle-aged man be enquiring for a young woman, especially one who had worked as a nightclub hostess?

Feeling ever more foolish, Rowlands was about to admit that he could not, when Loveless said, 'Dark. Petite. Five foot three or four. Pretty. A dancer's figure – although perhaps not tall enough for the Moulin Rouge chorus.'

'That might describe any number of girls,' said the manager. 'But I will ask around. If monsieur would leave his card . . .'

'I'm at the Hôtel Cécil.' Again, Rowlands was conscious of a certain increased alertness on the part of his neighbour.

'Then I will telephone you there,' said the man. 'Now I must leave you. There are things I have to see to . . . Madame. Messieurs.'

In the same moment, the house lights dimmed – or so Rowlands surmised, from the accompanying buzz of conversation, which was instantly hushed, in anticipation of the singer's return to the stage.

'Well, well,' murmured Celia Swift. 'It seems that we're *all* busy looking for someone in Paris.'

Chapter Seven

When the show was over – or at least the part of it that interested Rowlands, for whom the prospect of rows of statuesque dancing girls, clad in little more than a few strategically placed sequins and feathers, held little allure – the various members of their little party made a move towards going their separate ways. For Loveless, this was just a matter of walking a few hundred yards to his hotel, he said. 'It's only down the hill. Not worth getting a taxi. Good to see you again, Celia. Nice meeting you, Cochrane. Night, Rowlands old man. I'm here for another week or two. Let's meet at the Deux Magots soon.'

Rowlands suspected that his friend's reluctance to reveal exactly where he was staying was partly his natural secretiveness and partly embarrassment. From past experience of Loveless's insalubrious 'digs', he guessed that the hotel where his friend was putting up would be a run-down, if not actually sordid, establishment.

Lady Celia, who was returning to the Hôtel Crillon, had no such compunction. As the cab drew up, she merely pressed Rowlands's hand, murmuring, 'You won't forget to come and see me, will you, Frederick? We've a lot to talk about . . .'

After a brisk, almost cursory, farewell to Major Cochrane (Loveless having taken his leave some minutes before), she got into the waiting taxi and was driven away.

'Well,' said Cochrane, as the sound of the taxi faded away. 'It looks as if you and I are going the same way, Mr Rowlands.' He must have summoned a cab, for one drew up alongside almost at once – the Moulin Rouge being a good spot for picking up custom, Rowlands supposed. 'Tell me,' he went on, as the two of them settled back on the taxi's hard leather seats, 'just what is your interest in Amélie Mendl?'

When Rowlands hesitated, uncertain how much he ought to say, the other man laughed. 'Oh, don't worry! I know all about her. You could say I'm in the confidence of the "fair Rosaline" . . .'

'Then you know as much as I do,' said Rowlands. 'All she . . . Miss . . . that is, Rosalind . . . asked me to do was to make some enquiries at the nightclub as to Miss Mendl's whereabouts – you saw with what success,' he added wryly. 'She seems to have vanished off the face of the earth.'

'Indeed. Cigarette?'

'Thanks, but . . .'

'They're American, not those terrible French gaspers.'

Rowlands smiled. 'Then I'll have one.'

Having lit the cigarette – a Lucky Strike – for him,

Cochrane said, almost casually, 'So you think the girl's dead, do you?' He was speaking in English, but Rowlands still felt a twinge of unease. 'It's all right, he can't hear us,' said Cochrane, meaning the taxi driver. 'Even if he could understand us, the glass panel's shut. We're quite safe.'

Rowlands wasn't so sure, but he said, 'I don't know. It's a strong possibility. Especially as . . .' Again, he broke off.

'Especially as her alter ego – Clara Metzner – is dead. Whoever killed one might well have disposed of the other.'

It was what Rowlands feared. 'Perhaps,' he said.

'You knew the Metzner girl in Berlin, I understand?' Cochrane's voice was carefully neutral.

'I did,' was the reply. 'But it was twelve years ago. She was still at school. And since I'd only the vaguest idea what she looked like at that time, it was impossible to tell if the woman I saw at Fresnes Prison was the same person or not.'

'You'd have been hard put to identify her, even if you *had* been able to see,' said Cochrane grimly. 'Most of the deportees returning from the camps are in terrible shape. Living skeletons. Some of them can barely stand up. She won't have looked anything like the comely *Fräulein* you recall . . . nor indeed, like anything human,' he added, as if to himself.

'I rather gathered that,' said Rowlands. He didn't say that his blindness didn't prevent him from noticing other things about the people he met – their height, build and state of health, for instance, could be gleaned from a single handshake. In the case of Clara Metzner – if that had indeed been who she was – this contact had been of the briefest. But other impressions – the sourness of her breath, and the dead tone of her voice – had told their own story. This was someone who, if not mortally ill, had been very close to death.

'There are of course other ways of identifying a person,' said Cochrane, as if picking up on this thought. 'Matters of detail. Facts of which they, and they alone, are in possession.'

'Yes. And in that respect, Miss Metzner was word-perfect. She correctly answered all the questions she was asked about her family – even quite specific things, such as the apartment floor they'd lived on.'

'But you weren't convinced,' said Major Cochrane.

'No. It all seemed too pat, somehow . . . as if she'd learnt it by rote. I wish now,' said Rowlands sadly, 'that I'd asked her more about herself. The Clara Metzner I knew was full of life and energy. The young woman I spoke to at Fresnes seemed half dead.'

'That's the impression a lot of these deportees give off, I'm afraid,' said Cochrane. 'Even though they're alive – just – it's as if their spirit has been killed . . .' He was silent a moment. 'I expect my fair colleague, Rosalind, has told you a little about our reasons for wanting to find this girl,' he went on, still in the same laconic tone.

Rowlands said guardedly that he'd been given a bare outline.

'A "bare outline" is pretty much all we ourselves have to go on,' laughed Cochrane. 'The fact is, the French have been so cagey about letting us have sight of the records the *Sécurité* confiscated from the Germans – records of SOE agents captured by the Gestapo – that we've very little information as to what happened to them.'

'Night and fog,' said Rowlands.

'What? Oh yes. Exactly that. And it's not just our now-defeated enemy that's created this "fog" . . . Between you and me, Mr Rowlands, it's all a part of de Gaulle's attempt to diminish the role that the SOE played in the liberation of France. He'd much prefer it to have been the French alone who liberated the country. *Our* contribution has been conveniently overlooked. Which is why it's been so hard to find out what happened to our missing agents . . . Ah, here's the Parc Monceau! Won't be long now. Do you know the park? One of the most charming in Paris, in my opinion. Luckily, it wasn't too knocked about by the German Army's using it as a training ground.'

A few moments later, the cab drew up in front of the Hôtel Cécil. 'I've enjoyed our talk, Mr Rowlands,' said the MI6 officer, as they got out of the car. 'You might not think it, but you've already helped us in eliminating certain possibilities. It's a never-ending process, tracking down the disappeared . . .'

The offices at the Hôtel Cécil were on the first floor, Rowlands recalled, from his visit the previous day. Here, the various branches of the Service – call it MI6 or SOE – were housed. The living quarters were on the floors above. As he and Cochrane mounted the stairs (the lift was again out of order, the major said) someone came to the door of one of the offices. 'So you're back at last,' said Iris Barnes. 'Was it a good evening?'

'Well . . .' began Rowlands.

'It depends what you mean by "good",' interjected Cochrane. 'Gigi Gaspard was on good form, as were the dancers. But Mr Rowlands here didn't get much change out of Lefevre, the manager.'

Rowlands said that this was true. 'The trouble is, I've so little to go on,' he added. 'All you've given me is a name. I can't even *describe* the girl with any accuracy. Hardly surprising that people aren't very forthcoming.'

It wasn't like him to be irritable, but it had been a long and tiring day – beginning with the return visit to Fresnes prison, and the dreadful discovery they'd made there – and continuing, over the hours that followed, with what seemed to him like layer upon layer of confusion, lies and half-truths. The visit to the young woman who'd found the body – what was her name again? She'd known something, he was sure. But like many of those who found themselves caught up in murder, she'd chosen to keep that knowledge to herself.

Then there'd been the absurd incongruity of the fashion show: the meeting with Gaby Bonheur, and with the woman who'd haunted Rowlands's dreams for close on twenty years . . . It seemed to him part of the strangeness of that encounter that he should meet Celia Swift for the second time that day, at the Moulin Rouge, after hearing little or nothing of her for six years. In between the first and second meeting had come the – to his mind – equally pointless meetings with the so-called Schweitzer 'family', and with Edgar Hathaway, and Hathaway's wife. None of it made any sense. 'I can't see,' Rowlands went on, unable to keep the bitterness out of his voice, 'that I've been any use at all.'

There was silence for a moment. 'Why don't you come into my office, both of you?' said Miss Barnes at last. 'We can't hang about here on the landing all night.' She closed the door behind them. 'You're wrong, you know,' she said to Rowlands. 'Isn't he, sir? I mean about being useless.'

'I tried to tell him on the way here,' replied the major. 'What you've got to understand, Rowlands, is that it's only by asking questions that one makes things happen.'

'Like poking a stick into a wasp's nest,' said Iris Barnes. 'Someone out there has the information we're looking for. The only way to get it is to keep asking questions – poking the wasp's nest.'

'Don't you risk getting stung?' said Rowlands.

'It's a risk we have to take.'

They lit cigarettes, and then Miss Barnes said, 'I've a bit of news relating to the case, as it happens. The post-mortem report came back this afternoon. It makes interesting reading.'

'How so?' asked Major Cochrane. 'I don't suppose there can be any doubt about the cause of death when it's a case of hanging.'

'None,' was the reply. 'Except it wasn't that which killed her.'

'Then what . . . ?'

'Heart failure. It appears she was dead before she was "strung up", if you'll excuse the vulgar phrase.'

'I don't follow.'

'There were bruises on her arms that indicated she'd been subjected to rough handling,' said Miss Barnes. 'None around her throat – apart from the marks left by the ligature – so she doesn't appear to have been strangled.' She paused; exhaled a mouthful of smoke. 'Some of the deportees – Clara Metzner was one – are in very poor condition, after what they've been through in the camps. Emaciated. Their vital organs close to collapse. All it would take would be to put them under the slightest physical or mental pressure to bring them to the point of death. That seems to have been the case here.'

'It sounds as if you're saying that she was *frightened* to death,' said Rowlands.

'That's just what I am saying.'

'So one might infer that her death was from natural causes?' said Cochrane, in the tone of one making an interesting discovery.

'One might. But you're forgetting that whoever brought about those "causes" also took pains to make the death look like suicide. Technicalities aside, it's still a case of murder.'

With the grim revelations echoing in his mind, Rowlands expected to be kept awake that night – but in the end the combination of exhaustion and the effects of the alcohol he'd drunk sent him into a deep, mercifully dreamless sleep. His last waking thought was that he must try to telephone Edith in the morning. When he'd last spoken to his wife, as he was setting off to catch the boat train two days before, he'd said that he hoped he wouldn't be detained longer than three days, at most. Already, this prediction was starting to look optimistic. Edith had always been remarkably forbearing where her husband's sleuthing activities were concerned, but even she had limits to her patience . . . *I'll call her tomorrow*, he thought drowsily, as he drifted into unconsciousness.

He was awakened at just before seven, according to his

Braille watch, by somebody banging on the door. '*M'sieur! M'sieur!*' It was Madame Boucher, the concierge – an elderly woman, who kept guard in a little glazed-in cubicle by the hotel's front entrance. Now she stood on the landing outside his door, wheezing a little from climbing the steep stairs to that part of the establishment. '*Monsieur, c'est pour vous au téléphone*,' she explained, when Rowlands, having stumbled out of bed and put on his dressing gown, answered this summons.

'Who's calling? I mean . . . *Qui est à l'appareil?*'

'*C'est une femme.*' More than this the concierge would not or could not say. As he followed her slipshod footsteps down the stairs, Rowlands could not suppress a feeling of alarm. What on earth could have possessed Edith – for he was sure the caller must be his wife – to have rung up so early? Had something happened to one of the girls?

Entering the concierge's room just behind Madame Boucher, he seized the telephone receiver, which had been left dangling off the hook. 'Edith? Is anything wrong?'

There was a startled pause at the end of the line; then a voice he'd heard before but couldn't at once place said, '*M'sieur? Etes-vous l'Anglais?*'

He confirmed that he was. 'Who am I speaking to?'

'*C'est moi.* Claire Hubert.' The cleaner from Fresnes prison. Rowlands knew the voice now.

'What can I do for you, mam'selle?' he said, when the girl seemed to hesitate.

'I saw 'im,' she said bluntly, in her colloquial French. 'The man you *said* I might've seen . . .'

'Was this at the prison?'

'I'm telling you, aren't I? There was just this bloke,

wasn't there? Hanging about on the landing . . .' She lowered her voice, as if afraid of being overheard. 'It was that day . . . the day she was found . . . that girl . . .'

He knew it was Clara Metzner she meant.

'What time was this?'

''Bout five. I'd jus' started work. Saw 'im ducking into one of the doorways, like 'e didn't want to be seen . . .'

'And you'd never seen him at Fresnes before?'

'Not as far as I know.'

'Can you describe him?'

'Might be able to . . . Look, I can't talk now. *She's* prowling around.' She meant the directress, Madame Bodin, he guessed. 'I'll come to the hotel.'

'When?'

'I finish work at nine. I'll come then.'

'So . . . ten o'clock?' he said. But she'd already hung up.

The concierge, who made no secret of the fact that she'd been eavesdropping, said, '*Elle m'a demandé si l'Anglais était la. C'est vous, n'est pas, m'sieur?*'

'Oh yes,' said Rowlands. 'That's me.' Because even though he wasn't the only Englishman at the Hôtel Cécil, he was the one Claire Hubert had evidently selected as her confidant.

'So she asked for you?' said Iris Barnes, in an amused tone. 'You seem to have made an impression.' An hour had passed since the telephone call. Rowlands and the MI6 officer were sitting opposite one another in a café across the street from the hotel. 'Either that, or she took a dislike to *me*,' she went on. 'Not that it matters – the important thing is that she's owned up to seeing this man. I don't suppose she gave you a description?'

'No.'

'Pity. But it'll keep until she gets here. Ten o'clock, you said?'

'Or thereafter. She finishes work at nine.'

'It shouldn't take her more than an hour to get here by train and bus. Say a quarter past ten, at the latest.' She pushed aside her coffee cup. 'Unfortunately, I have to be elsewhere. But I'm sure you'll manage admirably without me. In fact, it'll be an advantage, my not being there. You've obviously a way with impressionable young females.'

'I've got daughters,' he said. 'That's all.'

'No need to take offence! It's a great skill, getting people to talk – one from which our organisation could benefit. Although we sometimes employ cruder methods for getting the same result.'

Iris Barnes got to her feet. 'I'll leave you to it,' she said, adding vaguely, 'There's not much doing until this evening, so you can amuse yourself for a while, after you've spoken to our young friend. I'll be back around lunchtime. Good luck with the interrogation.' Which was her idea of a joke, Rowlands supposed.

When she had left, Rowlands ordered another coffee and smoked a cigarette. From around him, in the quiet café, came sounds of those, like himself, who were idling away half an hour or so over the newspapers or a restorative glass of cognac. Men about to start work or those who'd just come off the night shift. There were no English voices.

He let his thoughts drift for a few moments, savouring the feeling of being there, in Paris, on a fine spring morning.

He could feel the sun warming his face, as it slanted under the awning that shaded the front of the café. The smells of tobacco and coffee were agreeable – as were the sounds coming in from the street: the whistling of an errand boy; the cheerful salutations of one shopkeeper to another, as they opened up their premises in readiness for the day's custom.

It seemed a bleak denial of all this benign activity that his presence there had been brought about by murder. Its dark stain seemed to colour everything: the quiet café, the whistling youth, the sparrows quarrelling on the pavement . . . But this was morbid stuff. Edith would have scolded him. The thought was a reminder that he had yet to telephone her. He finished his coffee and cigarette and went to do so.

It was Mrs Collins who connected his call to England. He'd asked Iris Barnes that morning if it would be all right to telephone his wife, and she'd agreed at once – 'I was about to suggest it . . .' – adding that he had better make the call from her office, as it was a better line and there'd be less chance of the concierge listening in. 'She's a nice old thing, but she will *hover*.' He'd already had evidence of this. And so he waited in the outer office, while the secretary made the necessary arrangements, remembering how, when he'd worked as a switchboard operator, calls to foreign countries, and even the remoter parts of the British Isles, could take several hours to connect.

To his surprise, no more than twenty minutes elapsed after he had put in the request before Mrs Collins put her head around the connecting door to say that the call was through. 'Thank you,' he said. 'You've been very quick.'

The young woman muttered something he didn't quite catch as she slipped past him into the outer office, pulling the glass door shut behind her. A moment later, as he picked up the receiver from Miss Barnes's desk, the sound of typing could be heard as she resumed whatever task she had been doing when he interrupted her with his request.

Edith didn't sound all that surprised to hear that his stay in Paris might have to be extended for another few days. 'I thought you were being a bit optimistic,' she said. It astonished him how clear her voice sounded over the line. She might have been standing next to him. 'What's the reason for the delay – or can't you say?'

'Rather not, old thing. But I can tell you that the news isn't good.'

'Oh dear. I'm sorry to hear it. Will Walter have to be told?'

'He's on his way. The news'll keep till he gets here. Edith, I can't talk for long . . .'

'Of course not. This must be costing you a fortune.'

'Don't worry about that. Everyone there's well, I hope?'

'Yes, we're all fine.'

'Good. I'll see you soon, all right?'

'Look after yourself, Fred.'

Then she was gone.

He checked his watch: a quarter to ten. Still plenty of time. 'Thank you,' he said again, having replaced the receiver in its cradle, and quitted the inner office. 'I've finished now.'

'I hope your call was satisfactory?' said Louise Collins.

'Entirely, thank you. Well, I'll leave you in peace.'

He descended the stairs and took a seat in the lobby to await his visitor.

Ten o'clock came and went. Thinking about it, Rowlands wasn't unduly put out. Fresnes was a good hour's journey by car. Getting to central Paris by train and bus or metro would be bound to take a good deal longer – even if there were no actual hold-ups. Trains cancelled. Buses delayed. It wasn't reasonable to expect Claire Hubert until at least half past.

It was an hour later than that before he was forced to admit that she wasn't coming. He'd smoked three more cigarettes and had walked up and down the pavement outside the hotel several times before it became obvious that she must have changed her mind. Either that, he told himself, or something else had happened to prevent her from carrying out her intention. He didn't let himself think too deeply about what this might have been.

It was ten past twelve when a taxi drew up in front of the hotel and Iris Barnes got out. 'I wondered if you'd still be here,' she said. 'You realise she isn't coming?'

'I suspected as much.'

She walked past him, through the glass doors of the hotel and into the lobby. As she started up the stairs she said to him, over her shoulder, 'A young woman's body was recovered from the line at Kléber metro station, two hours ago. They've taken her to the mortuary at the Hôtel-Dieu. I thought we'd go there after lunch. The post-mortem's at two. I was at the Quai d'Orfèvres when the news came in.'

Rowlands knew it was the headquarters of the Police Judiciaire de Paris to which she referred. 'Ah, Louise, do you have those letters for me to sign?' she said, as they reached the office. 'I've just time before Mr Rowlands and I have to go to the Hôtel-Dieu.'

'Yes, madame,' replied the secretary, in her clear, colourless voice. 'The letter to the minister is on top. And just to remind you that you are expected at the Paris Studios any time from five o'clock.'

'Thank you, Louise. Knowing your interest in cinema, Fred,' said Miss Barnes, 'I thought you might enjoy a visit to the Billancourt studios. Of course, they're not as grand as the ones at Babelsberg,' she added. The allusion was to the celebrated Berlin film studios which she and Rowlands had visited, twelve years before. It had been during the same visit that he had first become acquainted with the Metzner family. Clara's elder brother, Joachim, had worked at the studios as a runner; her younger brother, Walter, had been a dedicated film fan – a predilection that had almost cost him his life.

Thinking about Walter, now a fully qualified medical officer serving with the Royal Navy in South Africa, Rowlands wondered how much longer it would be before he arrived in Paris, to be confronted with the news of his sister's death.

He became aware that Miss Barnes was saying something. '. . . on second thoughts, I think we'll forgo lunch until after the post-mortem. It might not be the pleasantest of experiences.'

He'd had the same thought. It didn't take much imagination to work out that the injuries sustained by someone hit by a metro train would be horrific. Even though he would, perforce, be spared the sight of them, it would be bad enough hearing them described.

Chapter Eight

It was a twenty-minute drive from the Hôtel Cécil to the Île de la Cité, where the hospital was situated, diagonally opposite Notre-Dame Cathedral. At Miss Barnes's instruction, the driver dropped them off near the Pont d'Arcole, leaving them to make their own way onto the island. 'We've over an hour before we have to be there,' she said. 'Time for some Dutch courage. I know a bar nearby.'

As they took their seats in the cramped little *boîte*, Rowlands asked the question that had been troubling him ever since she'd told him the news about Claire Hubert. 'How did you know it was her?'

'Her *carte d'identité* was in her shoulder bag. *That* wasn't damaged. But the police will need a formal identification.'

'Who will they get to identify her?'

'Her next of kin, presumably.' That would be her mother, he supposed. His imagination baulked at the thought. 'Unless of course's she's mutilated beyond recognition,' Iris Barnes went on. 'In which case, they'll have to rely on other methods, such as dental records.'

Rowlands sipped his cognac. 'I can't help feeling that I'm to blame,' he said. 'If she hadn't been coming to see me, this would never have happened.'

'I wouldn't bet on it,' was the reply. 'If she was close enough to identify the man she saw at Fresnes, there's a good chance he saw her, too. They'd have tracked her down, sooner or later.'

'"They"?'

'The people we're up against. You didn't think – just because the Germans have gone – that the war's over?'

The Hôtel-Dieu, built on the site of a ninth-century religious foundation, and renovated during Haussmann's rebuilding of Paris, still retained a monastic atmosphere, thought Rowlands, as he and his companion were conducted along what seemed like miles of stone-floored corridors and down staircases that led to yet more corridors. Here, the pleasanter smells of the city – spring flowers in the window boxes, fresh bread from the little bakery they'd passed on the way; even the eternal smell of cigarettes – were obliterated by the pervasive hospital smell. A medicinal smell, not quite overlaying the grosser smells of mortality.

At length they reached a basement floor, where the hospital morgue was to be found. Of the spring sunshine, which had given an unseasonable warmth to the air, as they made their way through the narrow seventeenth-century streets of this most ancient part of Paris, not a vestige penetrated the thick walls of the Hôtel-Dieu. It was as if the presence of death had cast its cold shadow over the place.

'Wait here,' said Iris Barnes, as they reached the morgue at last. 'I'll just have a word with the pathologist.'

As he waited, nervously tapping his foot, Rowlands felt as if the chill of the stone floor had seeped up into his very bones. He would have liked a smoke, but thought that this might seem disrespectful – if not actually callous – and so restrained himself. After a few moments had elapsed, he became aware of two people approaching along the corridor down which he and Miss Barnes had come. One of the voices – a man's – was unfamiliar to him; the other was not.

'Where is she?' It was Madame Hubert. 'Where's my Claire? I want to see her.'

'All in good time,' said the man – perhaps a junior police officer – in a soothing tone. 'Now you just wait here, and I'll go and find the doctor to come and talk to you.'

'But . . .' protested Madame Hubert, as the policeman hurried off to carry out this mission. In the same moment, she recognised Rowlands. 'You're the man that come to our flat, with that woman,' she said.

'Yes. I'm so sorry about your daughter . . .'

'She was worried about something, was our Claire. It was after you was there, that day – you and that woman. "I've got to tell 'em what I know, Mum," she says. "It's only right." Now she's dead, they tell me – and all for trying to do the right thing.'

There was nothing he could say that would make a difference, and so he said nothing.

Just then, the rubber doors of the morgue flapped open, and Miss Barnes came out. 'It's her all right,' she said, apparently oblivious of the presence of the other woman. 'Her face isn't damaged, and so—'

'You'll remember Madame Hubert,' Rowlands cut across her.

'Oh. Yes, of course.'

'I remember *you*,' said Madame Hubert. 'If it hadn't been for *you*, my girl'd be alive today.'

It was a fifteen-minute drive from the centre of Paris to the Paris Studios at Billancourt – a journey that, by late afternoon, took them appreciably longer than that. So it was just on five o'clock when the Citroën pulled into the parking lot behind the studio buildings. These, said Iris Barnes, had originally been constructed as part of a factory to build aircraft cabins, and so were immense in scale. 'You could get a mock-up of the Colosseum under one of those roofs quite easily,' she said. 'Or a scale model of Montmartre. I believe it's been done, in both cases.'

Having announced themselves at the gate, they waited in the little lodge to one side of it while the gatekeeper made the necessary telephone call. Ten minutes passed. Rowlands, still preoccupied with the troubling events of the past few hours, paid little attention to what was going on around in this new setting, even though its details would, under different circumstances, have been of considerable interest to him.

So the comings and goings of studio technicians as well as those who were actively engaged – whether as actors, directors or producers – in making whatever films were being made here failed to engage his attention, caught up as he was in thoughts of the grim half-hour in the hospital morgue, and his last encounter (if you could call it that) with Claire Hubert. He recalled with a shudder the moment when the pathologist had raised the sheet, disclosing the dead girl's face, because it was then that Madame Hubert had said calmly, 'Yes, that's her. That's my girl.'

Nor was this the worst moment, as far as Rowlands was concerned. Ushered out of the dreadful room by the young policeman who had brought her there ('Come along now, Mother. Let's get you home . . .'), Madame Hubert had paused on the threshold. 'I don't blame you, you know,' she said, addressing Rowlands – or so it seemed to him. 'You was just doing your job. Same as my Claire was doing hers.'

'Of course, the Germans ran this place until a few months ago,' Miss Barnes was saying. 'Apparently Goebbels himself took an interest. You'll know all about *that*, I imagine?'

'What? Oh yes.' She was referring to those days they'd spent at the Berlin film studios in 1933 – Iris Barnes had been there in the guise of a journalist for one of the film magazines, while Rowlands had, to his own surprise, been conscripted as an 'extra'. . . And yes, Joseph Goebbels, Hitler's Minister for Propaganda, had indeed taken an interest in film – and film actresses . . . Rowlands shook himself out of his low mood. There was no sense in brooding about what couldn't be undone. Evidently his companion had found a way not to brood. 'I imagine that it would have been hard to keep him away,' he said. 'The combination of Paris and Parisiennes being a potent one.'

'Yes, it was he who set up the film company – it was called Continental, in those days,' said Miss Barnes. 'They produced over thirty films, starring some of France's favourite stars. Denise Delacourt was one. Constance Lumière another. Then there was poor Annette . . .' This, Rowlands vaguely recalled, was one of the actresses who had been put on trial for allegedly giving aid and comfort to the enemy. 'She was especially unwise in losing her head to a handsome officer of the Luftwaffe, ten years her junior. The others could get away with saying that *their* collaboration had been merely artistic. Hers was of the *horizontale* kind – unfortunately for her . . . Ah, here we are, at last.'

Because at that moment, a man came hurrying up to them. 'Madame. Monsieur. A thousand apologies for keeping you waiting. Maurice Laval at your service.'

This, Rowlands supposed, must be the studio manager or some other administrator – so he was surprised when Laval, leading the way towards the entrance of the main building, said, 'I am honoured that you wish to see my poor little film. Not that I can claim any artistic credit for *Eurydice*, you understand? I am merely the poor producer, who sees to all the less important but still useful details, such as making sure the whole thing comes in on time, and under budget . . .'

They entered what Rowlands guessed was a large atrium, beyond which a set of double doors led into a still larger space. This was instantly perceptible to him from the echo of the voices and other sounds that came towards them, and by the sensation of a large volume of air above his head. Shouts of 'Take care with the set, you idiot!' and

'Move that camera, can't you?' awakened memories for Rowlands of that long-ago time in Berlin, when he had (albeit briefly) experienced the thrill of making a film . . . 'They're just setting up in here,' explained Laval. 'A new picture, starring Camille Cambronne. Jean-Marie Rodin is directing.'

Iris Barnes gave a non-committal murmur; but Rowlands said, 'Are there many films in production at present, then?'

'Oh, six at least. There's a huge public appetite for cinema, now that things are more or less back to normal,' was the reply. 'Of course, we can't compete with Hollywood – the latest Donna Delaney vehicle was playing to full theatres in the first week – but we've enough homegrown stars to be able to offer some pretty decent competition . . . In here,' he added, as they came to a door on the far side of the giant studio. 'We shouldn't be disturbed.'

From the sudden diminution in the level of sound, Rowlands guessed that this must be a screening room – a supposition confirmed when the producer said, 'Take a seat wherever you like. It'll just be ourselves. It's not a film that's attracted a lot of interest – except from the Left Bank crowd . . . and that's because a lot of them are *in* it, if only as extras! All right, Paul . . .' This was to the projectionist. 'You can start the reel.'

With that, there came a whirring sound, familiar to Rowlands, as the film began to play. He supposed from the title that it must be a version of the Orpheus and Eurydice myth, but with a contemporary setting, if Laval's comment about the Left Bank extras was anything to go by. Not that he himself would be able to identify either the main players or any of the supporting cast, but it was helpful to know what kind of entertainment was in store. The music on the soundtrack was one guide: it was modern jazz.

'The first scene's set in Montmartre,' said Miss Barnes, in Rowlands's ear. 'The Artists' Café – or a mock-up of it. I imagine that the handsome brute in the blue jeans and paint-stained sweater must be Julien Corbeau's idea of Orpheus . . . Oh, Corbeau wrote and directed the thing,' she added. 'The actor playing Orpheus is his current "friend".' The last word was said with an ironic emphasis. 'But it's Eurydice – or rather, the actress who's playing her – I'm interested in. I wonder if she'll have any lines . . . or whether her presence will be as fleeting as her part in the original tale.'

And certainly the scene in the Montmartre café was dominated by masculine voices. These belonged to the artist, Orpheus, and his friends, who were also artists, to judge from the ensuing badinage. Rowlands's command of idiomatic French was just about good enough to follow what was being said:

'*Tu bosses sur quoi en ce moment?*'

'*Bof, pas grand-chose.*'

'*Et le portrait, alors?*'

'*J'ai laissé tomber.*'

'*Tu te fous de moi.*'

'Orpheus' had a good voice, thought Rowlands – it was deep and resonant. The voice of the actor playing his friend was less sonorous, but somehow more expressive. A voice for comedy rather than tragedy, perhaps. Now their conversation veered into a series of salacious jokes Rowlands couldn't follow – the abandoned portrait possibly standing in for the girl who'd been its subject . . .

Into this scurrilous cross-talk came sounds of a harsher nature – shouts and running footsteps; the beating of a drum. In the next moment, the café was invaded by another group – this one with violence in mind. Sounds of breaking glass, of furniture being overturned and of blows being struck, mingled with the cries of pain of those on the receiving end of the blows. Over this cacophony, there arose a single word, screamed by one of the agitators:

'*Traître!*'

It was a woman's voice.

'Ah, now it gets interesting,' murmured Iris Barnes. 'If I'm not mistaken, this is our Eurydice.'

And indeed this was confirmed a moment later when Orpheus, still panting from the rough and tumble, cried, in despairing tones, '*Non! Ce n'est pas vrai, Eurydice!*'

To which the eponymous heroine's only reply was a mocking laugh.

Then she was gone – or so Rowlands surmised, because at that moment Miss Barnes said, 'Stop the film. I'd like you to wind back a few frames, if you will – to where Eurydice enters . . . unless she's to appear again any time soon?'

'Not until the end of the reel – by which time she's dead,' replied Maurice Laval. He gave an order to the projectionist to wind back the film. 'What's your interest in the girl, anyway?' he said, while this was being done.

'I'm trying to trace her. I suppose you've no idea what became of her after this?'

'None. She's not a proper actress, you know – just one of Corbeau's hangers-on. He liked the look of her, I suppose, and decided to use her in the part. She doesn't have more than a line or two in the whole film. Just as well, because it put some of the real actors' noses out of joint – the fact that we were using someone with no acting experience.'

'When did she first appear?'

'I can't remember exactly. It must have been a couple of years ago – April or May of '43. She was just there one day, during filming. She did her bit, we paid her, and then she left. Why? Who is she?'

'Her name's Amélie Mendl. Your film gives us the best image we've got of her so far – at least of the way she looked until about six months ago.'

'Why, what happened to her six months ago?'

'Ravensbrück,' said Miss Barnes succinctly.

The producer shuddered. 'Christ. What a world.'

'Indeed. Run the film again, will you, from just before Eurydice's entrance? And then freeze it. I want to get a good look at her, to make sure it's the same girl.'

Chapter Nine

'I think we're making progress,' said Iris Barnes. They were back in her office; the sounds of a typewriter being vigorously put through its paces by the industrious Mrs Collins came through from the outer office.

Rowlands waited. It didn't seem to *him* that they had got very much further in their quest for Amélie Mendl. For the past few days they had pursued her phantom across Paris, and had talked to some of the people whose paths had crossed with hers. But of the knowledge that had got her killed, he and the MI6 officer had discovered nothing. 'We know she worked at Bonheur Modes from the spring of 1938 until the shop was closed the following autumn,' Miss Barnes went on. 'We can assume she changed her name, before getting a job as a waitress at the Moulin Rouge. During this time she attracted the attention of Diego Ruiz, and sat for her portrait sometime in 1941. She also frequented the Café de Flore around the same time – say, late '41 until early '42 – and was cast as

Eurydice in Corbeau's film the following year.'

She lit a cigarette and took a few drags before continuing, 'Shortly after the film was made – and before it was released – she disappeared. The next we hear of her, she is in Ravensbrück, where she meets Clara Metzner. What happened to her after that we heard from Clara herself, at Fresnes . . .'

'You mean that Amélie died in the camp?'

'If it *was* her.'

'I thought you said it was the same girl . . . the one in the film.'

'I merely assumed it. Without confirming documents – a passport or identity card – there's no proof it was her. Diego's portrait, wonderful as it is, is hardly a photographic likeness. As for our Eurydice, well it might have been Amélie Mendl, or it might not.'

'Are you saying it was actually Clara?'

'It could just as easily have been her. One pretty, dark-haired girl looks much like another . . . Yes, Louise, what is it?'

The secretary now stood in the doorway. 'I am sorry to interrupt, madame, but there is a telephone call for monsieur . . .'

'For me?' said Rowlands, wondering who it could be. Nobody apart from Edith knew where he was staying – and he hadn't given her the number of the hotel. '*Oui, m'sieur*,' was the reply. 'It was the English gentleman the lady asked for.'

Mystified, Rowlands followed Louise Collins into the outer office. The telephone receiver lay on the desk beside the instrument on which it rested when not in use. He picked it up. 'Hello? Frederick Rowlands speaking.'

'Oh, good. It *is* you. I wondered at first if I'd got the wrong Hôtel Cécil . . .'

'Lady Celia.' He was conscious of the secretary hovering nearby, and so kept his tone neutral. 'What can I do for you?'

The answer was a soft laugh. 'Why, what you've always done – which is to solve a problem for me. I'd hoped you would have come to the hotel before now, but I suppose you've been busy.'

'I . . .'

'No need to explain! I promise not to *interrogate* you about what you've been up to – you and the formidable Miss Barry . . .' For a moment he wondered who it was she meant, and then remembered that 'Rosalind Barry' had been the name Iris Barnes had employed during their visit to Bonheur Modes. 'I'd be delighted for you *both* to join me this evening, if you will . . . I thought an early dinner: say, seven o'clock? We've got theatre tickets for eight-thirty, but that should give us time to chat before we have to leave.'

He supposed that 'we' referred to herself and Major Cochrane.

'All right. But . . .'

'Ask for me at the desk,' said Lady Celia. 'Tell them I said you're to come straight up. My suite's on the second floor. We'll have dinner there. And don't bother about dressing. It's all terribly informal these days, as I'm sure you've found. Till seven, then.' Before he could ask her where it was they were to meet, she had rung off.

* * *

117

'It'll be the Crillon,' said Miss Barnes, when he passed on Lady Celia's invitation. 'It's where she always stays, isn't it? And no, I won't be joining you for dinner. It's you she wants to see. I've some things I need to do, as it happens.'

So, as the taxi dropped him in front of the famous hotel, Rowlands found himself on his own for the first time in Paris. Had he been left to his own devices, it might have been a moment to savour; as it was, mingled excitement at the thought of seeing her and trepidation as to what Lady Celia might ask of him overlaid any feeling of ease. He was glad he'd thought to arrive a few minutes early – glad, too, that (despite what she'd said) he'd taken the trouble to wear evening dress. It meant that he felt less like a fish out of water as he stood at the desk, waiting for the hotel manager to pay him some attention, while taking in the sounds of people coming and going around him.

'Oh my *dear*,' he heard one woman say to another, as both wafted past in an aura of perfume and rustling silks. 'They've lost *everything*, poor darlings. Now they sit there in that enormous house in the Rue de Rome, dining off boiled turnips, served on cracked Sèvres plates . . .'

'Good to be back in Paris, what?' said another voice – a man's, redolent of cigars and Scotch whisky. 'Not what it was, though, is it? No *style* . . .'

There was someone in front of Rowlands – a young woman – who seemed to be having difficulty persuading the manager of something.

'Please . . . it's important . . .'

'I've told you – deliveries must be taken to the trade entrance,' he was saying impatiently. 'The porter will show you where to go.'

'But Madame said I was to bring it straight to milady!'
The speaker sounded close to tears. Something about
her voice struck Rowlands as familiar . . . Yes. It was the
seamstress he and Iris Barnes had met at Bonheur Modes.
The one who'd known Amélie Mendl.

'Perhaps I can help?' he said, stepping forward. 'It's
Miss Dubois, isn't it?'

'Oh!' Sylvie Dubois seemed to notice him for the first
time. 'You are the Englishman – the friend of milady.'

'That's right,' he said. 'Now, what seems to be the
trouble?'

'It is milady's dress,' she explained in a rush. 'Madame
gave me instructions to deliver it into milady's hands. It is
for her to wear tonight,' she added. 'They are going to the
Comédie-Française . . .' As she was speaking, she laid what
Rowlands guessed was a large cardboard box containing
the dress on the desk in front of them.

At once the manager protested. 'I tell you, you cannot
leave that here! You must take it around to the side door.'

'Miss Dubois has explained why that is impossible,'
said Rowlands firmly. 'Her employer, Madame Bonheur,
wishes her to give it into the hands of the lady who is to
wear it – Lady Celia Swift.'

The mention of both names seemed to have the desired
effect, for the man muttered something about ringing
milady's room to see if she wished the dress-box to be
brought up by one of the pages. 'No need,' said Rowlands.
'I will be meeting Lady Celia myself in a few minutes. I can
take charge of the dress.'

Having made this arrangement to everybody's
satisfaction, Rowlands decided that the opportunity of

having a quiet word with Sylvie Dubois was too good to miss. 'Let's sit down for a moment, shall we?' he said quietly. 'There's something I want to ask you.'

'I have to get back. They . . . they will miss me.'

'What I have to say won't take long.'

'All right.'

There was a semicircle of armchairs on the far side of the lobby. Having ascertained that there was nobody sitting near enough to overhear them, Rowlands ushered Sylvie Dubois towards one of these and seated himself in another. 'You remember when we met, yesterday, that my friend, Miss Barry, asked you about Amélie Mendl?'

'*Oui, m'sieur.*' She sounded wary. 'I remember.'

'I got the impression that you knew Miss Mendl rather better than you said.' He was conscious of choosing his words carefully, not wanting to scare her off.

'I . . .' She hesitated; then seemed to come to a decision. 'She was my friend. We . . . we used to meet sometimes, after work. When we lost our jobs . . . I mean, when the shop was closed . . . we continued to meet.'

'When was this?'

'Oh . . . I don't know exactly. Three years ago, perhaps. We couldn't meet very often because she . . . Amélie . . . had to be careful. Being Jewish, you see. It was dangerous for her. Even after she changed her name, it was still dangerous.'

'When was this – that she changed her name, I mean?'

'Perhaps two years ago? She'd started working at the Moulin Rouge . . . serving drinks. They wouldn't have hired a Jew. Too many German Army officers went there.'

'Can you remember what name she used?'

She thought for a moment. 'Adèle. That was it. Adèle Morisot.'

'And you continued to meet, after she started working there?'

'Yes. We'd meet after she finished her shift. One night, she didn't turn up. I called in at the place, but they said she'd left. I never saw her again . . .' She hesitated. 'At least, not there.'

'Then you *did* see her again?'

Once more, the young woman hesitated, as if afraid she had said too much. 'I don't suppose it matters now,' she said. 'It was in the street – off the Boul' Mich'. . . She was with some people I didn't know. Two men and a woman. She'd cut her hair, but I recognised her, just the same . . .'

Rowlands said nothing, guessing there was more to come.

'I think they were *Résistance*, the people she was with,' said Sylvie Dubois. 'You got to recognise the type. They dressed like students, except they *weren't* students, if you know what I mean?'

Rowlands said that he did.

'There was one of them – a tall man, with red hair. He had his arm around Amélie. They went into a café. After that, I never saw her again.' She was silent for a moment. 'Do you think something bad has happened to her?' she said at last.

'I don't know. We're still trying to find out . . .'

'You and that woman you were with at Rue Cambon? The one in the chic grey costume?'

'Yes,' said Rowlands; adding with a smile, 'Although I couldn't tell you what she was wearing.'

121

'You're blind, aren't you?' she replied gravely. 'I didn't notice it at first. I had an uncle who was blinded in the Great War. At Verdun. He used to teach me card tricks. I never understood how he could tell which card was which, without being able to see them . . .'

Rowlands smiled to himself. Louis Braille's invention, which had stood Rowlands in good stead when it came to playing bridge, had evidently served a similar purpose here.

Suddenly, his young companion seemed to become aware of the time. 'I must go,' she said, jumping to her feet. 'They will be angry if I am late back.'

'Oh?'

'I have a room in the attic at Rue Cambon,' she explained. 'Madame has provided lodgings for those of her workers, like me, who have come to Paris from the country. It is much cheaper for us . . .' It also meant that the said employees were always available for extra jobs – such as delivering a dress to a client after hours, thought Rowlands. In the circumstances, he thought it was the least he could do to offer to pay her taxi fare – but she refused, saying she preferred to walk. 'It is not far. I like being out on these light evenings. Paris is so beautiful, isn't it?'

He agreed that it was, and having taken charge of the dress-box, bade her goodbye. It crossed his mind to tell her to take care – mindful of the terrible fate that had befallen Claire Hubert. But he told himself that nobody knew of his meeting with Sylvie Dubois, so she was probably safe enough. And it had been well worth talking to her – if only to learn the name Amélie Mendl had adopted during her last months of freedom.

'Monsieur!' It was the hotel manager. 'Milady has telephoned to ask you to go up. It is Suite 12, on the second floor. This boy will conduct you there.' With which he clicked his fingers to summon the pageboy; the latter relieved Rowlands of the dress-box and led the way to the bank of lifts.

'So, Frederick, I've got you to myself at last,' said Lady Celia, as the two of them sipped their drinks – whisky for him, champagne for her – in her private sitting room. They were alone, apart from her ladyship's maid, Hortense, who was busy in the next room hanging up the new evening gown, in readiness for helping her mistress to dress. 'Yes, this takes me back,' Celia Swift went on, 'to that time we were together in Dublin – do you remember?'

Of course he remembered. It had been six years since he and the woman who now sat opposite him had caught the Liverpool ferry to Dublin's North Quay, and had then been driven to the Swifts' townhouse in Merrion Square – yet it was as fresh in his memory as if it had been yesterday . . . 'You came to me *then* because I asked for your help,' she said. 'Now I need your help again.'

Rowlands waited, knowing she would explain in her own time. On the occasion referred to, when she'd brought him to her Dublin home, it had been in order to save a life; he guessed the reason for the summons today would be no less urgent. As he leant back on the comfortable sofa that stood at right angles to the one on which Lady Celia herself reclined, he thought of the years since he'd first met her, and of the times he'd tried to be of service to her. Once, teasingly, she'd called him her '*cavalier servante*'.

Well, it was true enough. He'd never expected anything in return – least of all her love. It was enough to know that she needed him.

'But we'll talk when we've dined,' she was saying. Because at that moment, a soft tap on the door announced the arrival of the waiter with the supper trolley, and, at Lady Celia's suggestion, she and her guest moved to the table in the alcove that was laid ready. 'I hope you like poached salmon,' she said, as the waiter took the covers off the dishes. 'No, leave it. I'll serve us,' she told this functionary, who then removed himself from the room.

The next few minutes passed in the agreeable business of consuming the meal, and the fine Chablis by which it was accompanied. Rowlands found to his surprise that he was hungry. He made short work of his plateful. His companion, he suspected, would merely toy with her food – pushing the plate away with most of it untasted.

When he'd eaten as much as he wanted, she touched a bell, and the maid appeared. 'You can get them to clear these things away,' she said. 'Mr Rowlands and I will be in my dressing room. I don't want to be disturbed for the next few minutes.'

'Milady.'

In the little boudoir next to the bedroom, she lit them both cigarettes. 'Another whisky?'

'I'll finish this wine, thanks.'

'As you wish.' She drew in a mouthful of smoke and then slowly exhaled. 'You'll remember a boy called Sebastian Gogarty?'

It was not what he'd expected. 'The young fellow who was cataloguing the library at Castleford?'

'That's the one. He had a bit of a crush on me, as you may recall.'

Rowlands did. The lad had made a perfect fool of himself, in his opinion. Not that he'd been the only one to lose his head over the beautiful Celia Swift, he reminded himself. 'Wasn't he going to join the RAF?' he said, casting his mind back to the last time he'd met Gogarty, when the young man – disappointed in love, and no doubt feeling thoroughly hard done by – had announced this intention.

'He was. And it's *because* of that that I'm asking for your help now. Sebastian Gogarty joined up in early 1940. Six months later, his plane was shot down over Germany. He's been a prisoner of war all this time.'

'How did you find out what had happened to him?'

'He wrote to me. They're allowed to have letters and parcels – through the Red Cross. He simply addressed the letters to "Mrs C. M. Swift, Castleford". Of course I wrote back,' she said.

Rowlands could see the rightness of that. It would have been a humane duty. 'And now?' he said. 'Hasn't he been released?'

'That's just it. He's disappeared. My last couple of letters were returned unopened. That was four months ago. I've heard nothing since.'

It struck Rowlands that there might be a reason for the silence – and not a good one – but he said nothing.

'I want you to find him,' said Lady Celia. 'I feel responsible for him, you see. If it hadn't been for me, he'd never have joined the RAF in the first place . . .'

'He might have done so anyway. I seem to recall that he felt strongly about doing his bit,' said Rowlands. 'For which I admired him.' Especially, he thought but didn't say, because Gogarty's native land had chosen to remain neutral during the war that had just ended.

'Oh, I know all that! But I feel to blame anyway. The poor boy had no one else to turn to, since his parents were dead.'

And he was in love with you, thought Rowlands, with a stab of pity for the unfortunate youth. 'What exactly do you want me to do?' he said.

'Well, *find* him,' she said, as if it were obvious. 'From the little we've been able to glean, it seems he was transferred to another camp – possibly in France. There are quite a number of them, you know . . .'

Just then the door opened. 'Sorry to barge in,' said a voice. It was Major Cochrane's. 'Only if we're to be in time for *Phèdre*, we ought to be leaving in fifteen minutes.'

'Heavens!' cried Lady Celia. 'I've still to dress. Help yourself to a whisky and soda, Nigel – and get one for Frederick, will you? I've just been putting him in the picture about Sebastian Gogarty.' With that, she opened the connecting door to the bedroom, and could be heard giving instructions to her maid: 'Don't fuss! There's plenty of time. Is my bath run? Good. I'll be five minutes . . .'

Left to their own devices, the two men returned to the sitting room, where Cochrane poured them both a drink. 'I take it you've met this Gogarty chap?' he said.

'I have – six years ago, so my chances of recognising him from just a few minutes' conversation are slim, to say the least.'

'*He'll* recognise *you*,' was the reply. 'But I agree that finding him in the first place will be difficult. The fact is, I suggested to Celia that you'd be the right man for the job. I can't allow her to put herself at risk, while things are in the state they're in. Even though the war's ended – or as near as dammit – the Germans aren't giving up without a fight. And they're doing their best to cover their tracks – with reason, if the stories I've been hearing of the way POWs have been treated are anything to go by . . . As the various camps are being evacuated, prisoners are being force-marched to other camps. It's a ghastly mess, frankly.'

'I see,' said Rowlands.

'If our young Irish hothead's been caught up in all that, then he's got himself into dangerous territory. I don't want Celia to be involved . . . nor, I might add, does her husband.'

'No, he wouldn't.'

'Ned Swift's a friend of mine,' the other went on. 'We served together in the Irish Guards during the last war. I promised him I'd look out for Celia, when she got this hare-brained scheme into her head of rescuing young Gogarty. To tell you the truth, I've got enough on my plate at the moment without having to chase after some stray POW.'

'Lady Celia said that she last heard from Gogarty four months ago,' said Rowlands. 'Has there been any further word since?'

'Nothing definite. He was in Stalag Luft III, in Lower Silesia – that's about a hundred miles south-east of Berlin. It was one of the camps set up by the Luftwaffe for Allied aircrews – run independently from those set up by the Wehrmacht. It appears there were a number of escape attempts during the three years it was operational. Some of the prisoners *did* escape and got back home. Others were recaptured and sent to different camps. When the place was liberated by the Russians in January this year, our boy wasn't among those still incarcerated.'

'Do you think he's still alive?'

Cochrane finished his whisky and poured himself another. 'I haven't the least idea,' he said. 'But if he's survived, I don't fancy his chances of doing so much longer. The fact is, the Germans have nothing to lose, which makes them desperate. Forced marches between camps aren't the half of it. Believe me, I've heard stories about some of the things that have been going on that'd make your hair curl . . . Ah, here you are at last!' he said, in a lighter tone, as the door to the bedroom opened.

'I'm ready, as you see,' said Lady Celia. 'With a good five minutes to spare.'

'I'll order a cab,' said Cochrane, picking up the telephone receiver.

'In a minute,' she replied. 'Have you put it to him?'

'Your rescue plan? I was just outlining the difficulties,' said Nigel Cochrane. 'I think it's only fair, if one's asking a man to risk his neck.' It was said in a humorous tone, but Rowlands was in no doubt that Cochrane meant every word.

He realised that both of them were waiting for his reply. 'I don't see what use I can possibly be in the circumstances – but I'm willing to try,' he said.

'Bravo!' cried Lady Celia. 'I knew I could rely on you, Frederick. When will you start?'

He must have looked startled at that, for Cochrane said, 'Give the man a chance, Celia! He's only just heard about all this . . . I thought it would make sense to start with some of the French POW camps,' he went on, addressing Rowlands. 'There's one near Strasbourg, close to the German border. From information gathered from Gogarty's fellow prisoners at Stalag Luft III, it appears that some of those who'd tried to escape were relocated there. It's a long drive, but we can do it in under five hours, if the roads are clear.'

Chapter Ten

They left Paris soon after six. There was very little traffic on the roads at that hour, and they reached the city's outskirts within a short space of time with the aid of the Citroën's powerful engine. The N4 took them towards Champigny-sur-Marne, passing through a number of small towns and villages in this picturesque region. Although it wasn't looking very 'picturesque' just then, said Cochrane. Many of the villages had sustained extensive damage from shellfire, having been the site of skirmishes between retreating enemy forces and advancing Allied troops. 'There was a good deal of fighting around here,' said Cochrane, as, nearing Montceaux-lès-Provins, they slowed to avoid a heap of rubble that had partially blocked the road. 'Some of these buildings have been reduced to nothing more than piles of smashed bricks and splintered timbers.'

Penetrating deeper into the rural region, they passed the ruins of a farmhouse and once, a roofless church. In the surrounding fields was further evidence that this had been a battlefield. The rusting hulk of a German tank lay abandoned in the middle of what used to be an orchard, while in a ditch outside the next village were the remnants of another vehicle – possibly a staff car, said Cochrane, to judge by the swastika painted on its side – that had been stripped of its wheels and doors, and anything else that could be salvaged for scrap.

But there were other yet more disturbing signs that the conflict – far from being over – was still raging here, far from the capital. The two bodies that lay at the roadside as they approached Saint-Dizier, for example. 'Collaborators,' said Cochrane, barely slowing the car to take a look. And in the market square of another nameless village, they came upon a sight that, to Rowlands, seemed worse even than this. A sobbing woman, surrounded by a baying mob, was being stripped naked, as a preliminary to having her head shaved – presumably for the crime of sleeping with a member of the occupying forces. 'She looks about eight months pregnant,' said Cochrane, in a neutral tone. 'So she couldn't have hidden things much longer, poor girl.'

'Can't we do anything to stop them?' said Rowlands, as the car moved slowly through the crowd which had gathered to enjoy the sport.

'*Voilà ce qu'on fait aux putes à Boches!*'

'What good would it do?' Cochrane honked the horn, in an attempt to facilitate their progress through the throng. 'Better to let them have their fun. Interfering would only make things worse for her.'

'But surely . . .'

'These people have scores to settle,' said the other,

accelerating, now that they were through the crowded square. 'One can't entirely blame them, barbaric as their methods are. Some of them have lost relatives. The SS weren't over-particular about who they made an example of for suspected Resistance activity. In one instance they massacred a whole village – children and all – before razing it to the ground. These folk – the French, I mean – have to find *somebody* to hold responsible.'

Rowlands said nothing, feeling sick at heart. The cries of the woman – '*Pitié . . . Je vous en supplie!*' – rang in his ears. What had they become, if such brutality had become the norm?

'Not long now before we reach Nancy,' said Cochrane, after both men had been silent a while. 'We'll get a bit of breakfast there before pushing on to Strasbourg.'

An hour later, the two of them sat over a hearty breakfast of *tarte à l'oignon*, smoked pork sausage and sauerkraut, washed down with plenty of black coffee. They were in the Brasserie L'Excelsior, near the railway station in Nancy – an establishment renowned, said Cochrane, for the excellence of its cuisine as well as for its flamboyant *fin-de-siècle* architecture. 'Really as good as anything you'll see in Paris.'

Rowlands, for whom the architecture was necessarily a closed book, was fully able to appreciate the food, reminiscent as it was of the meal he'd had with Iris Barnes and Percy Loveless at the Brasserie Lipp, where the cuisine was also from this region.

Cochrane pushed away his plate with a contented sigh and lit a cigarette.

'There's something you should know, before we get to where we're going,' he said.

'Oh?' Rowlands wondered what further surprises the other was about to spring. 'And what's that?'

'It's just that the camp we're going to – and where I think young Gogarty was last seen – isn't a prisoner of war camp, in the strictest sense,' was the reply. 'It was where they – the Germans – sent people who'd proved especially troublesome to them . . . members of the Resistance, SOE agents, and men who'd made escape attempts from regular POW camps. Our young friend would have fallen into the latter category, of course. I should imagine he was – and still is – a confounded nuisance,' he added. 'At least, judging by the trouble he's caused me already.'

Rowlands didn't respond to this quip. A growing suspicion took possession of him. 'What's the name of this place?'

'It's the only one of its kind on French soil,' said Cochrane. 'I suppose one would call it a concentration camp, given that it housed a variety of individuals the Nazis wanted to be rid of . . . a great many of whom were indeed eliminated by one method or another. We've only a rough estimate of the numbers – but it was certainly in the tens of thousands . . .'

Rowlands felt suddenly cold, although the day was warm. 'The name?'

'Natzweiler-Struthof,' was the reply.

So *that* was why Iris Barnes had seemed so relaxed about his leaving Paris, thought Rowlands – even though it might have made sense for him to remain, given that they now knew the name under which Amélie Mendl had been operating, up to the time of her arrest and deportation. But when he'd suggested that now might be the time to step up the search, Miss Barnes had been remarkably sanguine: 'Things'll keep until you get back. A couple of days more won't make much difference when we've waited so long.'

Once they'd left Nancy behind – its medieval Old Town was well worth a visit, said Cochrane, as were its grander eighteenth-century squares – the landscape through which they were passing began to change. Another hour's driving brought them to the foothills of the Vosges mountains. 'They're not as spectacular as the Pyrenees,' said his self-appointed guide, as they ascended what seemed to Rowlands like an increasingly steep series of inclines. 'But they have their dramatic moments. Some of the views across the valleys are quite lovely . . . It's a pity you can't see them.'

Rowlands agreed that it was a pity. 'But I can get a sense of what the landscape looks like from your descriptions,' he said. 'So I don't miss out altogether.'

'Yes, you seem to manage all right,' remarked the other, as the car slowed to navigate a sharp bend. 'I'm surprised that you don't rely on a stick – or a dog, for that matter.'

Rowlands explained that he'd had to leave his dog, Rex, at home, as it wouldn't have been practical to bring him to France.

'I can see that,' was the reply. 'I suppose as long as you've got somebody with you, you can get by.'

'That's right,' said Rowlands. 'Although it helps if whoever's with me gives me an idea of what's around . . .'

'Point taken. Well, we've just gone through one of the

mountain passes – I couldn't tell you which one, but I can see a line of mountains in the distance. I think the main one is called Le Grand Ballon. Below us is a mountain lake – they're very blue and deep here – surrounded by a lot of dense forest. It's mainly fir trees, but there are some deciduous species. Beech, mostly. It's quite a gentle landscape, compared to the Alps . . . although it's years since I was there. Used to do a bit of climbing, before the war.'

'Thanks,' said Rowlands. 'That's helped me get a better picture.'

'I suppose it must make you feel less adrift,' said Cochrane. 'Knowing what's around you.'

'Exactly that.'

He didn't add that he had already worked out some of the information just conveyed for himself. The precipitous nature of the road, for example, was evident from the protesting noises the Citroën's engine had been making; the increasing thinness of the atmosphere as they climbed was evident to him, too. He could have deduced the forested nature of the region from the smell of pine, and the fact that they were near water from a certain freshness in the air.

They continued to climb. The silence was profound. Once, Cochrane gave vent to an exclamation, as from somewhere above them a shower of small stones rained down, missing the car by inches. 'Chamois,' he said. 'They're insatiably curious beasts.'

'We must have reached quite a high altitude if there are mountain goats leaping around,' said Rowlands. 'My youngest daughter would be interested. She likes animals.'

Although he knew as he said it that he would say nothing to seventeen-year-old Joan of this or any other part of the trip.

Cochrane made no reply, except to say that they were nearly there. 'They couldn't have chosen anywhere more remote,' he said as the Citroën laboured up the stony track that passed for a road. 'Two and a half thousand feet above sea level, with impenetrable forest all around. Anyone who ended up here had very little chance of getting out.'

They'd reached the levelled-off area of ground that lay in front of the camp. Here, the car pulled up and Cochrane, having flexed limbs stiff from driving, got out. 'Well, this is it,' he said. 'Welcome to Natzweiler-Struthof, if "welcome" is the word I want.'

Rowlands followed suit. It was good to stretch his legs after hours of being cramped in the passenger seat. He drew a deep breath of the thin, pine-scented air. Even as he did so he was conscious of a feeling, not of liberation but of dread. Whatever they had come to find here, he knew it would be nothing good.

'It was the Yanks who liberated this place, at the end of '44,' said Cochrane, yawning and stretching. 'Although it's the French First Army who're in charge of it now. I expect it's their man we'll have to deal with. Let's hope he's not a Gaullist. They're not very well disposed towards the English.'

At the chain-link gates that led into what Rowlands guessed was some kind of compound, they were met by two military policemen, both of whom scrutinised the permits Cochrane produced before admitting them.

'There's not much to see,' said the major in an undertone to Rowlands, as they followed one of these officials across a yard. 'Just a collection of huts and a watchtower. One's always amazed at how banal these places look. If one didn't know what had happened here, one might think it had been used for some light industrial purpose – making buttons, or parts for radios.'

In one of the huts they found a French army officer who seemed to be the one in charge. He was far from delighted to see them, even though addressed in Cochrane's correct, if unidiomatic, French. '*Que voulez-vous ici?*' he demanded in an irritable tone. When the major explained the purpose of their visit, he replied curtly. 'You say you are looking for an Englishman – a pilot. I know nothing of this. I do not have the complete lists of those who were interned here, you understand.'

'You must have some record of the prisoners . . . if only an *incomplete* one,' said Cochrane. 'That is all we require, Colonel Duras.' Then, when the other did not at once reply, he went on, 'We are interested in any members of the RAF who were here – Mr Gogarty being one of them. Also in those SOE agents who were brought here – we believe there were several women . . .'

'I do not know about any women,' was the sharp rejoinder. 'My concern is with the French contingent – our *Résistance* people and others. Those incarcerated here were from more than thirty different nationalities,' he added. 'It will not be easy to find the ones you are looking for.'

'I realise that, Colonel,' replied Cochrane evenly. 'I'd like to look all the same, if that's all right with you?'

'You have the permission,' said Colonel Duras, in an indifferent tone. Rowlands could imagine the shrug with which he said it. 'I will get you the files you require.'

'I am grateful, Colonel.'

'Will there be anything else? Only I am busy, as you see . . .'

'I'd like to see more of the camp, if I may? Perhaps if you are too busy, one of your officers could show us around?'

'There is not much to see. The Boche destroyed most of it – along with the remaining prisoners – when they evacuated the camp in September last year.'

'Even so, I would like to see what remains.'

'As you wish.' The colonel lifted the telephone receiver from its cradle on the desk in front of him and spoke a few words into it. 'Captain Sorel will be your guide,' he said, replacing the instrument. 'After you have seen all you wish to see, I will have you brought to our records office. There you can look through the files for the names of those you seek.'

'Then we'll leave you in peace,' said Cochrane. The two army officers did not shake hands, Rowlands noticed. When they had exited the office, to find a junior officer waiting for them, the major said softly, 'I sometimes think we fought the war against the wrong enemy . . .'

Rowlands judged that this didn't need a reply. Although it was true that the Frenchman hadn't been particularly cooperative.

And there wasn't a lot to see. Lines of wooden huts, containing rows of rough wooden bunk beds. Some primitive washing facilities. A cookhouse with a row of iron stoves, on some of which were still to be found the large saucepans in which food for upwards of 50,000 prisoners had been prepared.

More sinister was what they found beyond the camp's perimeter. Here, a gallows – now dismantled – and a 'shower room' that had been converted for use as a gas chamber stood as grim testaments to what had happened here. 'As an operation, it was a lot smaller than those conducted at Belsen and Auschwitz – to name but two,' said Cochrane in a voice devoid of expression. 'But they managed to kill around twenty thousand here, nonetheless.'

Again, a reply seemed unnecessary. There was nothing Rowlands could say that would adequately express what he felt. Words such as horror and disgust didn't begin to cover it.

'And this, I suppose, is where it ended,' said Cochrane as, guided by the young officer, they reached another building, this one brick-built. It was the crematorium. Inside was a single oven, with a metal pallet protruding from its open mouth – like the kind that might once have been used for baking bread, said Cochrane. Around this grim structure stood several men. 'Resistance,' said Rowlands's companion, as they drew nearer. 'Come to see where their comrades perished, no doubt.'

The muttered conversation Rowlands could overhear seemed to confirm this:

'Hardly looks big enough to take a body, does it?'

'Oh, it was big enough, you can be sure . . .'

The young officer who had brought them to the place must have made a gesture indicating that the four men should move out of the way – for there was a burst of jeering laughter; then one of them said, 'And just who do you think you are, sonny? I'll have you know I've as much right to be here as anybody else – more, as it happens, since my brother died here.'

'We've no intention of stopping you,' said Cochrane, in his careful French. This provoked another outburst of sniggering.

'And what's *your* reason for being here, Englishman?' said the one who'd lost a brother.

'The same as yours, I suppose,' was the reply. 'To find out what happened here.'

'I can tell you that right enough,' said another man. 'Since I was here myself, from June until September '44. Some were worked to death in the mines. Some were shot while escaping, like Henri's brother here. Some were hanged. Some died of typhus. What more do you need to know?'

'I'm sorry about your brother,' said Rowlands to the man called Henri. 'We're trying to find out what happened to someone else who ended up here. He was with the RAF. An Irishman. His name was Sebastian Gogarty.'

Had he imagined the startled reaction – no more than a sudden intake of breath – from one of the men who had so far remained silent? He couldn't be sure. It was certainly the case that the man he'd addressed hesitated for a few seconds before replying, 'I do not know that name.'

'There was an RAF pilot hanged by the Boche,' said the third man, who sounded younger than the other two. 'An Englishman. He'd crashed his plane in the mountains, and hid out for a day or two in the *maquis*. Unfortunately for him, a Boche patrol found him, brought him back here and strung him up.'

'But he was a prisoner of war,' said Rowlands, appalled at the casual brutality of this.

'They said he was a spy,' replied the other. 'They could do anything they liked to spies.'

This reminded Rowlands of the other reason they had come. 'If you were interned here during the summer of 1944, you may remember some of the other British detainees,' he said. 'Four of them were women – SOE agents. Do any of you know what happened to them?'

There was a muttered exchange between the man called Henri – whom Rowlands supposed to be the leader of the group – and one of the others, before the former spoke at last. 'I cannot help you, m'sieur. I know nothing of these women you mention.' Then, to his comrades, 'Come. We have seen enough.'

With a clatter of heavy boots, they were gone.

'Charming bunch, weren't they, with their carbines slung across their shoulders and those jaunty little berets?' remarked Cochrane, who had taken almost no part in the previous series of exchanges. 'I knew we wouldn't get much change out of them.'

'They knew something,' said Rowlands. 'I'm sure of it.'

'Perhaps. Whatever it was, they weren't about to divulge it. Come on. I've had enough of this death chamber. Let's see what Colonel Duras's files have to tell us.'

The answer was, not much. The files in question were housed in rows of filing cabinets in one of the huts that had been set aside for this purpose. Here, Major Cochrane sat down at a trestle table and, under the watchful eye of the young French officer who had brought them there, began to peruse the lists of British prisoners of war who had been incarcerated at Natzweiler-Struthof between 1942 and 1944. Rowlands, who could offer no assistance in this task, left him to it, and went outside to smoke a cigarette – hoping by this means to expunge the taste of the crematorium from his lungs.

Having no desire to explore this dreadful place any further, he passed the next half-hour by walking up and down outside the hut. It seemed to him that the whole trip had been a waste of time. Maybe Cochrane would find the evidence he was looking for – maybe not. It didn't seem to Rowlands to make much difference.

The crucial information – which was the identity of the person or persons who'd betrayed the SOE women – was to be found in Paris, he was sure. It had to be somebody who'd known those women – who had perhaps been a member of the Palace network . . . A double agent, in fact.

It was the same person who had murdered Clara Metzner (for whether her heart had given out or not, it was still murder, to Rowlands's mind) and pushed Claire Hubert under a metro train. It was on finding *that* individual that they should have been concentrating their forces – not on searching through dusty files in search of names that might or might not be there.

He returned to the hut at last, to find that Cochrane was not much further forward than he had been at the start. He'd turned up the names of several RAF officers, including two men who'd escaped from Stalag Luft III and had then been recaptured by the Gestapo, and shot. 'So at least we can inform their families what happened to them,' he said. But of Flying Officer Gogarty, or indeed of the four SOE women, there was no mention.

Another hour went by. Rowlands smoked another cigarette and wished there was something useful he could do. At four o'clock, Cochrane gave a mighty yawn and pushed back his chair. 'I think I've found all I'm going to find here. Let's call it a day, shall we? If we start now we can do most of the journey in daylight.'

They accordingly took their leave of Colonel Duras, who showed no more interest in their departure than he had in their arrival, and having climbed into the Citroën once more, began to descend the mountain. On one side of the track was pine forest; on the other a sheer drop, said Cochrane, steering so close to the former that the lower branches of the trees brushed against the roof of the car. 'One wouldn't want to take a corner too fast up here,' he laughed.

'No indeed,' said Rowlands, heartily glad to be leaving this accursed spot behind.

'We'll pick up a bite to eat along the way,' went on the other. 'We should still be in Paris by . . . What the *blazes*?'

The car, which had been travelling at no great speed, now lurched to a halt, as the driver slammed on the brakes. Rowlands felt himself flung forward. 'Why have we stopped?' he said.

'Some bloody fool has left a heap of branches in the middle of the road,' was the reply. 'If I hadn't spotted it in time we'd have run straight into it.'

Chapter Eleven

Muttering under his breath, Cochrane got out of the car, with Rowlands following suit. 'We'd better shift this lot out of the way,' said the MI6 officer. 'Or we won't be going anywhere.'

But then came another interruption. Somebody who had been waiting by the side of the road now stepped forward, so that he was standing no more than a few feet away. 'W-wait.' The speaker was English. 'You w-were asking questions about me.'

'Who the hell are you?' growled Cochrane; but it was Rowlands who replied to the newcomer.

'Mr Gogarty, I presume?'

He found he was not entirely surprised by this encounter. So *this* was the man who'd remained silent during their talk with the Resistance group . . .

'Yes,' replied the man he'd addressed. 'I know you, don't I?'

'You do. The name's Rowlands. We met six years ago, at Castleford.'

'I . . . I thought I r-recognised you.' The circumstances of their last meeting had been acutely embarrassing ones for the young man, Rowlands recalled. No wonder he'd chosen to forget them. 'I w-want to know who sent you.'

Rowlands decided that there was no point in beating about the bush. 'You wrote to Lady Celia. It's she who asked us to find you.'

'Do I take it *you're* responsible for this unholy mess?' intervened Cochrane. 'Because if you are, I'd like to wring your neck, Mr Gogarty.'

'No, m'sieur,' said a voice Rowlands recognised as that of the Resistance leader, Henri, as he and what sounded to Rowlands like several others now emerged from the forest. 'It was I who caused these branches to be placed here.'

'Then you're a damn fool, too,' snapped Cochrane. 'If I'd been going any faster, we might have had a serious accident.'

'Happily, you did not, m'sieur.' Henri (if that was his name) gave an order, and two of his men began to clear away the branches from the road.

'One thing I d-don't understand,' went on Gogarty to Rowlands, 'is how you knew I'd be here? There are h-hundreds of POW camps scattered across France and Germany. I could have b-been in any one of them . . . in fact I *w-was* in one of the others – Stalag Luft III – until a few months ago.'

'It was a lucky guess,' said Rowlands. 'Wouldn't you say, Major?'

But Cochrane, evidently still annoyed by the way they'd been ambushed, refused to be drawn on the topic.

'If it's all the same to you, I'd like to get my car back on the road,' he said. 'This is hardly the place to be standing around discussing the whys and wherefores of our visit to KZ Natzweiler-Struthof.'

Then the man called Henri spoke up. 'The road is now clear, m'sieur. It was nothing but a few small twigs, as you see.'

'Then let's not waste any more time,' said Cochrane. 'I'm glad to have made your acquaintance at last, Mr Gogarty. I'll tell Lady Celia that her fears on your behalf were unfounded. And if you take my advice, you'll report PDQ to your squadron leader. The RAF takes a pretty dim view of its men going AWOL.'

He began to move towards the car, but Sebastian Gogarty forestalled him. 'Look, I'm s-sorry,' he said. 'I know it was a s-stupid idea to block the road like this, but it was the only w-way I could think of to stop you from leaving—'

'In truth, it was *I* who thought of it,' interjected Henri. 'It was the method we used in the old days, for ambushing the Boche. Only *they* would not have come out of it alive,' he added with a grim little laugh.

Cochrane ignored this, continuing to address Gogarty. 'Well, you've said what you wanted to say, so . . .'

'Actually I h-haven't,' was the reply. 'When you were in the crematorium, you – or rather Mr Rowlands – m-mentioned four women . . . British agents . . . the ones who've g-gone missing. The fact is, I know s-something about what happened to them.'

'Then you'd better spit it out,' said Cochrane coldly.

Rowlands thought it was time to intervene. 'We can't

talk here,' he said. 'Isn't there somewhere else we can go, where we can listen to what Mr Gogarty has to tell us?'

'There is a village a few kilometres from here,' said Henri. 'It is the place from which KZ Natzweiler-Struthof takes its name. There is a small bar there. I know the owner. You can talk there in private.'

With its zinc counter, cluster of small tables and cheap bentwood chairs, the bar was the kind that could be found all over France, and Belgium too, Rowlands supposed. He remembered places like this from his army days. They had provided a basic, but very welcome, refuge from the deadly realities of trench warfare, and a flavour – however diluted – of the country he and his comrades had been given the task of defending.

Now, as he took his seat at the table to which he and the other five men had been brusquely directed by the taciturn proprietor of the bar, he wondered if what he'd thought of at the time as the 'real France' would ever be the same after the horrors it had seen. That these had not come to an end with the 'war to end all wars', in which he and his fellow soldiers had been fighting, was all too apparent from what he had seen of the country so far – and no doubt from what he was about to hear.

Even after the proprietor had disappeared into a back room, having placed a bottle of brandy and six glasses on the table, and – at Henri's insistence – turned around the sign on the door that said *Fermé*, it was another minute or so before Sebastian Gogarty spoke. 'I s-saw them. Those w-women.' He took a sip of his drink, and half-choked at the fiery taste of it. 'It was s-soon after I c-came to the camp. That was in July, last year. I can't tell you the exact d-date, but it m-must have been sometime after we heard the news that there'd been an attempt to kill Hitler . . .'

'That was on the 20th of July,' said Cochrane.

'Yes. It failed, w-worse luck. Anyway, I'd been put to w-work mending the wire fence that ran along the eastern side of the camp. There'd been an escape attempt a f-few days before, and they – the camp authorities – wanted it r-reinforced. I was just g-getting on with it – working as slowly as I could, b-because it was a chance to be outside on what was quite a n-nice summer's day – when I heard the car pull up. It was the camp c-commandant's car – he was driving – which w-was unusual, in itself. Four w-women got out of the car. There w-were four SS officers lined up waiting to escort them. The whole thing seemed funny to me – I mean the fact that they were w-women, for a start, because it was a camp for men. Another thing I c-couldn't understand was why those four small women needed four big brutes to g-guard them . . .'

He took another sip of his drink. 'I noticed that none of the w-women were in uniform, so I guessed they must have been Resistance. M-most of the people that got sent here were. They all looked quite well dressed, and . . . c-confident, if that makes sense. I m-mean, they held their heads up, and s-seemed determined not to let their captors see they were afraid . . . W-which they must have been,' he added softly.

A silence followed.

'Then what happened?' said Rowlands at last.

'I don't know exactly . . . that is . . . I c-can only tell you w-what I heard from the others . . .'

'Go on.' Cochrane's voice was expressionless.

'There w-was a man . . . one of the prisoners. He w-worked in the crematorium. It w-was his job to stoke up the oven, w-when there had been an execution . . .' He had been speaking in his native tongue, for the benefit of the two Englishmen, but the meaning of what he said must have been intelligible to the Resistance leader, for he swore under his breath at this.

'W-we were told that we had to be in our h-huts by 8 p.m. that night. The blackout blinds had to be p-pulled down. No one was to look out, on p-pain of death. There were s-some who disobeyed, of course.'

His glass was empty. Cochrane refilled it. 'What happened then?'

'I d-didn't see what happened myself. The hut I was in didn't face towards the c-crematorium. But what I h-heard from s-some of the men who'd looked out was that the w-women were taken to a cell in that building at around 9.30 p.m. There was s-some shouting and protesting from the women before they were s-silenced. One man who w-was in another of the cells in the b-building that housed the crematorium said he heard groans and the s-sound of b-bodies being dragged towards the room where the oven was . . . That is all I c-can tell you,' said Sebastian Gogarty. 'Except to say that n-none of the women got out alive.'

Darkness was falling as the Citroën, with Gogarty now one of its passengers, set off on the return journey to Paris – at which Cochrane, who was once again driving, complained. 'I'd hoped to be further along than this while it was still daylight,' he said, as he steered the vehicle around the hairpin bends of the road that led down to the valley. 'But as it's turned out, our trip hasn't been entirely wasted.'

This allusion to Gogarty's presence, and to the information he had given them, was met with silence from the man himself, who had had to be persuaded, somewhat against his will, to return with them. 'You've important intelligence concerning four of our agents. I'll need you to file a full report before you get back to your unit,' Cochrane had said; adding, 'You'll be lucky not to be put on a charge for hanging about with a disreputable bunch of *maquisards*, instead of reporting at once to the British authorities. Only the fact that the whole country's been in such chaos these past few months gives you any sort of excuse.'

And so, having taken an emotional leave of his Resistance comrades, the young RAF pilot took his place in the back of the car next to Rowlands, with whom he also seemed disinclined to talk. Perhaps the memory of their earlier encounter in Ireland six years before had come back to haunt him, thought Rowlands, who was glad enough of the chance to reflect on what he had learnt that day. The horror of it was with him as he fell into an uneasy sleep in the back of the car.

It was almost midnight before they were back in Paris – too late to do anything but turn in, said Cochrane, as they drew up in front of the Hôtel Cécil. He'd find Gogarty a bed somewhere in one of the attic rooms, he said – obviously determined to let the young man out of his sight as little as possible until the latter's report on the events at Natzweiler-Struthof had been filed. But when the three men climbed the stairs, they found Iris Barnes waiting for them on the landing. 'I heard the car,' she said; then, on seeing his RAF uniform: 'You must be Mr Gogarty. Come into my office, all of you. I've a bottle of Scotch. You look as if you could do with a nightcap.'

'Mr Gogarty was at Natzweiler-Struthof during the period we're interested in,' said Cochrane, as they followed Miss Barnes into the room. 'He had information about what happened to our missing agents.'

'I see,' she replied. 'Then I'd like to hear what you've got to tell me, Mr Gogarty. These gentlemen will have heard it already, I know – but I'd like to hear it for myself.'

And so, once all four were seated, with glasses in their hands, Gogarty related the dreadful tale of what he had seen and heard that day. Miss Barnes listened in silence until he had finished; then she said, 'You say you saw the women arrive at the camp. Can you describe them?'

Gogarty took a sip of his whisky as he reflected. 'I only saw them for a few m-moments,' he said at last. 'B-but I did notice s-some things. One of them was tall, with r-red hair. I notice it because it c-caught the sunlight.'

'Celestine,' said Iris Barnes in a low voice.

'There was another w-with fair hair that looked as if it had been d-dyed. You could see the b-black roots. She was p-pretty, with large dark eyes . . .'

'Jacqueline.'

'There w-was a girl whose hair was tied back with a red ribbon. She was w-wearing a tweed coat and skirt. She looked very English . . .'

'Yvette.'

'The last girl was r-rather short. P-petite, you might

say. She had curly b-brown hair and she looked scared, I thought.'

'Paulette,' said Miss Barnes. She sounded suddenly exhausted. 'Yes, it's them, all right. Thank you, Mr Gogarty. You've made our job a lot easier.'

'I d-don't understand.'

'We've arrested the man who was the camp's executioner. Also the doctor who was in charge of administering the lethal injections the women were given before they were placed in the oven. So far, these men have denied ever seeing the women. Now we've some concrete evidence – yours – that will help to persuade them to talk.' She got up. 'I think that's enough for tonight. We'll reconvene here tomorrow first thing. I'll get my secretary to take down your statement, Mr Gogarty, and then you can sign it. Goodnight, gentlemen.'

An invitation had come for 'Frederick Rowlands Esquire and friend' to take tea at the Crillon Hotel. It was Major Cochrane who brought it, and read it aloud, at Rowlands's request. 'You see *I'm* not invited,' he said, when he had done so. 'It's you she wants to see, Mr Rowlands – and Mr Gogarty, too.'

The latter, when he was informed of this, became even more tongue-tied than usual. 'B-but I c-can't go like this!' he stammered when he could speak at all. 'I've only the uniform I s-stand up in and it's a p-perfect disgrace. I c-can't turn up looking like a s-scarecrow . . .'

'You'll do perfectly well as you are,' said Cochrane. 'Although you might have a shave. I'm sure Lady Celia won't give a damn what you look like,' he added, with what seemed to Rowlands a certain malicious satisfaction. 'She wants to satisfy herself that you're still in one piece, that's all.'

It was Major Cochrane who drove them from the Rue Saint-Didier to the Place de la Concorde – a route that took them along the Champs-Élysées. Gogarty, who had never visited Paris, seemed suitably impressed. 'Grand-looking place, isn't it? I've always w-wanted to see it. I should think it's a good deal b-bigger than Dublin . . .'

Rowlands confirmed this.

'Well, it's good to see that it hasn't been too kn-knocked about,' said Gogarty. 'Unlike some of the German cities. We really gave them a p-pasting.' Meaning he and his RAF comrades, Rowlands supposed.

'You haven't seen London,' he replied. 'That's taken a few knocks, as you put it.'

The Crillon itself elicited yet more admiring remarks from the young Irishman. 'It's more like a p-palace than any hotel I've ever seen,' he said. 'D'you think they'll let me in, looking as I do?'

Rowlands reassured him. 'Things have changed a good deal here, as they have everywhere,' he said. 'Six years of war have seen to that.'

As they entered the sitting room of the suite in which she and Rowlands had met two nights before, Lady Celia said, 'Ah, Mr Gogarty! It's been a long time since we met. But I'm glad to see you're looking well, in spite of your recent experiences.'

'Lady C-Celia . . . I . . .' Gogarty made a supreme effort. 'I h-have to thank you for all you've d-done . . .'

'And what's that?' she said. 'I suppose you mean replying to your letters?'

'W-well . . .'

'Believe me, that didn't require any great effort on my part. And in case you were in any doubt, my husband knew all about it.'

For a moment, Rowlands felt sorry for the young man. But then their hostess said, 'Oh do sit down, both of you! I haven't asked you here to make a fool of you, Mr Gogarty. I truly meant what I said – I was glad to write to you during all those months that you were in the prison camp. And I'm glad you're alive. That's about the best one can say to anyone these days, isn't it? Will you take China or Indian tea? They have both here, for a wonder . . . And then I *insist* on your doing justice to this marvellous spread. Only the Crillon could still be turning out *petits fours* of this quality.'

It seemed to Rowlands part of the general strangeness of the past few days – to be sitting here, on a chintz-upholstered sofa, sipping tea and making polite conversation, while only the previous day, he and his fellow guest had been face to face in the room where four women – and no doubt countless others – had met their terrible deaths . . .

He became aware that Lady Celia had asked him a question.

'I'm sorry,' he said, shaking himself out of his low mood. 'I was miles away.'

'So I gathered. I was only asking you, Frederick, how long you'll be staying in Paris?'

'No more than a couple of days, I should think,' he replied. 'It all rather depends . . .'

'Yes,' she said. 'I can see that it might. I myself will be returning to Dublin next week – stopping off in London en route. I've got to see our lawyers about some family business. We're adopting my husband's nephew . . . I don't know if you remember him, Frederick?'

'Of course I remember Reggie. Jolly little chap. He was about three when I last saw him.'

'He's nine, now. After his mother was killed in the Café de Paris bombing, we decided he ought to stay with us for good. It's taken an age to sort out the paperwork.'

Rowlands, offering his condolences for the death of Lady Celia's sister-in-law, thought that the late Mrs Jolyon Swift had died as she had lived, with a recklessness that took no account of others' feelings – least of all those of her young son. The bombing of the fashionable West End nightclub where she and her companions had met their end had caught the public imagination in a way many less showy incidents had not. The fact that the young, wealthy and privileged had fallen victim to one of the same bombs that were wrecking the East End had offered a moral lesson of a kind – if only that death spared no one.

Further conversation of an inconsequential kind followed, before Lady Celia, with a regretful sigh, said that she'd have to make a move as she was expected elsewhere for drinks and dinner. As he and Gogarty got up to take their leave, Lady Celia took Rowlands's hand in hers and held it for a moment. 'Promise you'll come and see us at Castleford very soon? I know Ned would be glad to see you – as would I,' she added, in a voice Rowlands hoped was audible only to himself. Privately he wondered if her husband would be as pleased to see him again as she'd claimed – given that the last time he and Rowlands had met was when Lord Castleford had been on trial for his life.

But he smiled and said that he could think of nothing he'd like more than to return to Ireland one day.

'Yes, you must come,' said Lady Celia. 'Ned said to remind you that he's still waiting to go for that ride with you.'

'I hadn't forgotten.' Which was true – every detail of that Irish trip was as sharply etched in his mind as if it had been yesterday. When they'd said farewell on the Dublin quayside, six years before, Rowlands had had no expectation that he and Celia Swift would ever meet again. And indeed it felt as if this more recent series of encounters were a kind of afterthought – a coda to what had seemed a final act. Perhaps it was better this way – to end on a dying fall.

Chapter Twelve

Emerging onto the windswept space of the enormous square, Rowlands was still absorbed in these valedictory thoughts. Once more he shook himself. That was the past; this was the here-and-now. There were taxis passing every few minutes; he put up a hand to hail one. As the cab slowed down in response to his signal, Gogarty said, 'Don't let's go back to that d-dingy hotel just yet. It's still early. And I've hardly seen anything of Paris. Tomorrow I'll be returning to my squadron to face the music. L-let me have at least one evening to myself. You know the city, Mr Rowlands,' he added eagerly, as the two of them climbed into the back of the waiting taxi. 'Where's the best place to go for a decent beer and a b-bite to eat?'

Rowlands thought for a minute. 'Le Select,' he told the cab driver.

He could equally well have chosen Le Dôme, La Rotonde, Closerie des Lilas, La Coupole – or any of the other bars and brasseries for which Montparnasse was famous.

Because it seemed to him that for a young man with literary interests, as he knew Sebastian Gogarty to be, this was the Paris he would most want to see. It was here, Rowlands knew, that American writers such as Edgar Hathaway and Gerda Epstein had congregated after the last war, in search of the literary and artistic freedoms for which the capital was celebrated; here, too, that one could find the cream of the French intelligentsia – the Schweitzers and Bertrands – arguing the night away over tall glasses of Pernod and shorter glasses of *vin rouge*.

Even though it was still early, the streets were already crowded: groups of students from the Sorbonne sauntered along the boulevard, loudly discussing where best to spend the evening. Girls clip-clopped past on their wooden-soled shoes, which had become the norm here (so Miss Barnes had informed Rowlands), because of the shortages of leather and rubber. 'Parisiennes have always been inventive, when it comes to fashion. They pride themselves on looking smart, even when they've had to resort to making do. They've become adept at running up a chic little two-piece from a man's worn-out suit, or fashioning an elegant turban from a scrap of curtain material.'

Rowlands, who had heard a good deal about such necessary ingenuities from his wife and daughters, had said he supposed such things took people's minds off the war.

'I s-say,' said Gogarty, interrupting these sartorial reflections. 'That f-fellow in the t-trench coat, g-going into that bar . . . looks a lot like Patrick Hackett . . .' – naming an Irish writer whose self-consciously 'difficult' work was beloved of the avant-garde. 'Isn't that where we're going?'

It was, and a moment later the cab pulled up in front of the establishment, and the two men got out. '"American Bar",' Gogarty read aloud; for this was what was written on the awning. 'Is this place m-mainly for the Yanks, then?'

'It's for anybody who wants to come here,' said Rowlands, as they went in, to be met by a cheerful racket, as those who had just arrived shouted greetings at friends already waiting at the bar.

'*Salut, mon ami!*'

'*Qu'est ce que tu bois?*'

'*Ouf! J'ai soif. Donne-moi un grand . . .*'

'What'll you have?' said Rowlands to his companion

'Let me g-get them. You've been v-very decent to me. B-besides,' added Gogarty, with the first sign of humour Rowlands had heard from him, 'I'm flush. The m-major gave me some f-francs to tide me over.'

'In that case, I'll have a beer.'

'So this is Parisian nightlife,' said Gogarty, as he and Rowlands waited to be served. In front of them was a long polished wooden counter, with high stools on which customers could perch while waiting for their drinks to be poured.

'It's certainly one aspect of it,' his companion agreed. 'I thought you'd like being among literary people – which I assume quite a lot of these folk are . . .'

'To be sure, if Hackett's here, there must be some p-poets around.'

'I believe you write poetry yourself, Mr Gogarty?'

'W-well . . . in a small way,' was the reply. 'At least, I used to . . .'

'Perhaps you'll take it up again?'

'Perhaps.' The youth was silent, quaffing his beer. 'To t-tell you the t-truth, Mr Rowlands, there doesn't seem much point in all that sort of thing now.'

'The war's made a lot of people feel like that.'

'It wasn't the war.'

Into the silence that followed Gogarty's remark, the voice of the man who was sitting on the other side of him came towards Rowlands.

'I tell you, business has been bad . . . Very bad . . .'

Now, where had he heard someone saying those very words, in just that lugubrious tone? 'Mr Gogarty,' he said, keeping his voice low. 'I'd like you to take our drinks to one of the tables a little way from the bar – ideally, facing away from it.'

'But . . .'

'Please. It's important.'

'R-right you are.' Having collected both the glasses, Gogarty led the way to a table in the middle of the room – one of a row set along a banquette. Here they sat down. 'So are you going to t-tell me what this is about?'

'There's something I want you to do for me,' said Rowlands. 'Do you see those two men sitting at the bar?'

'The ones who w-were on the far side of me?'

'That's right. I'm interested in the one nearest to where you were sitting.'

'Ah, that one. W-weaselly little feller. What's he done?'

'I'm not sure – yet. Now here's what I want you to do . . .'

A couple of minutes later, Gogarty – now sounding considerably the worse for drink – lurched up to the bar.

'I sh-shay . . . D-don't I know you?' He said in a loud, carrying voice, to the man Rowlands had pointed out.

'*Non, m'sieur,*' was the cold reply. 'You are mistaken.'

'B-but sh-shurely . . . You're the chap who runs the b-bookshop. D-don't tell me it's closed down?'

'*Non, m'sieur.* It remains open,' said the man. 'But I do not remember seeing you there.'

'You c-can't have forgotten! It's thanks to you and your R-Resistance chums that I'm alive today . . . Sh-shay . . . Lemme buy you a drink . . .'

'And I say I do not know you, m'sieur!' The little man was becoming agitated. 'I know nothing of any such activities . . .'

'Ah but you *do*, you know! It was after I'd c-crashed the crate during one of our moonlight "drops" . . . must've been spring of '43 . . . Lucky not to be p-picked up by the G-Gestapo. It was your chappies who found me . . . B-brought me to the jolly old bookshop. H-hid me in the c-cellar for a c-couple of days till the c-coast was clear . . .'

'M'sieur . . .'

'M-matter of fact, there was a girl in the case. Took a sh-shine to her, I did. N-name of Amélie . . . N-no . . . Tell a lie. It was Adèle. P-pretty little thing . . .'

The response to this was all Rowlands could have hoped for. The man he only knew as 'Marcel' leapt to his feet, almost oversetting the tall stool. 'M'sieur,' he almost spat. 'I do not know who you are, nor why you have come. And I know nothing of any such girl.'

Then he was gone, letting the door of the bar slam shut behind him.

'Well,' said Sebastian Gogarty, returning to the table

where Rowlands was sitting. 'Your man wasn't at all happy when I m-mentioned the lady.'

'No, but I am,' said Rowlands. 'Well done, Mr Gogarty. I owe you a very good dinner.'

'So our friend "Marcel" took exception to being questioned about Amélie Mendl – or should I say Adèle Morisot?' laughed Iris Barnes, when Rowlands, accompanied by Sebastian Gogarty, reported this exchange to her in her office the next day. Rowlands hastened to point out that it hadn't been he but Gogarty who'd put the question to 'Marcel'.

'Yes, yes, I know. Mr Gogarty was very quick-witted,' she replied. 'And Marcel isn't his name, by the way. It's Pierre Lafont. Although it's certainly the case that the Palace network used his bookshop in Rue des Écoles as an information exchange . . . although whether it was ever used to hide RAF pilots on the run I couldn't say.'

'It was the b-best story I c-could come up with,' said Gogarty sheepishly.

'And a very effective one, to judge by Lafont's reaction,' said the MI6 officer. 'Thanks to you, Mr Gogarty, it would seem that we're getting closer to finding our traitor.'

'D-do you mean to s-say that that little w-weasel was the man responsible for sending those women to their deaths?' demanded Gogarty, indignation making him more incoherent than ever. 'I w-wish you'd t-told me, Mr Rowlands. I'd have k-killed him with my b-bare hands.'

'Nothing's certain yet, Mr Gogarty,' said Iris Barnes. 'But I'll certainly be speaking to Lafont again about his activities during the period in question. And there's one other person I want to talk to – that young seamstress you ran into at the Crillon, Mr Rowlands . . .'

'Sylvie Dubois,' said Rowlands.

'That's the one. I'm hoping she'll be able to give us some more information about Amélie Mendl . . . or Adèle Morisot, as she was calling herself when she worked at the Moulin Rouge . . . which reminds me: we'll need to question the manager, Dominique Lefevre, again.'

'I can do that,' said Major Cochrane, who had just come in. 'I'm certain he was holding something back.'

'Thank you, sir. That would be a great help,' replied Miss Barnes. 'So that's settled: I'll take Sylvie Dubois and Pierre Lafont, and you can take Dominique Lefevre.'

'Perhaps you'd like to accompany me, Mr Gogarty?' said the major, in a more affable tone than he had hitherto used towards the young man. 'You ought to have a look at the Moulin Rouge before you leave Paris.'

Deciding to strike while the iron was hot, as Miss Barnes put it, they made first for the bookshop in Rue des Écoles. This, it turned out, was close to the Sorbonne, its popularity with the student population only too obvious from the crowd of young people lounging around in the street outside, blocking the entrance and jostling one another in the narrow passageways that led between the towering shelves.

In Paris, Iris Barnes explained, there were only two kinds of bookshop: the ones that were so crammed full of books, piled high on every surface, that it was almost impossible to move, and the ones – such as the elegant establishment two doors down – in which a modest selection of valuable volumes were displayed on velvet-lined easels in the window, with the price to be enquired for within.

Lafont et Fils was, needless to say, of the first kind. As they pushed their way through the throng, Rowlands felt himself back in the days when, as a part-time student at Ruskin College before the last war, he'd spent what little money he had buying books at Foyles on the Charing Cross Road. There, too (although on a much larger scale) had been the slightly chaotic shelving system, the profusion of books on every subject under the sun . . . He sniffed. How he loved the smell of new books! The crisp feel of their pages, too. Had circumstances been otherwise, he would have liked to linger – to savour the feeling of being surrounded by books, even though the only ones he was now able to read for himself were printed in Braille.

But they were here for another reason entirely, he reminded himself, as he followed Miss Barnes along the book-lined corridors, towards the back of the shop. Here, in a cramped little office, so crammed with boxes (presumably containing books) that there was little room to move, they found Pierre Lafont, seated at a desk on which stood a telephone, into which he was barking orders.

'I said six copies! Six! And I need them today!' Then, at a protest from whoever was at the other end of the line, 'Don't give me that about paper shortages! I know all about your paper shortages! Today! Or I cancel the order—'

He must have noticed the two newcomers at that moment, for he said apologetically, 'Distributors. Always some excuse . . .' Then, realising who it was he was addressing, he began to scramble to his feet, pushing back his chair with a scraping sound. 'Madame. To what do I owe the pleasure?' The conventional politeness of the greeting could not disguise the speaker's agitation, it seemed to Rowlands.

'I'd like to ask you some questions, Marcel . . . *Zut!* Can't seem to break the habit,' laughed Iris Barnes. 'You remember that when we last met I asked you about Celestine – the red-haired girl, who worked as a courier? You said you remembered her being in the shop. This would have been the autumn of 1941 . . .'

'What of it?' asked Lafont nervously. 'I have already said that I knew her – by sight, that is. I do not recall ever having conversation with the young lady. As I said before, there were many people who came to the shop.'

'I'm sure there were. But it was not about Celestine that I wanted to ask you. There was another girl – dark-haired, this one. Very pretty. Her name was Adèle.'

'I do not recall the name.'

'Unless it was Amélie. She used both names. And I am sure she visited your shop at that time. Early 1942, it would have been.'

'I am sorry, madame. I do not know this girl.'

'Think for a minute longer.' Iris Barnes's voice was cold. 'She belonged to the Palace network. You would have seen her with others from that group from time to time. We think it is possible that *she* was the one who betrayed the network . . .'

'I think I do remember her,' said Lafont eagerly. 'She went around with a crowd of artists and political types. She was with a man some of the time, I think. Yes, yes. It comes back to me now. Adèle. She was often in my shop. So you think she might have been the traitor?'

'It's one possibility,' said Miss Barnes. 'Well, I'm glad to have refreshed your memory, Marcel. I think that's all for now.'

She made as if to leave.

'Oh, one more thing . . . I don't suppose you've seen her recently – this Adèle?'

'I . . .' The bookseller seemed dumbstruck. 'No, madame.'

'Because we've reason to believe she's back in Paris.'

'I have not seen her.'

'Good. Then that's all. Come, Mr Rowlands, we'll leave this gentleman to his books.'

It was at that moment that Lafont must have taken a longer look at Rowlands, who had remained silent throughout the previous exchanges. 'It was you,' he said hoarsely. 'In the Select that night. With that drunken fool. He asked me about Adèle, too.'

Rowlands neither admitted nor denied it.

'I told you,' cried the bookseller. 'I have not seen this woman. She is nothing to me. Nothing!'

It seemed to Rowlands that he was very frightened. But of what – or of whom – it was hard to determine.

'He was lying,' the MI6 officer remarked to her companion, as the two of them stood face to face in the swaying metro carriage.

'Yes. I think so, too.'

'We'll give him time to think things over, before paying him another visit. He's mixed up in all this, I feel sure . . .'

Rowlands knew it was all she would risk saying while they were surrounded by people – although the likelihood that any of this motley assortment of students, housewives, American servicemen and businessmen would have been interested in what they were discussing was slim. But if he had learnt anything during the past few days in Paris, it was that appearances could be deceptive. Everyone he had met so far had had something to hide.

It was a twenty-minute journey from Saint-Michel Notre-Dame to Madeleine, during which – this one allusion aside – they spoke only of inconsequential things. Rowlands's imminent return to England being one of these. Tomorrow was Sunday – never the best day for making a journey, he knew; especially one with as many changes en route as he would have to make before reaching his destination. So he'd set out on Monday – at the thought of which he was far from sorry. His sojourn in Paris had not been without its pleasures, but over it all had been cast the shadow of Clara Metzner's miserable death.

At the Rue Cambon, they were admitted by one of 'Madame's' acolytes. 'She insists that they all dress alike in black dresses with white collars, like schoolgirls,' said Miss Barnes. When the latter stated her intention of paying a visit to the upper floor, the young woman seemed perturbed.

'One is not allowed to visit the atelier without permission from Madame,' she said. 'Since Madame is not here, it will be impossible to obtain her permission.'

'Then we'll just have to do it without,' said Miss Barnes, already mounting the stairs. 'You need not trouble your mistress at all. What I have to do will not take long.'

But when they reached the workshop under the eaves, it was to find that the young woman they sought was not to be found. 'Sylvie Dubois? I believe she has gone home for a few days,' said Madame Fournier, who seemed strangely unsurprised at the reappearance of the English intruders. 'She lives in the country. I have the address somewhere.'

She disappeared into the office at the far end of the long room, returning after a few minutes with a piece of paper, which she handed to Miss Barnes. 'Here you are. The village is called Morsang-sur-Seine. It is about forty kilometres from Paris. The family run a small hotel. It's a popular spot for summer visitors. Now if there's nothing else you want to ask me, I have to get on. We've a big order that's just come in. The Honourable Diana Hamilton-Vane's trousseau. My girls'll be working overtime.'

'So our bird's flown,' said Iris Barnes, as they left the building.

'Do you think she'll be back?' asked Rowlands, unable to shake off the unease he had been feeling since learning of the girl's defection.

'Hard to say. The only way to find out will be to telephone the parents . . . or we could go there. Forty kilometres isn't so very far. But there's nothing more to be done today,' she added, as they descended once more to the metro station, to take the line to George V. 'We'll go back to the Cécil now and see whether Major Cochrane and Mr Gogarty have had better luck this afternoon than we have.'

On being asked whether he had ever employed a young woman called Adèle Morisot, the manager of the Moulin

Rouge had admitted that he did recall someone of that name. One of the temporary staff. A waitress. They'd tried her out for a week or so, but then she'd just disappeared, without warning. It had left him short-staffed, at a very busy time. Oh, yes, he remembered her now. Where she had gone, he had no idea. People disappeared all the time in those days. One never knew if they were alive or dead. Sometimes it was better not to know.

'So it was rather a wasted journey,' said Major Cochrane, when they met in Miss Barnes's office later that afternoon. 'Although Mr Gogarty here enjoyed himself, I think.'

'I . . .'

'He was a great success with the dancers,' Cochrane went on gleefully. 'All the nice girls love a man in RAF uniform.'

'I h-hardly s-said a word to any of those g-girls,' protested Gogarty. He didn't sound too put out at being teased, however. 'The m-major did all the t-talking.'

'Well, you've had more success that we did,' said Miss Barnes, having recounted the substance of their visits to Lafont et Fils and Bonheur Modes. 'If Lafont doesn't contact us in the next few days, we'll have to pay him another visit.'

'Yes, and then there's the Dubois girl,' said Cochrane. 'It sounds as if a trip to Morsang-sur-Seine might be in order.'

'It would, but not today. We've another engagement,' said Iris Barnes. 'I'm sure the major will lend you some evening clothes, Mr Gogarty.'

Chapter Thirteen

The apartment was on the third floor of the mansion block – one of those built in the 1870s, during the last phase of Haussmann's twenty-year renovation of Paris. Here, on the Île Saint-Louis, the pale stone buildings were of a uniform size – four storeys, with mansard roofs and tall windows overlooking the Seine. 'They're being snapped up for a song,' said Miss Barnes, as she and her party, having been dropped off on the Quai des Célestins, walked across the bridge onto the smaller of the two boat-shaped islands that were such a feature of this part of the city. 'Of course they've always been desirable places to live, but it's only those with the money to maintain them who can afford them, these days.'

Their host that evening being one of this fortunate few, she hadn't needed to add.

Reaching the place, they climbed the broad stone staircase and came at last to the third-floor landing where a door stood open. An English butler relieved the men of their coats and Miss Barnes of her wrap. 'Mr Harrington is in the small drawing room,' he informed them in sonorous tones. 'To your right, madam, and through the glass doors.'

Rowlands's impression as he entered the first of the rooms – each of which led to the next, with only the intercession of the said doors, all of which now stood open – was of a large, airy space. Polished wooden floors, scattered here and there with what he guessed were antique rugs, threw back a volume of sound – voices, laughter, the chinking of glasses – so that at first it was difficult to orient himself. 'It's this way,' said Iris Barnes softly, touching his arm to guide him in the right direction. 'I think it must be the room where the drinks are, because that's where everybody's gathered. There isn't much in the way of furniture,' she added, knowing that this would be welcome information. 'That is, there *is* furniture – some very nice pieces, as one might expect – but it's been pushed back against the walls, out of harm's way.'

Two enormous windows stood open, admitting a warm breeze. It almost felt like summer, he thought. 'It's a splendid view,' murmured his companion. 'The river, with Notre-Dame on the far bank.'

'One couldn't wish for anything more Parisian,' said Rowlands. He was still trying to work out what was behind this visit to the plutocrat's pied-à-terre. He didn't believe for a moment that it could be without any ulterior motive.

The room they had just entered was full of people, and redolent of cigarette smoke and perfume. There was a lot of laughter coming from one of the groups clustered near the door. At the centre of this was their host. Catching sight of the latest arrivals, he broke off what he was saying – 'I believe you, old sport! Thousands wouldn't . . .' – and came towards them. 'Glad you could make it, glad you could make it,' he exclaimed; then clicked his fingers to summon the waiter. 'What'll you have? Champagne? Or there's Scotch . . .'

'Champagne for me,' said Iris Barnes.

Rowlands and the major chose whisky, while young Gogarty, perhaps determined to enjoy as much of the authentic French experience as he could, accepted a glass of the sparkling wine. Rowlands hoped it wouldn't go to his head. He was in an excited enough mood as it was.

'I'm afraid you find me in a huddle with some of my esteemed compatriots,' said Boyd Harrington, sounding unrepentant. 'We Americans do tend to stick together – even in Paris. Say, Gerda . . .' – addressing one of the group that was standing nearby. 'You know Miss Rosalind Barry, from the Foreign Office, don't you? She goes to all the literary parties, so I'm sure you must have run across each other . . .'

'I haven't had that pleasure,' said a gruff voice Rowlands recognised as belonging to the celebrated poetess and art collector, Gerda Epstein.

'Delighted,' said Iris Barnes. Rowlands wondered how she managed to remember which of her alter egos she was employing at any one time.

'And this is my companion, Miss Torville . . .' This would be the taciturn 'Avis' who had been at the Ruiz show, thought Rowlands, as the former made some inaudible reply.

'Major Cochrane I know,' Boyd Harrington went on.

'But I don't think I've met these two gentlemen . . .'

'This is Frederick Rowlands, a friend from England,' said Miss Barnes, remedying this omission. 'And this is Sebastian Gogarty. He's with the RAF.'

'Good to meet you both,' said Harrington. 'I'm a great admirer of your Mr Churchill.'

'We rather like him ourselves,' said Rowlands.

'Yes, we've found we can do business with him rather better than with the General,' replied the American. '*He* doesn't seem to think much of Americans . . .'

'Or indeed of the British,' said Miss Barnes.

'Yes, it'll be interesting to see . . .' But just then, Harrington was distracted from saying what it would be interesting to see by the sound of voices from the next room.

'Boyd, you old devil! Where are you hiding?' It was Edgar Hathaway. With a murmured excuse, Harrington left them and went to greet the writer.

'Dear Edgar!' said Gerda Epstein. 'Always so full of masculine *vigour*. Avis and I find him quite a tonic, don't we, dear?'

Over the course of the next hour, the rooms where the party was being held filled up, as more and more guests arrived. Most of these were unknown to Rowlands – members of that international fraternity, he supposed, which could be relied upon to turn up on any occasion combining a great deal of money with an interest in art. From time to time a familiar voice floated towards him out of the crowd. Edgar Hathaway, who had come with his journalist wife, was one such; another was Percy

Loveless. 'You here, old spy? How delightful!' exclaimed the latter. 'I don't often come to these things – too many Americans – but I thought I'd make an exception for this one . . . Mmm, real caviar,' he murmured appreciatively, as a waiter came by with a tray of hors d'oeuvres. 'And *good* champagne. Harrington always does one proud in the way of refreshments . . . I see Hackett's here. What that chap wouldn't do for a free drink is nobody's business! He's with the Schweitzer mob, of course. Old Jacques is another one who seldom baulks at the notion of drinking the filthy capitalist's champagne . . .'

'Do you know Patrick Hackett?' Rowlands asked, interrupting this tirade. 'Only I know somebody who would very much like to meet him.'

The young man in question had been hanging about on the fringes of a heated debate as to whether art could survive into the latter half of the twentieth century, now that the fraudulence of Western civilisation had been exposed by the exigencies of war. Having collected him, they went in search of the Irish writer, finding him in conversation with Iris Barnes.

'So if you hear anything, I'd be grateful if you'd let me know.'

'To be sure.'

'Because time's running out if we want to . . .' She broke off what she was saying. 'Hello, Loveless. I suppose you've come to admire the latest addition to Harrington's collection?'

'I have, as a matter of fact. Paddy, it's good to see you. What have you been up to these past few years?'

'This and that,' was the laconic reply.

'I'd like to introduce Sebastian Gogarty – a compatriot of yours and a fellow alumnus of Trinity College, I gather. Mr Gogarty has been flying planes across enemy territory on our behalf.'

'Have ye now?' said Hackett softly. 'Then I'll shake your hand, Mr Gogarty.'

'I . . . I'm a g-great admirer of your w-work,' said the young man, sounding quite overcome at being thus noticed.

'D'ye write yourself?'

'I . . . That is . . . a little.'

'Send me something, then,' said the other. 'I'm in Montparnasse. Rue des Favorites. The postman knows me.'

'Thank you, s-sir. I'm honoured.'

'No more o' that,' said the writer sharply. 'Just send it, man.' Then, with what in anyone else would have seemed like deliberate rudeness, he turned away, and could soon be heard talking to Major Cochrane about cricket.

For the rest of the evening, the conversation flowed as freely as the wine – both having a dizzying effect on Rowlands's consciousness. It was always an effort to keep track of all that was going on around when one couldn't see who was speaking or receive clues as to how what was said was being received by those around . . .

As he stood, lighting up a cigarette, he found himself tuning in and out of a number of different conversations – each forming a theme in the concerto that was the party. The one about the relevance or otherwise of art in the post-war world had given way to a discussion of the sculptures of Giacometti. 'Too, too haunting,' opined a woman who'd been to see the show. 'I really think he *captures* something . . .' What it was, she didn't say.

Another partygoer had been to the recent exhibition at the Louvre. 'Quite marvellous . . . all these exquisite little dolls, dressed in haute couture. It's to raise money for war victims . . . and to showcase the fashion industry, naturally.'

A third exchange, conducted in an urgent undertone, was on a more intimate topic than either of these. 'I told her, "Honey, he's the very *last* man on earth you should be with." But would she listen? No.'

'That gal's her own worst enemy.'

'Shh. She'll hear you.'

Suddenly, he'd had enough of this brittle chatter.

Stepping across the threshold of the open French windows onto the balcony, he drew in a breath of the cool night air. Sounds of voices from the street below mingled with the soft rustle of the breeze in the branches of the plane trees along the embankment. Resting his elbows on the ornamental iron balustrade, he wondered anew what it was he was doing there. He felt he had achieved nothing. Two young women had been killed and the person – man or woman – who had done so was still at large. Whether this individual was also responsible for delivering the four SOE women to their deaths was still uncertain. He felt a surge of anger – with himself, and with what seemed an impossible situation.

With a stifled exclamation of disgust, he flung the stub of his cigarette away.

'You seem a bit out of sorts,' said a voice he knew. 'Shall I go away again?'

'No need, Lady Celia.' He forced a smile. 'I'm just tired

of my own company, if you want the truth.'

'I get like that sometimes. It passes, after a while. But I'm sorry if you're feeling blue . . . Only I wanted to thank you for what you did . . . finding poor Mr Gogarty for me, I mean.'

'Major Cochrane did that.'

'Oh, I think the credit should rightfully be yours. To begin with, Nigel hadn't the faintest idea what Gogarty looked like. If he – Gogarty, I mean – hadn't recognised *you*, and decided to trust you, he'd still be languishing in the forest with those *maquisards* . . . Oh yes, Nigel told me all about it!' She laughed. 'The ambush on the forest road . . . with the Resistance people armed to the teeth, in their berets and leather jackets . . . It does sound fearfully exciting.'

So Cochrane hadn't mentioned the earlier meeting – the one in the crematorium – for which Rowlands was glad. 'Yes, I suppose it did have its exciting moments,' he said. From the room behind, the sounds of laughter and chatter seemed to him to have increased in volume.

'Well, well,' said Lady Celia, as if she, too, had just noticed this. 'Look who's here! The guest of honour, one supposes . . . Boyd does like to spring these surprises. I suppose it's what makes his parties so successful.' She touched his arm. 'Shall we go in?'

They stepped back into the room, to find their host in the middle of making a speech of welcome. 'Very glad you decided to come, after all, old sport,' he was saying. 'It wouldn't have been the same without you.'

'You invited me. I have come,' said Diego Ruiz.

It struck Rowlands that, in this distinguished company,

which included powerful individuals such as Edgar Hathaway, Jacques Schweitzer and Patrick Hackett, Ruiz commanded attention in a way the others did not. Was this star quality? If so, it wasn't something that could be measured in terms of wealth or achievement, but had more to do with sheer force of personality.

Harrington was still speaking. 'Yes, I wanted you to be here, Diego, on this night of all nights, because it's a special occasion. The unveiling of a great work by a great master . . .' He took a step towards the wall on which, Rowlands surmised, something was displayed – something hitherto concealed by a curtain. Into the anticipatory silence that had fallen over the room, there came a faint swish as the curtains parted – then an outburst of clapping and cheering from the watching crowd.

'So *that's* what all the fuss was about,' murmured Lady Celia in Rowlands's ear. 'A painting.'

But Harrington wasn't finished. 'A toast!' he cried, as waiters circulated with fresh glasses of champagne. 'To *The Little Seamstress* – and her creator, Diego Ruiz! The greatest artist of the twentieth century . . .'

There was renewed applause at this. But a man who was next to Rowlands muttered something that must have been inaudible to anyone standing further away. 'Traitor.' It was said in French, and Rowlands was reminded of the last time he'd heard the word spoken. It had been during the film he'd watched, a few days before. Then, it had been the actress playing Eurydice who had said it – an accusation against her lover, Orphée. Now the taunt was echoed by the man who'd written the script for the film – Julien Corbeau.

* * *

'What do you think he meant?' said Rowlands to Iris Barnes.

'I should have thought it was pretty obvious.'

'You mean he was insinuating that Ruiz was a collaborator? Is there any actual evidence for that?'

'Not as such. Although Diego has been criticised in some circles for . . . shall we say . . . keeping his head down during the Nazi era.'

'Yes, but that's hardly . . .'

'There are different kinds of treachery,' she said.

They were on their way to Morsang-sur-Seine. It was Sunday. Miss Barnes was driving. It was a beautiful spring day. Had things been otherwise, Rowlands would have been basking in the unaccustomed warmth, in the fresh smell of the meadows through which they were driving; in the general feeling – call it liberation – that being out of the city instilled.

But things were as they were.

'What do you mean?' he said.

'Simply this: Diego Ruiz has a reputation – not only as a very fine painter, but also as a man who likes women. It's well known that he sleeps with his models. Amélie Mendl was one of these, and probably one of his conquests, too. He must have seen her around during the making of *Eurydice*. It was filmed all around the streets of Montmartre, where Ruiz has his studio. No doubt he asked her to pose for him, one thing led to another, and Julien's leading lady transferred her affections to someone else . . .'

'Ruiz.'

'Exactly.'

'And Corbeau was in love with her.'

'One must suppose so. Although . . .' She reflected a moment. 'I'd always supposed his interests lay in quite another direction . . . No matter. Whatever the reason, his accusation of treachery was not the kind of insult one would want to have thrown at one in these febrile times.'

'No.'

'Light me a cigarette, would you? There's a pack of Pall Mall in the glove compartment. And help yourself.'

He did so, and having lit her cigarette, lit his own. For the next few minutes the two of them smoked in companionable silence. The miles rolled past. 'Are you familiar with this region?' she said at last. 'It's rather pretty. Mainly farmland, you know – and some rather nice woods along the river.'

'The fighting never got this far,' said Rowlands, 'so I never got to see this bit of country. But I imagine it must resemble the landscape one used to see in French paintings before the war. People in striped jerseys and straw boaters enjoying themselves in pleasure boats, or drinking wine in riverside restaurants . . .'

'Yes, it's very like that,' said Iris Barnes.

At length they reached the little town, which consisted, so Miss Barnes informed her companion, of a church, a *mairie* and a few shops. There were several inns, catering to the weekend visitors with whom the area was popular during the summer months. Having enquired at a nearby épicerie, they were given directions to Le Vieux Bateau Hotel – a venerable establishment fronting the road with a garden sloping down towards the river, Miss Barnes said.

'According to the woman who runs the grocery,

it's Sylvie's grandfather who owns the place,' she went on, pushing open the gate and leading the way along a flagstone path to the front door. 'Her parents have taken over the running of the hotel, since Monsieur Dubois senior became too infirm.'

She paused a moment, with her hand on the bell-push. 'It doesn't look as if it's been modernised, either. Still the same roughly plastered walls and old-fashioned wooden shutters as it had when it was first built a hundred years ago.'

With its appetising smells of cooking and its uneven, quarry-tiled floor, smelling faintly of lavender polish, the place had the homely feel of a family-run business, thought Rowlands – an impression confirmed by the pleasant-sounding proprietress who now came to greet them. *Would madame and monsieur be wanting lunch?* she wanted to know. If so, they had a 'special' that day of grilled trout. 'Caught this morning,' she added, with pardonable pride.

'Thank you. That sounds most agreeable,' replied Miss Barnes. 'But first I must ask you . . .'

'*Maman*—' It was a young girl's voice. She broke off, on seeing the strangers.

'You must be Sylvie's sister,' said Iris Barnes. 'You're very like her.' Then, to the girl's mother, 'Is your elder daughter about? I'd like a word with her, if you can spare her for a few minutes.'

'But . . . madame . . . my Sylvie is in Paris. She works for Bonheur Modes. Perhaps you have heard of it?' Again, there was the note of modest pride.

'Are you saying she is not here?' said Iris Barnes, ignoring the question.

'Yes, madame. Why should she be here?' said the woman. 'I have said: she is in Paris.'

'And you haven't had a letter, saying she intends to visit?'

'A letter? No. I have had no letter.' The implications of these questions suddenly seemed to strike Madame Dubois, for she said, in a voice made sharp by alarm, 'What has happened? Why are you asking questions about my Sylvie?'

'What do you think has happened to her?' asked Rowlands, when he and Miss Barnes were once more seated in the Citroën on their way back to Paris. There had, of course, been no agreeable lunch of grilled trout on the banks of the Seine – nor had they stayed at Le Vieux Bateau any longer than it took the MI6 officer to press her card into the hand of the anxious mother, with instructions to get in touch as soon as she heard from her daughter. 'Not,' she'd remarked to Rowlands, as they quitted the place, 'that it seems very likely that she *will* hear anything.'

Now, she considered the question for a moment, as the car gathered speed (no more dawdling along the highways and byways of the Île-de-France for *them*). 'I couldn't say,' she said at last. 'She's vanished, that's all I know. Although that policeman said there's been no reports of bodies turning up in the past few days – which is something, you'll admit.'

He didn't dignify this with a reply.

And it was true that the sergeant in charge of the local police station, where they'd called in on the way back – having left disaster in their wake, thought Rowlands – had said he knew nothing of any missing girl. He'd keep an eye out, he said – he knew the Dubois lass by sight; nice little thing – and he'd telephone the minute she appeared. *If* she appeared.

'Do you think Madame Fournier was lying – about Sylvie going to visit her parents, I mean?'

'I don't know. I'll need to take it up with her. I don't, as a rule, like being lied to,' said Iris Barnes with a lack of emphasis that was more chilling than an obvious display of anger. 'Of course, it's possible that the girl *meant* to visit and got delayed en route . . . seeing a boyfriend, most likely.'

'It's possible,' he echoed, not believing it for a moment.

'Yes, we could do without another one,' murmured Miss Barnes. Another dead girl, he supposed she meant. 'But I'm rather afraid that we'll be hearing from that policeman before long – what was his name? Sergeant Lenoir.' Rowlands was afraid of that, too. It seemed to him that his trip to Paris had done little or nothing to further the investigation with which he'd been asked to assist, but had in fact only made matters worse.

London, May 1945

Chapter Fourteen

May 1945. The war was over. The monster was dead, by his own hand. All Europe – and America – was rejoicing. London, on that day – 8th May – was given over to what at any other time would have seemed like a kind of insanity. People dancing in the streets and jumping into the fountains in Trafalgar Square. Crowds streaming along The Mall, and massing in front of Buckingham Palace – waiting for a glimpse of the King and Queen and the two young princesses (one still in uniform) and the Prime Minister. An equally vast crowd thronging Whitehall, to hear the great man address the people. Piccadilly and the West End turning itself into one enormous nightclub, with 'society' people mingling with the commoner sort, to the evident enjoyment of both . . .

For Frederick Rowlands, the elation he was feeling – in common with the rest of the population – at the ending of a long and gruelling war was tempered by an immense sadness. So many lives had been lost. So much that was precious and beautiful had been destroyed. Cities – not least his own – had been smashed to smithereens, along with millions of their citizens. Historic alliances had been torn up. Neighbour turned against neighbour. Added to these painful realisations (which he kept to himself for the most part) were troubling thoughts of the time he'd spent in Paris, not a month before, and the feelings of guilt and suspicion that had blighted his memories of that city.

London, although bearing the physical evidence of years of aerial bombardment, had at least escaped the horror of years of forced collaboration with the enemy. It seemed to Rowlands that this kind of wound went deep. Buildings could be repaired, or rebuilt. The scars of betrayal could never be erased.

His two elder daughters had earlier announced their intention of joining the crowds in Trafalgar Square. Margaret would go straight from her government job in Buckinghamshire, she said (what that job was remained vague; although her father, at least, had a pretty good idea). Anne was going with a party of fellow WAAFs from their station in Suffolk. He himself, although thankful that (in Europe at least) the fighting was over, had no desire to join the celebrations, except remotely. He'd pour himself a glass of beer to toast the King, and light himself a cigarette to smoke with it, while listening to Mr Churchill's speech on the wireless.

But when he said as much to his wife and youngest daughter, they reacted with dismay – loudly, in seventeen-year-old Joan's case. 'It's so unfair! Why can't *I* join the fun? A lot of the girls from my school are going – that's why they've given us a half-holiday.' Joan was boarding with her uncle and aunt in Richmond during school terms – an arrangement that had meant her education had been less disrupted when the family had moved to Brighton, after being bombed out of their home in Kingston. She'd arrived home a couple of hours earlier, however, owing to the said half-holiday.

'It *does* seem a bit unfair that she should be the only one of our girls to miss out on such an historic occasion,' said Edith to her husband, when Joan had stormed out, saying bitterly that if they weren't going to celebrate the end of the war, she was going to feed the rabbits.

'There'll be celebrations in Brighton . . .'

'It won't be the same. And you call yourself a Londoner!'

'All right, you win,' he said resignedly, knowing that if he didn't give in, he'd never hear the last of it. 'You'd better look up a good train. I'll see about ordering a taxi to the station.'

'God bless you all. This is your victory! It is the victory of the cause of freedom in every land. In our long history we have never seen a greater day than this. Everyone, man or woman, has done their best. Everyone has tried. Neither the long years, nor the dangers, nor the fierce attacks of the enemy, have in any way weakened the independent resolve of the British nation . . .'

Standing in the densely packed crowd that filled the street in front of Whitehall, Rowlands listened to the simple but powerful words of the man who had led the country to victory. He recalled as he did so the last time he had heard the voice – now booming out from the loudspeakers – when, for a few memorable moments three years before, he had been face to face with Winston Churchill.

As the sonorous phrases rolled out, greeted with cheers at every interval (for the speaker had been schooled in the classics, and knew the value of a rhetorical pause), Rowlands felt his heart lift. For those few brief moments, surrounded as he was by tens of thousands of his fellow Londoners, and with his wife and daughter beside him, he could forget the horrors of the past six years, and think only of the future, and of a world without war, which had been promised by their leaders for so long.

He remembered standing in a crowd in Trafalgar Square as large as this one. It had been on Armistice Day, 1919. That had been a silent crowd – all the more impressive because of its silence. There had been no cheers, no flag-waving, as there was now. When the maroon sounded, the transformation was immediate. The roar of traffic died. All the men removed their hats. Men and women stood with heads bowed, unmoving.

For fully two minutes the silence was maintained – there and across the country. Everyone and everything stopped: buses, trains, trams and horse-drawn vehicles halted. Factories ceased working – as did offices, shops, hospitals and banks. Schools became silent, court proceedings came to a standstill; prisoners stood to attention in their cells. Only the sound of a muffled bell tolling the hour of eleven broke the silence.

Rowlands himself had not been there, in November 1918, to hear the guns fall silent on the Western Front, since he'd been invalided out of the army the year before.

He and other St Dunstaners still undergoing rehabilitation had listened to the news on the wireless. There had been little rejoicing then, he recalled; just a sombre feeling of relief that the war for which all those present had given their sight was over at last. Nor had Rowlands and his comrades joined in the victory parades that had been held the summer after the war. It had seemed to him, as it had to others of his generation of servicemen, that there was precious little to rejoice about.

Even now, as the Prime Minister had just reminded his listeners, the war was still going on in the Far East. It seemed to Rowlands, as the band struck up and the strains of 'Land of Hope and Glory' echoed around Whitehall, that war, in some shape or form, had been going on for almost his whole life. And while the Russians – now Britain's allies – would be commemorating their victory the day after this one, there would be some in Eastern Europe who would not be celebrating on 9th May. The Poles, for instance.

After the Yalta Conference in February, and the installation of a provisional government – essentially one controlled by Stalin – the dream of a free Poland had effectively died. 'Betrayal' was the word on the lips of all those who had taken part in the struggle for that now unattainable dream. One of these had been Anne Rowlands's fiancé, Jan Wawrzkowicz, who had died when the plane in which he had been accompanying the Polish prime-minister-in-exile, General Sikorski, had crashed in the sea off Gibraltar – sabotaged, it was said, by the Russians.

'They've been cut out of things completely – the people who've been fighting for Poland,' Anne had said furiously, on one of her (increasingly rare) visits home. 'It's the Russians who are in control. There's no hope for that country now.'

It had been in vain for her father to point out that there would soon be elections, when the Poles could make their own choice of government. 'You don't believe *that*, surely?' she had replied. 'The whole thing will be fixed by Stalin's lackeys. The country's been sold down the river. Betrayed – by those who should have stood by her.'

It had seemed to Rowlands that, allowing for the difference in their respective political views, his daughter was sounding more and more like his sister, Dorothy. She, too, would never countenance any opinion other than her own. Rowlands wondered if Anne's growing estrangement from her parents – or rather from him, because she'd never been close to her mother – had come about because at some level she blamed him, and the older generation in general, for failing to stand up for her dead lover's country. Of course it wasn't true, or even fair – what, after all, could he have done? But he was sad to think there was now this rift between them . . .

Now he had a further reason to worry about Anne.

Tired and footsore after their day in London, the Rowlandses had returned to the house in Dorset Gardens, with Margaret, their eldest, whom they'd met at Victoria Station. She'd been granted a couple of days' leave, she said. 'We're not wanted by the powers-that-be at present. They're too busy tearing everything down,' she'd explained, mysteriously.

'But I thought Anne would be with you?' said Rowlands, as the four of them boarded the packed Brighton train.

'So did I,' was the reply. 'But you know Anne. She didn't turn up.'

Margaret had arranged to meet Anne by the Victoria Memorial opposite Buckingham Palace at two o'clock, she said. 'I waited and waited, but she didn't come. Or if she did, I didn't see her. There were thousands of people milling about.'

'Maybe she's run off with that American airman she was so keen on,' put in Joan innocently.

'Do I know about this?'

'Oh Fred, don't be so stuffy!' said his wife. 'You've forgotten what it was like to be young. Goodness, I'm tired after all that standing about. I'll be glad of a nice cup of tea . . .'

It wasn't until they'd had the tea, and the sandwiches that would do for supper, Edith said, that the topic of Anne's whereabouts was raised again – this time by her mother. 'I worry about that girl. She oughtn't to have gone off without letting Margaret know. She's become far too casual in the way she treats others.'

'Oh I don't mind,' said Anne's sister, adding philosophically, 'that's just the way she is. She was with a gang of her RAF friends. They're great ones for making a night of it.'

'Anne's a sensible girl at heart,' put in Edith's mother, Helen. 'She's probably just having fun. These poor young people have been through a lot in recent years.'

Which was certainly true, thought Rowlands, but the fact remained that Anne wasn't happy – hadn't been happy since that man of hers went missing. When she deigned to come home at all, she sat around smoking and playing those eternal jazz records of hers – or went for long, silent walks with her father and the dog. 'I'm fine, Daddy – really! Just tired. They keep us pretty busy at the station, you know.' These being her superior officers at RAF Mildenhall.

'Well, you'd tell me if anything were the matter, wouldn't you?' he'd said, knowing she probably wouldn't. His lively, cheerful daughter was no more – replaced by this coolly detached young woman who seemed, increasingly, a stranger.

London in the days following the celebrations had the air of a person waking up on the morning after a very good party: a little rueful that the fun had come to an end; a shade embarrassed by remembered indiscretions. Had people really climbed up lamp posts, splashed in fountains and kissed perfect strangers in the street? It all seemed a hectic dream, from which one had awoken to a more sombre reality. The clearing up after the party had begun.

Nor was it merely a matter of pulling down bunting and sweeping up litter, after the many street parties that had been held across the capital, and beyond it. A greater reconstruction had to begin. For London was no longer the city it had been. The physical evidence of this was all too obvious: the bomb sites, with their ruined houses; the cratered streets and mounds of debris; the deterioration of the civic fabric one encountered everywhere. 'It's a verra guid thing ye canna see it, Fred, and that's a fact,' said Alasdair Douglas, when the two men met in the superintendent's office at Scotland Yard. 'It'd break your heart to see the mess they've made of the old city – the area around St Paul's has been completely flattened. As for the East End . . .'

He broke off, to light his pipe.

'I've a fair idea of how it must look from what you and others have told me,' said Rowlands. 'And it's rather wonderful that they didn't hit St Paul's itself, although not from want of trying, I gather.'

'Indeed,' said the other. 'Drat this pipe! It never draws well in damp weather . . . Aye, those V2s at the end of last year did some of the worst damage . . . I was called out to the New Cross incident, ye know. Carnage is the only word for it.'

'Yes, I heard about that,' said Rowlands grimly. 'It hit a Woolworth's, didn't it?'

'It did. Just after midday on a busy Saturday. One hundred and sixty-eight people killed outright – thirty-three o' them children.' Douglas was silent a moment. 'The blast was so fierce that bodies were flung up in the air, like rag dolls, so eyewitnesses said. What I saw mysel' was bad enough. Buildings reduced to rubble. Streets ankle-deep in broken glass. People covered in blood, staggering around, blinded by the dust and smoke and deafened by the noise . . . I tell you, Fred, it was worse than anything I saw at the Somme – and that's saying something.'

After another silence, the policeman went on, with an attempt at levity, 'So you've just come back from Paris, Fred? Must've made a nice change. No bomb sites there, I reckon!'

'No,' agreed Rowlands. 'No bomb sites. But . . .' He broke off, wondering how to express what it was he'd felt about the place. 'It's not what it was.' He was conscious that it sounded lame.

'Och, nowhere is, if it comes to that. I mean, look at poor old London . . . But you mean something else, apart from burnt-out buildings and broken water mains . . .'

'It's the *atmosphere* that's all wrong,' said Rowlands. 'The people. It's as if . . . I don't know . . . they're all constantly looking over their shoulders, afraid that somebody's listening . . .'

'That comes from living under Nazi occupation for the past five years,' said Douglas. 'People don't know who they can trust any more.'

'I suppose that's it. At least *here* everyone's pulled together . . .'

'Aye, for the most part. Although not everybody is as public-spirited as you seem to think. There are always a few rotten apples.'

'I dare say. But when things were at their worst, with the bombs raining down, people looked out for each other.'

'And some didna. You're telling me Paris has changed for the worst, and I'm saying that London has, too. For every story you can tell me of bravery and self-sacrifice, I could tell you one that shows the opposite. People stripping the brooches, rings and watches from the dead bodies of those killed in the Café de Paris bombing, for instance . . . That shows another side to human nature, you'll agree?'

'It does.' Rowlands recalled what Lady Celia had told him about the fate of her wayward sister-in-law, Henrietta Swift. He hoped the ugly story Douglas had just recounted hadn't reached her ears.

'But let's not argue over such matters,' said the other.

'You still haven't told me what took you to Paris in the first place – or is it too hush-hush?'

'Not really. I was asked to help identify someone I'd known years ago, that's all.'

'And did you?'

'No. I couldn't decide if it was the same person or not.'

'I shouldn't worry about it,' said the superintendent. 'We . . . the police . . . would always rather a witness made absolutely certain before committing himself either way.'

'Yes, but then the person was killed. So I've lost my chance of providing a positive identification.'

'Ah. That's a pity,' said Douglas. 'Was it murder, d'ye ken?'

'It seems likely. There's been another death since.' Maybe *two* deaths, he thought; he'd had no word from Miss Barnes as to whether or not Sylvie Dubois had been found.

'Hmm,' said Douglas. 'And this *pairson* . . .' His Scottish accent became more pronounced the more interested he got. 'Man or woman, did ye say?'

'Woman. German Jewish. Name of Clara Metzner.'

'Indeed?' Douglas thought for a moment. 'Metzner. Wasn't that the name o' the laddie ye brought back wi' ye from Berlin?'

'Her brother. He's in South Africa with his unit.' *Or he might be in Paris by now*, thought Rowlands.

'I see. Then it'll be a nasty shock for him to learn that his sister's dead.'

'He hasn't seen her since he was a child. But yes, it'll be a shock.'

'Blast the thing! It's gone out . . .' Douglas prodded

fruitlessly at his pipe. 'I have the feeling,' he went on, 'that there's more to this than ye've told me.'

Rowlands admitted that this was so; then went on to relate the story of Clara's 'twin' (as he thought of her): Amélie Mendl.

'So you see it's a conundrum,' he said, when he had summarised, as briefly as he could, the facts about the missing seamstress. 'With Clara dead, there's no one who can say what happened to Amélie after she was arrested and sent to Ravensbrück. Did she die there, or did she get away, somehow, in all the confusion that followed the Liberation? Nobody knows – or is prepared to say. What seems clear is that she had become a danger to someone, perhaps someone in a position of importance. Hardly surprising that she's gone to ground.'

'Hmm,' said Douglas again. He had given up the attempt at relighting his pipe. 'A conundrum, as ye say. Still, it's a lot more interesting than the kind o' thing I've had to deal with these past few weeks. Sad, sordid little cases, for the most part. Cases that show the very worst of human nature. A man comes home on forty-eight hours leave to find his wife with a young child he doesn't recognise as his own. He kills both wife and child. The child, it may not surprise ye to know, isn't his wife's at all, but the child she happened to be minding for a neighbour. Sad, and sordid, like I said.'

'Jealousy's a terrible thing,' said Rowlands.

'Aye, that's as may be. But I fear this war has had a bad effect on people – making them hard and cruel. I'll be glad when they let me retire at last,' said Douglas. 'I'm sick to death o' the lot of 'em.'

Chapter Fifteen

Rowlands's visit to London – the city where he was born, and where he had lived for most of his life, until a German bomb had landed rather too close for comfort to the family home in Kingston – had not been solely for the purpose of looking up his old friend, Superintendent Douglas. Because now that the war was over, and things were returning to normal, there might be a chance that the house in Grove Crescent could be restored, so that he and Edith, and Edith's mother, and seventeen-year-old Joan, might return there at last. His two elder daughters, he knew, might very well have other plans. Margaret would be getting married soon. As for Anne . . . but he had no idea what Anne would want to do.

And so he'd taken a few days off work – there wasn't much doing anyway – and he and Edith had taken the train to Richmond, to stay with Edith's brother and his wife, with whom Joan had been staying during term-time, in order to attend the local girls' school. From Richmond, it had been a short bus ride to Kingston, and a few minutes' walk from the bus stop to the door of their former home. It had been many months since they'd last set foot there, and then it had only been to oversee the removal of their furniture to storage.

So it was an empty shell they contemplated now: a house that, although swept clean of the fallen plaster and broken glass that had littered the floor, and stripped of its ruined carpets and curtains, still had the musty smell of an abandoned dwelling, and the hollow echo of rooms long uninhabited. Even though it was not the first time Edith had seen the place in its present state, she couldn't repress a cry of dismay: 'Oh! My poor garden! The rose trellis has blown down since we were last here, Fred. And the kitchen garden's a mass of weeds.'

'That shouldn't be too difficult to put right,' he said. He had always done most of the gardening. Although a broken rose trellis and a few weeds were minor problems compared to the large crater left by an unexploded bomb that had destroyed most of the lawn. The bomb had been removed, the crater partially filled in and covered over with planks, but it was still an eyesore. 'What I'm more concerned about is the structural damage to the house. How bad does it look to you?'

'Well, there's still that great crack running across the right-hand wall . . . But it doesn't seem to have got any worse.'

'That's something,' he said. 'I'll get Tomkins to come and take a closer look.' This was the local builder. 'He'll give me an estimate for how much it's going to cost to fix . . . always assuming it can be fixed.'

The two of them had been strolling along the brick path that ran down the side of the garden and had paused so that Rowlands could inspect the condition of his fruit trees – the apple trees were in bloom, and the pear tree had almost finished flowering, while the cherry blossom was about to come out. Rowlands's guide dog, Rex, had been let off the lead, since his master could rely on his wife to guide him. The former had insisted, however, that Rex should accompany him to Kingston. The dog would need to get used to the place if they were to come back here, he said. It would be a big change from Brighton, but he was an intelligent animal and would adapt.

Now, as Rowlands drew a spray of apple blossom towards him in order to sniff its delicate smell, the Labrador, which had been nosing about in the shrubs that bordered the garden on its far side, suddenly let out a sharp bark. 'He's found something,' said Edith. 'I hope it's not some horrible dead animal . . . Drop it, Rex! Oh . . .' Because the dog had obediently dropped the object he'd retrieved at her feet.

'What is it?'

'A toy rabbit. It must have belonged to little June.'

'Yes.'

Both were silent, remembering the night of the raid that had destroyed their neighbour's house, killing June's father, Donald Watson, who had left the air-raid shelter to fetch a blanket for the child. Now nothing was left of the house next door but a heap of broken bricks and smashed timbers, overgrown with nettles and ground elder.

'Do you know where they're living now?' Rowlands said at last – meaning Mary Watson and her child.

'Durham, I think. She has family there.' Edith picked up the toy from where Rex had dropped it. 'What a terrible time this has been. I suppose we've been lucky.'

'We have.'

There was half an hour's wait before the next bus back to Richmond, and so, having locked up the house, they went for a walk. Grove Crescent was a quiet cul-de-sac off the main road, with the river on the other side, separated from the road by a steep bank. As he and Edith prepared to cross, Rowlands let go of his wife's arm. 'Rex can take me across. He'll have to get used to doing it, once we're living here again.'

'Oh, Fred. Do you think we will?'

'I'm sure of it,' he said.

It was peaceful strolling along the towpath, with only the occasional sound of a passing vehicle from the road above to disturb the quiet. A warm breeze blew in their faces, bringing with it a smell of freshly cut grass. A skiff came gliding towards them, its oars cutting through the water with a swishing sound. The rhythmic shouts of the cox, urging the rowers on, stirred memories for them both. 'I remember when I used to keep time for you,' said Edith, tucking her hand into the crook of her husband's arm.

'And very good at it you were,' he replied. 'Maybe I'll take up rowing again . . .'

'You'll have to cut back on the cigarettes, then. You're not as young as you used to be.'

There was no denying the truth of this.

They walked on for another few minutes. 'I forgot to tell you,' said Edith. 'I had a letter from Dorothy a couple of days ago. In all the fuss of coming up to London, it slipped my mind.'

'How are they?' Rowlands's sister and her husband ran a small hotel in Cornwall. After the bombing of Portsmouth and Southampton, it had been requisitioned as a hostel for those made homeless by these events – a fact which might have been irksome to some women, Rowlands thought, but which had been entirely to Dorothy's taste. She'd always been a zealous social reformer. Providing shelter for those dispossessed by the war would have been right up her street.

'They're fine. She and Jack are looking forward to the boys coming home, of course.'

'Any idea when that'll be?'

'The demobilisation starts next month, accord to the report I read in the *Telegraph*. But it'll depend on age and length of service as to who gets sent home first. No doubt Billy'll come home covered in glory,' she added, with the faintly acerbic note that usually entered her voice when Dorothy's eldest son was the topic.

'Yes, he's had a "good war",' said Rowlands. 'Promoted to squadron leader, no less! Dottie must be very proud.'

'Oh she is! Although Danny's done very well in the Marines – so Billy won't have *all* the glory to himself.' Danny was Dorothy and Jack's adopted son. Given the dreadful start he'd had in life, the lad had indeed done well, thought Rowlands. Nice young fellow, too. No 'side' to him.

'Any news of Walter?' He kept his tone neutral, but Edith knew him too well to be deceived.

'Fred!' she admonished him. 'I've *told* you you're not

to blame for what happened to that poor girl . . .'

'If I'd only been able to identify her that day, she might still be alive,' he said stubbornly. 'And now Walter has lost the only relative he had in the world.'

'Just put it out of your mind,' said Edith. 'There's nothing you could have done. We'd better turn back,' she added. 'Or we'll miss our bus. You know Diana hates people being late for lunch.'

Edith's sister-in-law combined a breezy manner with a decidedly old-fashioned dislike of what she called 'bad manners': 'Of course it couldn't matter *less* when you turn up! *I* don't give a hoot! I'd be *just* as happy with a sandwich for luncheon! It's just that Cook *insists* on a hot meal at midday – and she *does* get very huffy if the food is allowed to get cold . . .'

'Yes, we certainly mustn't be late for Diana.'

The next few weeks were busy ones for Rowlands. Peacetime, it seemed, was every bit as demanding of time and energy as war. For a start, there was all the administrative work that had to be done, before St Dunstan's men who had been temporarily housed in the organisation's property in Church Stretton – or at Melplash Court in Dorsetshire, which had been made available to St Dunstan's for the duration – could return to the purpose-built residential building on the cliffs at Ovingdean, which had been in use as a hospital since the beginning of the war.

Then there was sorting out what St Dunstaners were going to do now that there was no longer a need for camouflage nets to be manufactured, or mats for anti-aircraft guns to be produced. Would they be welcomed back to their peacetime jobs in factories, offices and shops, or would they be found surplus to requirements (as had happened in 1918), now that tens of thousands of sighted and able-bodied men were returning from the war? And what about the younger generation of newly blinded men who would need to be trained for whatever their future careers might be? It was – to use a word Rowlands had recently employed in another context – a conundrum.

There were times during those weeks when – exhausted by fielding telephones and dictating letters at the After-Care Unit in Brighton – Rowlands began to feel an affinity with Mr Bevan and his cohorts, similarly engaged in the seemingly impossible task of getting millions of British servicemen and women back to civilian life after the exigencies of war.

Between these work-related matters and the renovation works (now proceeding apace) on 44 Grove Crescent, Rowlands had little time to dwell on what had happened in Paris a month before. He had heard nothing more from Iris Barnes, who seemed once more to have vanished into the shadows in which she and her fellow MI6 operatives seemed always to dwell. He wondered if he would ever learn the fate of Amélie Mendl, or that of her friend, Sylvie Dubois. The investigation, with all its promising leads, had come to a dead end.

In the meantime, he – along with the rest of the country – was getting used to post-war life. The blackout had ended, with the resumption of full street lighting and the illumination of the clock on Big Ben – a token, for those able to appreciate it, that the nation had emerged

from the darkness of war into the light of a better world . . .
or so one hoped. For Rowlands, for whom darkness was
a permanent condition, the resumption of this aspect of
normal life could only have a symbolic value – although it
was one he was happy to celebrate along with his nearest
and dearest. 'Just think! No more putting up those filthy
blackout blinds every night!' said his daughter Joan. 'Ugh!
I used to hate the feel of them. Nasty, scratchy stuff.'

Food and petrol rationing continued. 'One would
think we were still at war,' grumbled Edith, faced with
the challenge of providing Sunday lunch for the whole
family when the Rowlandses' three daughters chose the
same weekend to arrive, so that, with all six of them in
residence, including Edith's mother, the little house in
Brighton was full to capacity.

'You'll manage,' said Rowlands. 'You always do.' And
indeed, by the time the family was assembled around
the table in the cramped little dining room of 6 Dorset
Gardens, his wife had contrived a very acceptable meal
of roast pork and apple sauce (Edith belonged to a local
'pig club'), roast potatoes and greens, with jam roly-poly
and custard for afters. Sitting in his accustomed place at
the head of the table, Rowlands felt himself blessed. Here
were those he loved best in the world, safely back under
his roof.

It was true that there had been changes – not all of
them happy. He was conscious of Anne, already lighting
up a cigarette after pushing away her plate; and of Edith's
intake of breath as she started to say something about
this and then decided not to. But Margaret seemed
happy enough, chatting away to her grandmother about

arrangements for the wedding; and Joan . . . was just Joan. 'Does anyone want the last roast potato?' Yes, on the whole, they had been fortunate . . . as many had not, he reminded himself.

There had been so many deaths – both of those known to him and those who were strangers. In the former category was Donald Watson, who had been their neighbour at Number 44, and Henrietta Swift, who had left the safety of neutral Ireland for the thrills of London's West End . . . to her cost, as it turned out.

Then there was Jonathan Simkins, Margaret's former admirer, from the days when the Rowlands and Simkins families had shared holidays in Cornwall. Jonty Simkins's Wellington had been shot down over Germany in the spring of 1943. Also among the dead that year were the crew of the Lancaster bomber D-Donald, with whom Rowlands had become acquainted while working on a case at RAF Mildenhall. Led by their dashing skipper, Rupert Moncrieff, the seven-strong crew had made it through thirty missions, only to find their number was up on the thirty-first.

A casualty of a different kind of war – one that was secret, and being fought against an enemy who did not always declare himself – was Jan Wawrzkowicz, the Polish Resistance fighter, to whom Anne had briefly been engaged and for whom she was now eating her heart out. Clara Metzner, too, had been a victim of this kind of war – as had the four SOE women who had vanished into the uncertainty of night and fog, and who were known to Rowlands only by their code names . . .

Yes, there had been too many deaths, he thought.

'Fred . . .' He became aware that his wife was speaking. 'I've asked you three times if you'd like a cup of tea.'

'Sorry. I was miles away. A cup of tea would be splendid, thanks.'

'I'll make it,' said Joan, springing to her feet. 'You sit still and rest, Mummy.'

'Now why does that make me feel a hundred?' said Edith, when their daughter had gone to fulfil this generous offer; but she was laughing as she said it. *She's happy too,* thought Rowlands.

'You wait till you *are* nearly a hundred,' said Mrs Edwards. 'You'll appreciate being made a fuss of then.'

'Mother, you know you don't look a day over sixty!' replied her daughter. 'Whereas *I* seem to be getting more lines every year.'

'Yes, I've always looked after my skin,' said Helen Edwards placidly. 'In my day, we didn't go in for sun-baths, as you young people do. And we didn't smoke – women, that is.'

If Anne took this remark as directed at herself, she gave no sign of it, but – having stubbed out the offending article – said she was going for a walk.

'Let's all go,' said Edith, as Joan returned with the tea-tray. 'I could do with a breath of air.' And so leaving Mrs Edwards to rest ('I won't join you, dears, if it's all the same to you. I've already had my little constitutional.') they set out on the short walk that led from the house to the sea.

The seafront was as busy as Rowlands had ever known it to be – this being a fine Sunday in what had only recently become peacetime. The beaches were of course still out of bounds, with tangles of barbed wire and tank traps barring the way to the sea. The sea itself regularly threw up unexploded mines, which had to be defused in order to be made safe. West Pier and Palace Pier were still partially dismantled (a precaution taken early in the war to deter enemy landing craft). Piles of sandbags lined the base of the promenade, where Rowlands, Edith and the girls, accompanied by Rex, now strolled – although the giant Bofors guns which had been placed at intervals along this stretch of the coast had now been removed.

There was a smell of frying fish in the air, and the vinegary tang of whelks and cockles from the stalls along the front. People thronged the pavements, clustering thickly outside the seafront pubs, from which heady aromas of beer and cigarettes mingled with the sounds of talk and laughter to produce a festive feeling. Someone was beating out a popular tune on a piano, with which voices of varying tunefulness joined in.

'Roll out the barrel,
Let's have a barrel of fun . . .'

Even Edith – who usually disdained the more plebeian amusements of her fellow citizens – seemed affected by the general air of relaxed goodwill. 'You know, I'll rather miss this place,' she said to her husband. 'It'll be strange to be back in Kingston after so many years living by the sea.'

'It might be a while before the house is fit to live in,' he reminded her. 'It all depends how long the underpinning takes. And then there's all the decorating to do . . .'

'I realise that. But after four years, I think I can stand another few months' wait.'

From up ahead, the voices of their daughters drifted back to them.

'I can't *believe* you're still hungry, after that enormous lunch.' This was Margaret to her youngest sibling.

'That was *hours* ago! Besides, I *like* fish and chips!'

'You'll get fat.' This was Anne. 'Then no one will marry you.'

'Who says I want to get married? And *you're* too thin, if it comes to that. Men like a well-rounded figure, Granny says.'

'I hope,' said Rowlands in an undertone to his wife, 'that they don't all rush off and get married. I feel I've hardly seen anything of the two older ones during these past few years . . . and not much of Joanie, either, since she's been staying at your brother's.'

'Oh, Joan'll be at home for another few years yet,' said Edith. 'As for Anne . . .' She broke off. 'She will be all right, won't she?' she added softly. 'I worry.'

'So do I. But I think she'll be fine,' he said, not sure if he believed it.

Chapter Sixteen

Another week passed before Rowlands was again able to visit the house in Grove Crescent. The 'cost of works' grant he'd been awarded by the War Damage Commission had specified that this was to cover the cost of returning the property to the way it had been before it had sustained bomb damage. Not a penny more would be offered once this had been achieved, and so he was anxious to make sure that the building costs were kept within this limit.

It was Anne who came with him on this occasion. She'd accumulated some leave, she said, as a result of which she'd been granted a whole week off. 'I've spent the past six weeks working non-stop. They're letting the married women go home first, so the unmarried ones like me are in demand to provide cover.'

'Hmm.'

This time, he didn't make the mistake of asking her if she was all right; after a moment, she said, 'I'm looking forward to seeing the old place again. It must be four years since I was last there. I remember it looked a complete wreck.'

'It's looking a bit better now.'

'Yes, I think it was the day after it was hit that I came. I'd just decided to join the WAAFs.'

He remembered that day only too well.

'I sometimes regret it . . . giving up the Ruskin, I mean.' This was the diploma in Fine Art she'd been doing at the Slade – which had been moved out of London by then, to Ruskin College in Oxford. 'But there wasn't really a choice, with everyone else joining up.'

'Of course not.'

'And then, if I hadn't joined the WAAFs, I'd never have met Jan,' she said.

'No.' Again, he refrained from further comment.

It was the first time she'd mentioned her lover since the news of his death had been conveyed to her by her father, who had heard of it first from Iris Barnes. 'It's all right, you know,' Anne went on. 'I don't think about him very much any more. One can't live in the past.'

'That's true.'

'I learnt that from you,' she said; then, as the train began to slow down, 'I say, I think this must be our stop. Rex knew it right away, didn't you, old boy? What a clever dog you are! You can lead the way to dear old Grove Crescent.'

When they arrived at the house, it was to find it clad in scaffolding, from the top of which the builder, Wilfred Tomkins, hailed them. 'Hi! Mr Rowlands! I was hoping you'd come today! Brought the young lady wiv yer, too, I see . . .'

Rowlands introduced Anne.

'Very nice, too, miss, if I might say so. Bin doin' yer bit for the country too, I reckon.' This was doubtless because Anne was in uniform. 'Tell yer what,' bellowed the affable Tomkins from his Olympian height, 'why don't I come down there, seein' as you can't come up 'ere . . . an' I'll let you know 'ow I've bin gettin' on wiv mending this 'ere roof . . . Stanley!' This last was to the silent youth who was Tomkins's assistant and who, as far as Rowlands could tell, did most of the work. 'You can make us a nice cuppa tea while I talk to Mr Rowlands 'ere . . . Tha's right, you make yerself comfortable, like, Mr Rowlands. There's a packing case right be'ind yer. Lovely dog, this.' He bent to fondle Rex's ears. 'Stanley! Bowl o' water for Mr Rowlands's dog while yer abaht it . . . Nah then, about these joists . . .'

While her father was thus engrossed, Anne, declining the offer of tea, had wandered along the road a little way – perhaps to look at what remained of the house next door, or just to remind herself of what life had been like when she was growing up in this pleasant neighbourhood before the war. Yes, one shouldn't live in the past, thought Rowlands; but sometimes it was good to remember what had been.

'. . . so what I reckon is, we only have to replace the damaged sections,' Tomkins was saying. 'Which'll keep costs down, you'll agree, and means there'll still be some money left over for doin' up the inside of the property.'

'That is good news,' said Rowlands distractedly. Because he'd become aware, as they were sitting there, each perched on a packing case and nursing a tin mug of powerful sweet tea, of the voices of two people – at first some way off, then coming closer. One of them belonged to his daughter. The other . . .

'Good afternoon, Mr Rowlands! I am sorry to intrude upon your conversation. But I have been up and down this street in search of the house. Then, by fortunate chance, I happened to meet Anne . . .'

'Walter.' Rowlands got to his feet. 'I'm very glad to see you.'

'Oh, so you know this young gennelman, do yer?' interrupted Tomkins. 'Only I saw 'im from up above – hangin' abaht, 'ee was – an' I fort to meself, "What's the Navy doin' 'ere?" No offence meant,' he added hastily.

'None taken, I assure you,' said Walter Metzner.

'But . . .' Rowlands was struggling to take in the appearance, out of the blue, of the young man with whom his thoughts had been preoccupied in recent weeks. 'Where did you come from?'

'If you mean today, then from the Cliff House Hotel. I have been staying with dear Mr and Mrs Ashenhurst, who have always been so kind to me. Before that, I was in Simonstown – which is the port for Cape Town, you know. My ship arrived in Portsmouth ten days ago.'

'Then you haven't been in Paris?'

'Paris? No.'

'And you didn't receive the telegram?'

'I did not. Mr Rowlands, what means this? I can see by your face that something is wrong . . .'

'I fink,' said Wilfred Tomkins, 'that it's time you an' me was gettin' back to work, Stanley, an' leavin' these folks to their private conversation. Come along, me lad, don't dawdle!'

'Thank you, Mr Tomkins. You're doing a grand job,' said Rowlands. 'I feel sure I can leave the works in your capable hands.'

Once the builder and the builder's mate had returned to their lofty eminence at the top of the scaffolding, Rowlands turned to Walter Metzner. 'I'm afraid I've some bad news for you. Perhaps it's best if we find somewhere we can talk without interruption.'

A short walk from the house brought them to the Ram, a pub on the river, where the landlord was on the point of taking down the shutters. Apart from a crew of thirsty rowers, who had just disembarked onto the towpath, Rowlands and his two companions were the only customers. 'What'll you have?' he asked the young naval officer.

'A pint of bitter,' was the reply. 'I have not tasted English beer for a long time. In South Africa, you know, the beer is like our German beer.'

'Anne?'

'Half of the same, please.'

All three seemed reluctant to broach the subject that must have been uppermost in all their minds. 'I must say, you're looking very brown and fit, Walter,' said Anne, as her father returned with the drinks. 'All that South African sun, I suppose?'

'Yes. You, however, are rather pale. A consequence of the English weather, no doubt . . . So tell me,' said Metzner, abruptly changing the subject, 'what it is you have to say, Mr Rowlands? Have you news of my mother?'

Rowlands winced. This was worse than he'd feared. 'I'm afraid I've no reliable news about your mother,' he replied. 'But what I've heard isn't good, I'm afraid. Although with things being as uncertain as they are these days, one probably shouldn't jump to conclusions.' He took a breath, to give himself the courage to say what he had to say. 'It's your sister I need to talk to you about. You see . . .'

'But this is very strange!' interrupted Metzner. 'I have had a letter from Clara.'

'What?'

'Yes – it was waiting for me at Cliff House when I returned there a few days ago. I have it with me. See?'

He must have taken the envelope from his breast pocket, for Anne said, 'It's got a French stamp. May I see?'

'Certainly.' He handed it to her.

'Posted two weeks ago,' said Anne, in a puzzled tone.

'That's impossible,' said Rowlands.

'No, it's quite clearly postmarked 8.5.45.'

'I don't care what the postmark says – it can't have been posted by Clara . . .'

'Will somebody please tell me what is going on?' said Walter Metzner. 'I show you a letter I have received from my sister – which, by the way, I am willing to swear is in her handwriting – and you tell me it cannot be so. You must explain please, Mr Rowlands.'

'All right,' said Rowlands. 'I'll tell you what I know.'

When he had done so, Metzner was silent for a long moment. 'I do not understand,' he said at last. 'You tell me my sister is dead – perhaps murdered. You do not know for certain that this is so, however. You are also unable to say whether the woman you met and spoke to, before she died, was Clara . . .'

'I've told you. She is – was – very much changed. But she knew certain things about your family, and the life you had together in Berlin, that suggested she might have been who she claimed to be.'

'And I am telling you that she must have been lying, whoever she was,' said Metzner. 'Read the letter if you need proof.'

'Read it, Anne.'

She withdrew the letter from the envelope and unfolded it. 'It's in German.'

'Naturally, since my sister and I grew up speaking that language. I will translate for you.' He cleared his throat and read aloud: '"My dear Walter, I hope this reaches you in Cornwall. I have no other address to which to send it. I am well, as you see. I am living for the moment in Paris – a temporary address. If you wish to write to me, you can send it c/o Poste Restante, Box No. 252. I have much to tell you. Write soon, little brother. Yours ever, Clara." So you see,' Metzner concluded, having folded up the letter and put it away, 'my sister is alive and well. Whoever that woman was that you met, it cannot have been Clara.'

Then who was it? wondered Rowlands; but he said nothing.

'You will think me very rude,' went on the young naval officer. 'I have not asked how you and your family are. Forgive me. This business with Clara has put everything else out of my mind. I trust you and dear Mrs Rowlands are well?'

'Very well.'

'And Margaret and little Joan?'

'Both well.'

'That is good,' said Metzner. 'I can see for myself that Anne is well . . . although rather pale, as I said. You have been working too hard, perhaps, Anne? Burning the midnight oil, as you say.'

'You know me,' said Anne. 'I never turn down an invitation to a party.'

'Well, there has been reason to celebrate, has there not? The end of this terrible war . . . although of course, it is not over yet. Only for us in Europe . . . those that survive,' he added under his breath. Something seemed to strike him for the first time. 'But where are you and the rest of your family living? For it appears that the house where you used to live, and where I was fortunate enough to find you, is no longer habitable.'

Rowlands told him. 'It was rather a stroke of luck, your finding us here,' he said. 'The house had stood empty for the past four years.'

'It was indeed lucky.' The young man finished his drink, and got to his feet. 'I must go,' he said. 'I am expected back at the ship tomorrow.'

'Where will you stay tonight?'

'I will find somewhere. A station hotel.'

'You'll come back with us,' said Rowlands. 'You can catch the train to Portsmouth first thing in the morning. Mrs Rowlands would never forgive me if I let you spend your last night of leave in an hotel.'

They arrived in Brighton to find that Margaret's fiancé, Lieutenant Frank Dawson, had also been granted leave from his ship, so a general mood of celebration prevailed. Edith had, for a wonder, managed to procure a joint of beef for their meal that evening, which, accompanied by horseradish sauce, as well as plenty of roast potatoes and green peas, made a suitably satisfying repast for the seven of them. The only family member missing was Joan, who had begged to be allowed to spend the weekend at her uncle and aunt's in Richmond, in order to attend a summer fête.

As their little party sat around the table in the tiny dining room, Edith – having extracted as much information as she could from Walter, concerning the well-being or otherwise of the family in Cornwall – plied both the naval officers with questions as to how soon they could expect to be demobbed. 'Surely, now that the war's over they'll be letting you go home?'

'The war isn't over yet, Mother.' This was Anne. 'There's still fighting in the Far East.'

'I know that! But it seems only fair that they should release the ones who've been serving nearer home . . .'

'You're looking brown as a berry, Walter,' said Margaret, perhaps to deflect attention from this likely topic of contention. 'Unlike Frank here.'

'Yes, most of my postings were to cold northern climes,' laughed Dawson. 'I'd hoped for Gibraltar, but it didn't happen – or at least, it hasn't so far.'

'Do you intend to stay in the service, then?' said Metzner.

There was an awkward silence.

'More potatoes, Frank?' said Edith, with whom her prospective son-in-law was a favourite. 'Or another slice of meat?'

'Yes, please, Mrs R,' was the reply. 'The fact is, we've

been discussing various possibilities, Margaret and I,' he went on, when his plate had been refilled. 'My job remains open at Bray and Hollingsworth' – this was the solicitor's office where he had been doing his articles – 'and then there are Margaret's studies to consider.'

'Yes, when I last saw you, Margaret, you were still at Cambridge,' said Walter. 'Studying mathematics, I think.'

'Oh, a lot has happened since then,' replied Margaret.

'A world war, for one,' put in Anne sardonically.

'The fact is, I'm not sure I want to return to academic life,' went on Margaret, ignoring this interpolation. 'Especially now that Frank's got his promotion. He's lieutenant commander now, you know . . .'

'You'll be given a ship of your own, next,' said Anne, still in the same ironic tone. 'I can just see you as a commander's wife, Meg.'

'Oh, I doubt it will come to that,' said Dawson quickly. 'There are far too many deserving fellows ahead of me in the queue.'

'I think this calls for a toast,' said Edith. 'We can have it before the summer pudding. Fred, there's that bottle of sherry in the sideboard. Anne, you can fetch the glasses. Now we've two things to celebrate – Frank's promotion and your safe return home, Walter.'

Toasts were accordingly drunk; the summer pudding was brought in and served out; a contented pause followed. Then Margaret said, 'Delightful as it is to sit around drinking, the washing-up won't do itself.'

'I'll help you,' said Dawson, getting up.

'I'd offer to help, too – but you two lovebirds won't want me getting in the way,' said Anne. The bitterness in her voice saddened Rowlands. 'I suppose you'll be carrying on with your doctoring, won't you?' she said to Metzner. 'There'll always be plenty of opportunities for doctors.'

'That is true,' he replied simply. 'I do not think I will be short of work in the days to come.'

Paris, June 1945

Chapter Seventeen

Passing under the great arched roof of the Gare du Nord, the train began to reduce speed as it moved towards its designated platform. Rowlands felt the young man at his side give a start. 'Paris . . .' breathed Walter Metzner, in a tone of subdued emotion. 'I am glad to be here again after so long.' The allusion, Rowlands knew, was to the time, now a dozen years ago, when the lad, then aged twelve, had passed through the city after leaving his native Berlin – a journey necessitated by the increasingly dangerous conditions for Jews in Germany. Now, with the danger having largely receded, he was returning in the hope of reconnecting with that past, and with the life he had been forced to abandon.

As the train came to a halt, Metzner was already on his feet, lifting down their luggage from the rack. It had been a week since the telephone call, in which the young man, his voice trembling a little with excitement, had announced his intention of making this journey: 'Herr

Rowlands . . . forgive me . . . I am forgetting my English. I have heard from her . . . from Clara. She has replied to my letter. I will read it to you . . .'

'It's Walter,' said Rowlands to his wife, who had been hovering at his shoulder as he stood in the hall with the telephone receiver in his hand. Not for the first time, he found himself grateful that the St Dunstan's houses had telephones installed as a matter of course. 'Hello . . . Are you still there?'

'I am here. I was just finding the passage in the letter. It does not say much, but . . .'

'Three minutes, caller,' said the operator.

'Yes, yes. A minute more, if you please . . . This is what she says: "Ask for me at the Hôtel Saint-Denis in Rue Lepic. It is near the Cimetière de Montmartre. I will meet you there. It will be safer, thus." You see?' he had cried, as the 'pips' began to go, 'It is as I said. She is safe and well.'

Perhaps not as 'safe' as all that, thought Rowlands, if such secrecy was necessary. 'When do you leave for Paris?' he asked.

'Another minute, operator, please! I leave as soon as I can. But I must ask a favour, Mr Rowlands. I should like you to come with me. Clara knows you . . . and she has not seen me since I was a child.'

Metzner was all for going straight to the Rue Lepic, and the hotel where he hoped to find his sister; but as it was now midday, Rowlands suggested that they should first get something to eat, and perhaps seek out a place to stay for the night before proceeding further. It seemed to him that after a separation lasting twelve years, another few hours wouldn't make much difference.

Metzner thought differently, of course. 'I have already wasted another week since I received Clara's letter,' he said, as the two of them emerged onto the Boulevard de Magenta. 'My commanding officer was not at first convinced that I could be spared. If we delay any longer, I am afraid that Clara will think I am not coming . . .'

In the end, they compromised by walking as far as Barbès-Rochechouart metro station (since neither was overburdened with luggage), pausing on the way at a pavement café for a cup of coffee and a ham and cheese baguette to take the edge of their hunger. From here, Line 2 took them as far as Pigalle, from which metro station a short walk along Rue des Abbesses brought them to Rue Lepic. For most of the journey – whether on foot or by metro – Metzner said little, only breaking his silence to ask for directions when they came to an intersection.

The contrast with the talkative Sebastian Gogarty, so loud in his appreciation of all things Parisian, could not have been sharper. Instead of the enthusiastic cries of 'Oh, I s-say! D-do look at that! H-how m-marvellous . . .' which had punctuated Rowlands's walks and drives around the city with the young Irishman, there was only a morose silence.

He himself was enjoying the sensation of being once more in this most enchanting of cities. The smells of baking bread and pastries wafting from nearby shops, mingled with the distinctive odour of French cigarettes, and the occasional snatch of conversation: *Non! C'est vrai! Ma foi! C'est incroyable* . . . All this, and a great deal more, contributed to his general feeling of . . . call it *joie de vivre*.

Coupled with this agreeable emotion was a less pleasant feeling of unease. Because he was here, wasn't he, under false pretences? Instead of making contact with Miss Barnes, on returning to Paris with the young man whom she needed to identify a body, he was . . . well, wandering around, soaking up impressions like a blessed tourist. Although, he told himself, it was really her responsibility to make contact . . . not that she could do so without knowing that he and Metzner had arrived. Should he report to the Hôtel Cécil, then? He wasn't sure of the etiquette of *that*, either . . .

They had reached the Hôtel Saint-Denis. 'It looks rather a shabby place,' said Metzner dubiously. 'I hope Clara is not short of money.'

'I'm sure it's perfectly fine. Well . . .' Since the young man appeared to be hesitating, 'shall we go in?'

'You go,' said Metzner suddenly. It struck Rowlands that, far from looking forward to the encounter with his long-lost sibling, he was actually dreading it. 'You can prepare her.'

'Walter, I really think . . .'

'Please,' said the other. 'You will know what to say. You always do.'

'All right.' But he found, as he entered the mean little building, whose entrance hall smelt of bad drains and boiled cabbage, that his heart was beating rather too fast. In the foyer, Rowlands found the proprietor, busying himself with some routine task behind the desk. His question as to whether Mademoiselle Metzner was in residence was met with silence, accompanied, he guessed, by an indifferent shrug. He repeated the question. This time it brought a response: '*Il n'y a pas une telle personne ici.*'

Then, as Rowlands was about to turn away:

'*Attends. J'ai une lettre.*'

The letter – a single sheet of cheap paper, perhaps torn from a notebook – was as cryptic in what it said as the earlier missives had been:

Meet me at 5 p.m. at Wilde's tomb in P.L.

'Père Lachaise,' said Rowlands, when Metzner puzzled over this. 'The cemetery. It's nearby.'

'But that means we've almost three hours to wait,' said Metzner, sounding both disgruntled and (Rowlands thought) somewhat relieved that the meeting was to be postponed a little longer.

'It'll give us time to find somewhere to stay,' replied Rowlands, who had already decided that this would not be the Saint-Denis. They accordingly retraced their steps, and after a few minutes found themselves outside what appeared to be a more salubrious establishment in Rue des Abbesses. Here, they were able to secure two small but clean rooms and make arrangements for dinner that evening.

Although whether they would require a table for two or three persons remained to be seen, thought Rowlands. He couldn't suppress a feeling of apprehension – no doubt on account of the cloak-and-dagger nature of the arrangements. He wondered whether these were merely the result of a taste for intrigue on the part of Clara

Metzner (if it was indeed she they were going to meet) or because she felt herself under some genuine threat.

Given what had happened to the woman who had claimed to be her – and indeed to the other two young women caught up in the case – this seemed not unreasonable.

Then there was the question of whether – or how soon – he should inform Miss Barnes of their presence in Paris. When he had last seen her, almost two months ago, she had been expecting young Metzner to arrive, in order to confirm that the dead woman they had thought to be Metzner's sister was indeed who they supposed her to be.

But when he put this to Metzner, the latter seemed reluctant to perform this task (one might even have called it a duty). 'I don't see what it's got to do with me. That woman – whoever she was – can't have been Clara. Clara's alive – and here, in Paris. How else do you explain her letters? There's no way anyone but the real Clara could have written them – or known the address to send them to in Cornwall.' Which wasn't quite true, thought Rowlands – she could have obtained the information in the same way as she had the details of the Metzner family's life in Berlin; but he supposed the young man had a point.

In the end, they agreed on a compromise: Rowlands would telephone Miss Barnes at the Hôtel Cécil with the news of Metzner's arrival in Paris. The decision as to whether or not to bring the young man in to identify the body of the unknown woman would then be hers alone. And so, after depositing their bags at the Hôtel Juliette, they crossed the street to the little bar where, having settled his companion at one of the tables with a glass of wine, Rowlands purchased a number of tokens for the telephone from the bar's proprietor and entered the cabin to the side of the bar to make his call.

He had the number in his head, having trained his memory to retain such things during his days working as a solicitor's receptionist. He dialled and was rewarded with the sound of the connection being made; then of the ringing tone: once, twice, three times . . . ''Allo?' said a voice he knew. There was a note of suspicion in the voice, as the number he'd dialled was the direct one for MI6.

'Madame Collins? It's Frederick Rowlands. I wonder if I might speak to Miss Barnes, if she's there?'

There was a moment's delay, followed by a silence, as if the receiver had been covered while his request was relayed to another. Then: 'Frederick? You're in Paris, I gather?' It seemed to Rowlands that Miss Barnes didn't sound altogether surprised at this.

He explained.

'Ah, so you've got Walter Metzner with you. Better and better! Tell me where you are, and I'll send a car for you.'

At the Hôtel Cécil, Rowlands and Metzner were met at the door, then ushered up the stairs and into Iris Barnes's office by the ever-efficient Mrs Collins. 'There you are, Fred!' said the MI6 officer breezily, as if she and Rowlands had met only the previous day, instead of nearly two months before. 'And you must be Mr Metzner.' They had in fact, met some years earlier – something which neither chose to remind the other. It was only later that Metzner said, 'She was in Spain that time, wasn't she? I knew her at once . . . although she looks different. She's done something to her hair. Changed the colour, I think. And those glasses make her look older . . .'

'Some tea, Louise, if you'd be so kind,' said Miss Barnes; then, when the three of them were alone, 'I'm glad you've decided to turn up at last, Mr Metzner.'

'I didn't—' he began; but Rowlands cut across him.

'It appears there's some doubt as to the identity of the girl we found dead at Fresnes prison,' he said.

'Oh?' Again, she didn't sound surprised. 'Then who was she?'

'Whoever she was, it wasn't my sister Clara,' said Metzner. 'Because I'm meeting her this evening.'

'Even so,' replied Miss Barnes, after a moment. 'I'd like to make absolutely sure. You won't object, I hope, Mr Metzner, to accompanying me to the mortuary. It shouldn't take up much of your time,' she added, perhaps seeing from his expression that he was about to protest. 'I can have you back in Paris within the hour.'

'I'm supposed to be meeting Clara at five,' said Metzner. 'In Père Lachaise cemetery.'

'Don't worry, you'll manage it with time to spare. Ah, thank you, Louise.' For the secretary had entered with the tea-tray. There was a brief hiatus while tea was poured out and cups dispensed; then Miss Barnes went on, 'So when did you last hear from your sister, Mr Metzner? Or may I call you Walter?'

Fresnes Prison was as grim as Rowlands remembered it: there was the same oppressive feeling as one entered the gates; the same disagreeable smells of carbolic, urine and institutional food hung in the air. The morgue was in the basement. Guided by the prison governor – not Madame Bodin, this time, but a man – who had been expecting them, they descended a flight of stone stairs into a chill netherworld. Here, the smells were masked – although not entirely obliterated – by still more powerful disinfectant, and sounds were muted. Rubber doors flapped open as they entered, and closed again behind them. Rubber-soled shoes padded noiselessly across tiled floors.

In the room to which they came at last, an orderly slid a metal drawer from a cabinet. A cloth was pulled back.

'God in heaven,' said Walter Metzner, after a shocked silence. 'What happened to her to make her look like that?'

Iris Barnes ignored the question. 'Do you recognise this woman?' she said sharply.

'No. I . . . I've never seen her in my life.' His voice sounded choked with horror. 'Who is she? What did they *do* to her?'

'Can you say positively that this is not your sister Clara?'

'No . . . I . . . It *can't* be her.' Metzner sounded close to tears. 'I've told you. My sister's alive.'

'But you're not absolutely certain it isn't her?' The MI6 officer's tone was relentless.

'How *can* I be certain? I haven't seen my sister since I was twelve years old. And this . . . this woman's nothing but a bag of bones . . .'

'Do you recognise this?' Iris Barnes must have held something out to him, because Metzner gave a gasp. 'It was taken from around her neck when she was found.'

'It's her locket. It belonged to my mother. But how . . .' He broke off, then went on, 'How did it come here?'

Iris Barnes was silent a moment; then she said, 'So you still insist that this can't be your sister, Clara?'

'I . . . I can't be sure. It might be. But then . . .'

'Then whoever you're going to meet at five o'clock tonight must be somebody else,' she finished for him. Then, when he seemed incapable of replying, 'I believe the woman you're intending to meet is called Amélie Mendl. She was your sister's friend. They met in Ravensbrück concentration camp. It was while they were there that they must have agreed to exchange identities.'

They entered Père Lachaise by the main gate. It was a quarter to the hour. The place shut at six, the guardian of the cemetery had warned them as he ushered them in, and so they couldn't afford to waste time. As it was, said Metzner, breaking a long silence, they'd be lucky to get to the appointed meeting place by five. He hadn't realised, he said, how enormous this place was. Since their return from Fresnes, he had been even more taciturn than usual – preoccupied, Rowlands guessed, by thoughts of what he had seen there.

Only once, during the hour that had passed since they'd left the confines of the prison in the back of the official car, had he touched upon this. It had been when he and Rowlands, having been dropped off at the metro station at Madeleine, were waiting for the Line 12 train that would take them to Abbesses. 'Those people standing over there,' he said abruptly. 'The ones that look like death . . . with such terrible eyes . . . Was she one of them?'

'I think so.'

These were the people who'd returned from the

camps, Rowlands knew. The Jews who'd survived to tell the tale . . . They had been described to him in much the same way by Iris Barnes on his arrival in Paris. He couldn't of course see what they looked like for himself, but he'd been able to ascertain enough from that one meeting at the prison with Clara Metzner – if indeed that was who she had been. He remembered the feel of her hand in his, like a little bundle of bones; her listless manner and the sour smell of her flesh.

'What was done to them?' cried Metzner – to which there was no answer that Rowlands could give.

From the gate – 'like the entrance to Hades' said Metzner – they walked along the main avenue, consulting the map the young man had been given by the cemetery's custodian. 'Rossini . . .' he murmured, as they passed the elaborate tomb of the famous composer. 'Alfred de Musset . . . Haussmann . . .' The latter, as prefect of the Seine region, having been responsible for the transformation of Paris into its present glory.

After walking for a few more minutes, in a silence interspersed by Metzner's appalled comments on the vulgarity of the memorials – the weeping angels and plump cherubs . . . above all, the mausoleums, with their ornate decorations 'like something you'd find on a mantlepiece' said Metzner – they came at last to the chapel. 'What a monstrosity,' he muttered. 'This place gives me the creeps. We go right here, I think . . .'

It was very quiet in this city of the dead; only the rustling of the wind in the treetops and the cawing of rooks broke the unearthly silence. Once, they passed an old man – a gardener, Rowlands supposed – wheeling a barrow full of garden refuse. Rotting lilies, from the smell of them. Metzner hailed him: 'Which way to Wilde's tomb, Grandpa?' But he made no reply. 'Deaf,' muttered the young man. 'I think it's this way, however . . .'

Now, they wandered in a maze of interconnecting paths, running between graves of those – both famous and obscure – who'd dedicated their lives to the visual arts. Gustave Doré, Ingres, Lalique . . . Metzner read the names inscribed on the tombs aloud. It seemed to Rowlands that they were making little progress. Surreptitiously, he checked his watch. Three minutes to five.

They had entered what seemed to be a relatively unpopulated area – or maybe it was that Metzner had grown tired of reading out the names of the dead. 'Good God, what's that?' exclaimed the young man suddenly, as they came upon a tomb that was set a little way apart from the others. 'It looks like a kind of angel – or an avenging Fury . . .'

The words had scarcely passed his lips when the sound of a shot rang out, shattering the silence. Instinctively, Rowlands flung himself flat on the ground, dragging his companion down with him.

Chapter Eighteen

For a long moment, as they lay there in the dust, Rowlands's one thought was that they must get out of the open. As it was, they were sitting ducks for the marksman – whoever he might be. 'Listen,' he said to Metzner in an undertone. 'Can you see anywhere we can take cover?'

The answer to this was a stifled groan; then Metzner said, forcing the words out through gritted teeth, 'There's that . . . monstrous tomb . . . with the angel . . . We could hide . . . behind that . . .'

'You're hurt,' said Rowlands.

'Bullet clipped my shoulder.'

'Can you run?'

'Think so.'

'Then . . . let's go!'

With which Rowlands scrambled to his feet, hauling Metzner after him. In another moment, they stumbled against what felt to Rowlands like a wall of smooth stone. He caught his breath. 'We must get you to a doctor,' he said.

'Yes.' The other emitted a laugh that was more of a gasp of pain. 'To think . . . I got through the war . . . without a scratch . . . and now . . .'

'Quiet! Someone's coming.'

His sharper hearing had picked up the sound of hurrying footsteps on the gravel path. Was this the assassin, come to finish the job? If so, they were done for.

'*Est-ce que ça va? J'ai entendu un coup de feu . . .*' The voice – a man's – was warm and concerned.

Rowlands replied that his friend was hurt, but not badly. '*As-tu vu qui l'a fait?*'

'*Non . . . mais . . .* You are English!' said the stranger. 'I am sorry that you should have been attacked in our city.'

'Who *are* you?' demanded Metzner. 'How do we know that it wasn't you who shot at us?'

'I have no gun,' replied the other. 'See?' He must have held up his hands, or made some other placatory gesture. 'You are free to search me if you wish. But it was not I . . .'

'All right. I'll take your word for it,' said Metzner grudgingly. Suddenly he remembered why they were there. 'But where is she?' he cried. 'It's past five o'clock.'

The thought had struck Rowlands at the same time. 'Have you seen a young woman about? We were supposed to meet her here.'

'A woman? No. Although I did see somebody running away . . . perhaps the one who shot at you.'

A dreadful suspicion crossed Rowlands's mind. Maybe Metzner hadn't been the gunman's only victim . . . 'Was it just one shot that you heard?' he asked the newcomer.

'I think so . . . *Attention!* Your friend looks as if he is about to pass out.'

'I'm perfectly fine,' protested Metzner feebly; but the other, whoever he was, paid no attention to this.

'Let me look,' he said to Metzner; then, after a moment, 'I do not think the wound is deep . . . Have you a handkerchief, monsieur?' he added to Rowlands. The latter produced one, and their rescuer proceeded to tie it tightly around Metzner's upper arm, making a temporary tourniquet. 'My medical school studies came to an end when the Germans moved in,' he said. 'But I still remember some basic first aid. There! That will hold for the moment.'

'Thank you,' muttered Metzner.

'It is nothing. You look a better colour. Do you think you can walk?'

'Of course.'

'Good. Then I will take you to my house. It is just over there . . .'

'I'm not leaving this spot,' said Metzner stubbornly. 'Clara . . . my sister . . . might still come. I cannot let her down.'

So he still clung onto the thought that it was his sister – and not the woman impersonating her – whom he had come to meet, Rowlands realised.

'That wound must be properly cleaned and dressed,' said the other. 'If you wish, I can bring you back here once I have done this. Or I can take you to a registered doctor, if you prefer . . .'

'No. I have to stay here.'

'I think the best solution is that *I* should stay here – at least for the next hour, until the cemetery closes,' said Rowlands. 'It may be that Clara will appear, once she knows it's safe to do so.' *Or she might already be dead,* he thought, but did not say. 'I think you should go with Monsieur . . .'

'Diop,' said the stranger. 'Jerome Diop.'

'Frederick Rowlands.' The two shook hands. From this brief contact, Rowlands received an impression of a lithe, muscular young man, slightly below average height. His hand was thin, but strong. 'As you may have noticed, Monsieur Diop, I am blind . . .'

'Yes, I see it now,' said Diop. 'Although you disguise it well. Some men carry a stick.'

'I usually do. And I have a dog at home, in England.' Rowlands shrugged. 'But I can find my way without either, if the route is not too difficult . . .'

'It is not. From here, you must follow the Avenue Circulaire – that is the main path that runs around the perimeter of the cemetery – until you come to the gate onto Avenue Gambetta. My house is in the Rue des Rondeaux. It is about a hundred metres to your left when you come out of the gate. I am on the second floor. Above a wine shop. You cannot miss it.'

With this, he and Metzner began to walk away, moving slowly and haltingly on account of the latter's injury. 'Tell Clara I'm sorry not to have waited,' called Metzner, his voice betraying the pain he was in. 'Tell her I want to see her, more than anything.'

'I will, don't worry.' *Always supposing she turns up, whoever she is,* thought Rowlands. If he felt a qualm about letting Metzner go off with the remarkably helpful Jerome Diop, he swiftly dismissed it. There had been no choice, with Metzner in the state he was in. As Rowlands knew only too well from his soldiering days (and as Metzner himself would have known), an untreated wound could turn bad very quickly, leading to fever – or worse. And Diop – an African name, he guessed – had certainly been a Good Samaritan. Although how he had come to arrive on the scene so soon after the shot had been fired was something Rowlands wasn't yet prepared to put down to coincidence . . .

When the footsteps of the other two had died away, he took stock of his surroundings. He was still standing with his back to the Wilde memorial. If he stretched out his hand he could touch the wings of the angel – a Modernist being, to judge from its stylised form. On both sides of the monument were other, less elaborate tombs, he discovered. Even though he was tempted to search a bit further afield to see if he could find a clue as to what had happened here – an abandoned gun, for instance – he knew it would be foolish to stray too far away from the arranged meeting place.

There was still a chance that Clara Metzner – or her doppelgänger, the elusive Amélie Mendl – would appear.

He checked his Braille watch. It was half past five. There was still half an hour before the cemetery closed. Cautiously, taking care to count his steps (a technique he found useful in unfamiliar territory), he walked a short distance along the path in one direction; then turned and retraced his steps a few paces beyond the memorial in the other. 'Clara,' he called softly. 'You can come out, now. It's quite safe.'

He strained his ears to hear a sound – a rustle in the shrubbery that bordered the path, perhaps – that would betray the presence of another. 'Clara,' he called again.

'It's me, Frederick Rowlands . . .' But there was no sound, except that of the wind in the trees.

After a few more minutes of this sentry-go, Rowlands decided there was no point in remaining any longer. He'd make his way to the Rue des Rondeaux, and see how young Metzner was doing. The latter would be disappointed that his sister had failed to keep the appointment – but there was no help for that.

His decision was, in any case, hastened by the arrival of the cemetery's custodian, brandishing a bell, which he was wielding with some energy. 'Monsieur! The cemetery will be closing in ten minutes,' he cried, as he drew nearer, panting a little from the steep climb. 'You must make your way to the gate. The Gambetta exit is the nearest . . .' All this was conveyed in rapid French, the sense of which Rowlands was able to grasp without too much difficulty. The past few days, combined with the two weeks in April that he'd spent in Paris, had evidently polished up his rusty language skills.

'I was just going,' he replied. 'But before I do, perhaps you can tell me if you have seen a young woman about, within the past hour?'

'A woman, eh?' said the old man suspiciously. 'What does she look like, this woman?'

'I'm afraid I am not in a position to tell you – other than that she may have dark hair.'

'Hmph!' said the other; then, peering closer, 'You are blind, are you not? Was it the war?'

He was of the generation – as was Rowlands – for whom this meant the First War, not the Second. When the latter agreed that it was 'the war' that had left him blind, the custodian said, 'Ah, that terrible war! I was at Verdun, me. I lost many comrades there.'

'That was indeed a terrible battle. Your army fought very bravely.'

'We did. And we killed many Boche,' said the old man; then, when Rowlands produced his cigarettes, 'Thank you, monsieur. I will accept one in memory of that time . . . And no, I have not seen any young woman, dark or fair. They are mostly old women who come to tend the graves, you understand?'

Rowlands said that he did. The two of them lit up, and stood smoking their cigarettes in companionable silence for a minute or two. 'Well,' said Rowlands at last. 'I had better be going. The Gambetta gate, you said?'

'Yes, monsieur. But you have forgotten your cigarette lighter,' said the custodian. 'See? It is on the ledge below the angel. An old trench lighter, is it not? I had one very like it when I was in the army.'

Rowlands was about to say that the lighter was not his, and that it must have been left by some other visitor to the tomb. But an instinct that there must have been something deliberate about the placing of the object restrained him. He took it from the old man's hand. 'Thank you,' he said.

The Rue des Rondeaux was a cobbled street that ran along the cemetery wall for a short distance, and then forked right at the corner wine shop Diop had mentioned. Here, finding the door on the latch, Rowlands climbed a rickety flight of stairs, following the sound of voices to the second floor. He found the two young men sitting over a bottle of wine – evidently the ice had been broken, to judge from their animated conversation. As he entered the room, Metzner leapt to his feet. 'Mr Rowlands! Oh.' His disappointment was obvious from his voice. 'I see that you have not found my sister. I had hoped . . .' He broke off.

'We can try again tomorrow when the cemetery opens. Or there might be another message at the hotel.'

'Yes, yes. You're right.' He brightened. 'Diop here has fixed my shoulder so that it is as good as new.'

'Hardly that,' laughed his new friend. 'But the sling will support your arm for a day or two until the shoulder's healed up.'

'I tell you, we could have used him in the Navy's Medical Corps,' said Metzner, who had clearly got over his earlier suspicion of Diop. 'I couldn't have done a neater job myself.'

'I believe you,' said Rowlands; then, 'Have you lived in this part of Paris long, Mr Diop?'

There was a moment's silence; then the other said, with a laugh, 'That was a polite way of asking me if I belong here! I am French, I assure you – although my parents were from Senegal. It is, as you know, a French colony.'

'Indeed,' said Rowlands. 'And I hope I haven't offended you. It's just that I was intrigued by your name – and your accent, slight as it is. It's how I distinguish one person from another – by voice.'

'No offence taken,' said the young man. 'Although of course there are as many different accents in France as there are in England – especially in our respective capital cities, where there are most "incomers" . . .'

'That's true – especially since the war . . . I mean the last war.'

This reminded him what it was he had to ask Metzner. He took the lighter from his pocket and held it out. 'Does this mean anything to you, Walter?' he said.

Metzner reached for the lighter, using the arm that wasn't tied up in the sling. 'It does look familiar,' he said after a moment. 'Rather an ugly thing, with that dull black case.' He flipped open the top with his free hand and span the wheel, to ignite the flame. 'Looks as if it still works, though . . . Where did you find it?'

Rowlands told him.

With which the young man must have taken a closer look, for he said, in a changed voice, 'There are some initials engraved on the back – look!' Forgetting that this was impossible for Rowlands. '"J. M." – that could stand for "Jakob Metzner". My father's name. I believe that this must be his lighter! He had it with him in the trenches. I remember, now . . .'

Rowlands must have looked sceptical, for Metzner went on, with rising excitement, 'This proves it, don't you see? It *must* have been Clara at the cemetery, and not the other one.'

'Have I missed something?' said Jerome Diop. 'Who is this "other one" you mention?'

'A woman my sister knew in the camp,' said Metzner. 'It seems that they swapped identities – for what reason I do not know.'

Because one of them feared for her life, thought Rowlands. It seemed to him that, whatever Metzner believed, it was by no means conclusively established that the woman who had left the lighter on the tomb was Clara Metzner.

'Hmm,' said Diop. 'It is not the first such story I have heard since the Liberation. Paris is full of people with something to hide – people claiming to be who they are not . . . Well, I hope you find your sister, Monsieur Metzner – or may I call you Walter? Take care of that shoulder of yours. The dressing will need to be changed in a day or two. If you wish, you may return here and I will do it.'

'I'm very grateful,' said Metzner. 'And yes, we must henceforth be "Walter" and "Jerome" to one another. I was fortunate that it was you who came along when you did. I mean, what were the chances that you should have been a fellow doctor?'

Diop laughed. 'I told you, I'm not a doctor . . . or not a qualified one, like you. My real profession is very different – but it suits me rather better than medicine ever did.'

'And what profession is that?' said Rowlands, who was not entirely sure that Diop was who he said he was, either. There had been something almost too 'pat' about the way he had appeared on the scene, at the moment of the shooting. Rowlands disliked coincidences. And Jerome Diop, with his medical training and his smoothly affable manner, seemed a little too good to be true.

'Why, I'm surprised you haven't already guessed,' was the reply; then the young man broke off, in some confusion. 'Forgive me. I was forgetting . . . You *do* hide it rather well – your blindness, I mean. Here, give me your hand.'

Rowlands did so and, a moment later, felt the cold touch of metal upon his palm. Guided by the other, he ran his

242

hand along the smooth brass bell and up the body of what he now realised was some kind of musical instrument, with its complex arrangement of keys. 'The tool of my trade,' said Diop. 'My saxophone. If you like,' he added carelessly, 'you can come and see it in action, at the club where I play, most evenings. Cabaret Au Lapin Agile. I've a set tonight at eight, as it happens,' he added.

It was a quarter to eight when they set out from the Hôtel Juliette, having first availed themselves of what the establishment had to offer in the way of an evening meal, which was not much, as it turned out – a ragout of rabbit and onions – but something was better than nothing, in Rowlands's opinion, especially if alcohol was likely to be consumed.

Cabaret Au Lapin Agile was a ten-minute walk from Rue des Abbesses. 'What a funny little place,' was Metzner's comment. 'It looks like a bit of a dive.' This certainly seemed an apt description of the cramped little bar, which was housed in a two-storey cottage, halfway up a steep cobbled street. This might have belonged to some more remote rural area, thought Rowlands, as they pushed open the wicket gate, rather than being located in the heart of a great city.

Inside it was crowded, smoky and hot. People sat at tables set out across the room, or on benches pushed back against the wall. Someone was playing the piano. As Rowlands and his companion entered, shouldering their way through the throng that was gathered around the bar, there was a burst of applause; a moment later, other instruments – guitar, double bass and saxophone –

joined in, contributing their respective layers of sound to the melody. Rowlands recognised this as 'Cotton Tail' – a favourite of Anne's. Duke Ellington, wasn't it?

They found seats at the end of a bench, a few feet from the stage. While Metzner fetched drinks, Rowlands lit a cigarette and settled down to listen. The saxophonist was good, he thought, realising in the same moment that this must be Jerome Diop. 'Cotton Tail' segued into 'Take the "A" Train'. With no possibility of carrying on a conversation, Rowlands allowed his thoughts to drift. He was aware only of the rhythms of the music and of Metzner beside him, nervously tapping his foot in time to it.

On returning to their hotel, they had called first at the Hôtel Saint-Denis, in the hope that there might have been another message from Clara – or the woman who was claiming to be her, Rowlands amended to himself. But there was nothing. 'We'll try again tomorrow,' he said to Metzner. 'After what happened earlier, she's probably lying low.' With which Metzner had had to be content.

'I just don't understand why she didn't show herself, once she knew the danger was past,' he said querulously. Rowlands forbore from pointing out that she could not have been certain of this. Clara – if it was Clara – had every reason to be cautious.

Even if she had recognised Rowlands, and the brother she had not seen for so many years, it would still have been reckless to break cover with a gunman about. Two women had been murdered already – and a third, in all probability, he reflected, taking a sip of his beer.

Thinking of the young seamstress he'd talked to at the Hôtel Crillon a few weeks before reminded Rowlands that he'd yet to ask Iris Barnes if there had been any news of her. He resolved to do so as soon as possible, the next day. All these loose threads and missing persons were connected, it seemed to him – if he could only work out how.

He became aware, above the music – it was 'Do Nothing Till You Hear From Me' – that a fresh group had entered the little bar. These were American voices, and familiar to him. 'You gotta try it at least the one time,' said Boyd Harrington. 'Cherries in wine. It's the local speciality.'

'Thanks, but I'll stick to beer.' This was Edgar Hathaway. 'That sweet stuff turns my stomach.'

'Well, I'm game,' said Mildred Gelber. 'I always say you have to drink what the natives drink if you really want to get the feel of a place.' As the drinks were being ordered, she must have spotted Rowlands. 'Say, haven't we met before?'

'Good evening, Miss Gelber,' he replied, raising his voice above the music. 'Yes, we have met. It's Frederick Rowlands.'

'The soldier, right?'

'That's right. Although "old soldier" might be more accurate.'

'Oh, you're not *that* old,' she laughed, squeezing into the vacant place beside him on the bench. 'Gee, what a swell place! Eddie insisted that we should visit what he told me was one of the major hang-outs of his youth. Now I've seen it, I can understand why. Eddie always was big on atmosphere.'

The music, which had risen to a crescendo, now dwindled into silence, which was itself broken by a burst of applause.

'What about you?' said Rowlands, remembering that she, too, had her professional status. 'Aren't you researching an article?'

Mildred Gelber gave a throaty chuckle. 'Not me,' she said. 'Tonight is strictly for fun. My last night in Paris. We go to London tomorrow . . . Now *there's* a story I'd like to write!' He must have looked enquiring, for she went on, '"A Tale of Two Cities at War" – don't you think that'd be a great title? Showcasing two very different kinds of resistance . . . The British with their backs to the wall, throwing everything they've got at Hitler . . . and the French, resisting in the only ways they could . . . secretly, silently, right under the enemy's nose . . .'

'That sounds as if it would make a very interesting article,' he said. He was conscious as he spoke of a certain restiveness on the part of the young man sitting on his other side. 'Miss Gelber . . .'

'Mildred.'

'Mildred, then. Do let me introduce my friend, Walter Metzner.'

'Lovely to meet you, Walter.' Then, as Metzner murmured a response, 'Say, haven't we met someplace before? Your face looks awfully familiar.'

'I do not think so,' replied the young man gravely. 'I have only visited Paris once before, as a child. And I have never been to America.'

'No, it wasn't in the States that I saw you . . . or somebody very like you. It's a thing I have,' she explained. 'I recognise faces. Yours is like another face I've seen, quite recently . . .' She thought for a moment. 'I've got it!' she cried, as the music struck up again. Rowlands recognised the tune as 'Round Midnight'. 'It's that portrait. The one Boyd's got hanging in his apartment. *The Little Seamstress.* The resemblance is uncanny. Are you sure you don't have a sister?'

Chapter Nineteen

Before Metzner could reply, they were joined by the other members of Mildred Gelber's party. 'Why, if it ain't my old *compañero*!' cried Edgar Hathaway, giving Rowlands a hearty slap on the back. To judge from his whisky-scented breath, he had already imbibed pretty freely before arriving at the club. 'Say, Harrington, I want you to meet Fred Rowlands. Fred was in the war, too . . . I mean the first, not the second, go-around . . .'

'Oh, Mr Rowlands and I have met,' said Boyd Harrington, who was perfectly sober, as far as Rowlands could tell. 'Nice to see you again, Rowlands. I hadn't realised you were still in Paris.'

'I left, and I've come back,' replied Rowlands; remembering in the same moment why it was he'd returned. 'This is Walter Metzner, a family friend. He and I have some business to do here, and so . . .'

'Can you see it, Boyd?' interrupted Mildred Gelber. 'The likeness. It's uncanny, don't you think?'

But Harrington was momentarily distracted by the matter in hand, which was buying drinks. As before, he seemed to relish the role of master of ceremonies, thought Rowlands. 'Scotch for you,' he said to Hathaway. 'Another of those wine cocktails for you, Mildred? Or do you want something else? And a beer for you two gentlemen, am I right?'

'The portrait,' insisted Mildred Gelber. 'He's the living image . . . if he was a she, I mean.'

'He? She? What damn-fool thing are you talking about now, honey?' demanded her husband, in a tone of affectionate raillery. 'My wife lets her imagination run away with her,' he added, seemingly addressing the room at large. 'I tell her, "Honey, there's only room for *one* imagination in a marriage . . ."'

'Shut up, Eddie,' said his spouse. 'Boyd, I'm talking about that precious portrait of yours. The "Seamstress" thing. Take a look at this boy here, and tell me if you don't think that he and your girl are as like as two peas in a pod.'

Having issued his commands to a passing waiter, Harrington now turned his attention to Metzner. 'Yes,' he said after a moment. 'I see what you mean. Although my girl's a lot prettier . . . and she doesn't have her arm in a sling. What happened there, Mr Metzner?'

'An accident,' the young man replied quickly. 'So you think your painting might be a portrait of my sister?'

'Could be. But then again, it could just be Mildred's overactive imagination getting to work.'

'I resent that!' laughed the journalist. 'I've got a good eye for faces, as you know, Boyd.'

'You do. And Metzner here is certainly a similar type

to my little seamstress . . . Of course, Diego's painted a lot of people,' the American art collector went on. 'Including some of the patrons of this very establishment. "Au Lapin Agile" – that was one of his early pieces. I've been trying to buy it for years, but he won't sell.' He chuckled reminiscently. 'He told me to go boil my head, in so many words, as I recall. Seems my money's not good enough for old Diego . . .'

The music started up again – it was 'A Night in Tunisia' – so that conversation became difficult. It didn't stop Hathaway, however. 'So what brings you to my old stamping ground?' he yelled at Rowlands, who gestured towards the stage, where Jerome Diop was just then playing a solo.

'The saxophonist invited us,' he shouted back.

'Who? Oh, the African fellow? He's good – but not as good as "Bird" . . . Ever hear him play?'

Rowlands said that he had not.

'You missed a treat. Say, can we get some more drinks here, or what?'

It was very late by the time they left the cabaret, and Rowlands for one was glad to get back to the hotel. After the quartet's set had ended, there had been more drinks bought, and more talk of musicians, past and present, who had performed at the club, and whose photographs, Diop pointed out, now graced the walls around them. Sidney Bechet. Coleman Hawkins. Benny Carter. 'My hero,' said Diop, of the legendary saxophonist. Had circumstances been otherwise, Rowlands would have enjoyed such talk, and relished being in the company of such celebrated bohemians as Edgar Hathaway and his companions, with their stories of Paris between the wars.

As things stood, he could only feel that he and Metzner were wasting time that might otherwise have been more profitably spent in chasing up what leads they had. He determined that he would get onto this first thing in the morning. At least, he thought, as he fell into a heavy, dreamless sleep, their experience in Pére Lachaise cemetery had proved – if proof were needed – that the person who had been trying to prevent Walter Metzner from finding his sister was still at large – and dangerous.

He presented himself at the Hôtel Cécil before nine o'clock the next morning, having travelled by metro from Abbesses to Arc de Triomphe – a route with which he was now familiar. His stick offered support of both a physical and psychological kind, so that, with the additional advantage of his sharp hearing, he was able to navigate both the metro tunnels and the streets at either end with relative ease.

He'd left Walter sleeping. The previous day's events – not least being shot at and wounded – had left the young man shaken and exhausted. Rowlands thought that he'd be better off spending the next few hours recuperating. He accordingly left word with the concierge that the gentleman in Number 5 was not to be disturbed, and that he himself would return within a couple of hours.

It was the concierge, Madame Boucher, who let him in. She rang to announce him, and a few moments later, Mrs Collins came down. Rowlands's greeting was met with an embarrassed silence. She really was a shy young woman, he thought. 'Is Miss Barnes in her office?' he asked. 'I'm afraid I don't have an appointment, but . . .'

'I will enquire, m'sieur.'

She must have retraced her steps, because a moment later, Rowlands heard the office door open, and the muffled sound of voices from within. After this brief exchange, she returned, her footsteps noiseless on the tiled floor, so that it was only when she spoke to him that he realised she was there. 'Madame has someone with her. But if it would please you to wait . . .'

'Of course.'

He found a seat and sat down. From the floors above him came sounds indicating that people were already at work. Telephones rang and were swiftly answered; footsteps hurried to and fro. Evidently people started their working days early at the Hôtel Cécil – unless it was that some of them had been here all night?

A few more minutes passed; then Mrs Collins stood in front of him once more. 'Madame asks if you would be so good as to join her.' She led the way upstairs and, having tapped once upon the door, opened it, and stood aside to let Rowlands pass. 'She will be with you shortly, m'sieur.'

He could hear Iris Barnes's voice coming from the inner office. 'Yes, I think we're closing in. But it might take—' She broke off, as if at a signal from the other.

'I suggest we don't count our chickens, just yet.' This, too, was a voice Rowlands knew. It was the Irish writer, Patrick Hackett. A moment later, the glass door between the inner and outer offices opened, and he came out.

'You know Frederick Rowlands, I think?' said Miss Barnes.

'To be sure. We met at Harrington's flat. You were with a young countryman of mine, I seem to recall.'

'Mr Gogarty.'

'That's the feller. He sent me some of his poems,' Hackett went on. 'Not bad, a few of 'em – if a little too reminiscent of the work of the late, great Willie Yeats . . . Nice young feller, I thought him,' he added, meaning Sebastian Gogarty, not W. B. Yeats, Rowlands guessed. 'A brave one, too. Shot down over Germany, wasn't he?'

'He was.'

'Coffee, Louise, if you'd be so kind,' said Miss Barnes, interrupting these remarks. 'Do join us, Patrick – although I know you're pressed for time, what with this other business to see to . . .'

Hackett said that he would stay for coffee, and that the 'other business' could wait. 'I hear ye've been in the wars a bit yourself, Mr Rowlands,' he went on. 'Lucky to escape with your life, were ye not?'

'Oh, I was never in any danger,' said Rowlands, wondering why he was still surprised by how fast news travelled here. 'It was my young friend, Walter Metzner, who came off worst.'

'Yes, I was sorry to hear what happened at the cemetery,' said Iris Barnes. 'I hope Mr Metzner has suffered no lasting ill effects from his injury?'

'He'll live,' said Rowlands.

'Ah, thank you, Louise,' said the MI6 officer, as the secretary returned with the tray of coffee cups. 'Put it down there. I'll do the rest. If you could let me have those letters for signing by the end of the morning, I'd be grateful.'

'Madame.'

Mrs Collins withdrew to the outer office, and a few minutes later could be heard tapping away on her typewriter.

'I suppose what this means – the attack on poor Mr Metzner – is that our quarry is getting rattled,' Miss Barnes went on. 'Trying to scare you both off. I don't suppose,' she added, taking a sip of her coffee, 'you got a look at the gunman?'

'Unfortunately not.' Rowlands hesitated a moment. 'A certain Mr Diop came along at that moment – luckily for Walter. He – Mr Diop – had had medical training, and so . . .'

'He was the right man for the job,' Pat Hackett finished for him. Once more, Rowlands had the uncanny feeling that the Irishman knew more than he was saying.

'But it wasn't about that incident that I wanted to see you,' he said, addressing Miss Barnes. 'It was about Sylvie Dubois. I wondered if there'd been any news?'

The MI6 officer was silent a moment, as if considering how much she should say. 'We haven't had a positive identification yet,' she said at last. 'But the body of a young woman of about the right age was pulled out of the Seine at the Pont de l'Alma two days ago. It was badly decomposed, as you might imagine, after more than a month in the water. We're waiting for her parents to arrive from Morsang-sur-Seine before we take the investigation any further.'

At the thought of the ordeal that was in store for these unfortunate people – and of the fate that had, in all probability, been suffered by the gentle young woman he had met that evening at the Crillon – Rowlands felt a burning anger. She'd have been about the same age as Anne. If it was the last thing he did, he'd find the man who killed her, and make him pay . . .

'If it does turn out that the body recovered from the Seine is that of Sylvie Dubois, then it points to the fact that the murderer must be the same person who killed the other two women – the cleaner, Claire Hubert and the woman we now know to have been Amélie Mendl,' said Miss Barnes.

'Of whom I know a little more than I did – if not everything there is to know,' put in Pat Hackett.

He must have looked at Iris Barnes for approval of what he was about to say, for she said, 'Go on. I think Mr Rowlands should hear the full story, don't you?'

'Indeed I do. Amélie Mendl – or Adèle Morisot, to give her the name under which she operated at the time I am about to tell ye about – was a member of the Palace Resistance network. We think that she was recruited in the spring of 1942. This would have been soon after she left her job at the Moulin Rouge, having been sacked eighteen months before from her job at Bonheur Modes – where she and the Dubois girl had met, as ye know. It's likely that she was recruited by one of the Schweitzer crowd, during her visits to the Café de Flore. During this time, she was taken up by Julien Corbeau, who put her in his film. She also sat for her portrait – I believe ye've met Diego Ruiz, Mr Rowlands?'

Rowlands said that he had.

'Charming feller, isn't he? I admire his work – his manners, not so much. Anyway, Amélie/Adèle may have become Ruiz's mistress at this time, although Ruiz claims not to remember any such thing . . . What is certain is that, in August 1943, the Palace network was betrayed.'

Hackett was silent a moment, then continued, 'Among those who were arrested and deported to concentration camps were the four women known by the code names Paulette, Jacqueline, Yvette and Celestine, whose fate you yourself were instrumental in discovering, Mr Rowlands.'

Rowlands nodded, recalling with a shiver that day at the Natzweiler-Struthof camp, when he and Major Cochrane had learnt the truth from Sebastian Gogarty about what had happened to the women.

'I can speak with authority about this episode, because I was meself involved with one of the Paris networks – the Giselle – and had the task of liaising with other networks, both in Paris and elsewhere. My own network was, sadly, compromised a few months later. It was impossible,' he added wryly, 'to weed out all the traitors . . . Anyway, to return to Amélie/Adèle. For a time, we believed that she might have been the one to betray the network. She was in the right place, at the right time, you might say . . .'

'And what time and place was that?' interrupted Rowlands.

'Lafont et Fils – the bookshop in Rue des Écoles,' was the reply. 'It was an information exchange, you understand. Couriers, such as "Adèle" and her comrades, could deposit and pick up messages and documents, too, to forward to other agents in the field. Sometimes these were hidden in books; at other times, they might be secreted – in microscopic form – in matchboxes, or tubes of toothpaste. I did a bit of that kind of thing myself.' He gave a laugh that was not quite a laugh. 'Boy Scout stuff.'

'But very dangerous, if you were caught,' said Iris Barnes. 'The Gestapo didn't look kindly on such activities.'

'They did not. Anyway, we assumed – that is, I and my colleagues in the British Intelligence service assumed – that Adèle, or Amélie, or whatever one wants to call her, was the one responsible for betraying her comrades in the Palace network. After the network was "blown", one hundred and sixty-seven people were arrested and deported. Three were shot trying to escape. Two died as a result of maltreatment . . . Torture,' he added grimly. 'Two escaped from a train that was taking them to Germany. One of these was a friend of mine,' he went on. 'Code name "André" . . . although I don't suppose we need bother with code names now. He said the girl we suspected of treachery had been sent to Ravensbrück camp, north of Berlin. That was the last we heard of her, until she – or rather, a woman claiming to be Clara Metzner – turned up in Fresnes prison.'

'It was then,' interjected Iris Barnes, pouring herself another cup of coffee from the jug on the tray, 'that things took an interesting turn. Because that, you will remember, Frederick, was when you came in.'

He did indeed remember. 'Go on,' he said.

'Here was a woman, lately returned from a concentration camp, who claimed to be someone she was not – or so we suspected. The reason why she had assumed the identity of someone else might have been because she feared being unmasked as a traitor by the French authorities – or indeed, by British Intelligence. That is, ourselves.'

She put down her cup. 'The penalty, in either case, would have been severe. But then you were brought in, at our request, to corroborate, or disprove, her story.' She lit a cigarette. Its acrid aroma filled the air. 'This you were unable to do, although you had doubts, did you not, as to whether she was who she claimed to be . . . Do smoke, both of you,' she added. 'There are cigarettes in the box on my desk. French and American. Anyway,' she went on, 'while you were still deliberating, "Clara" – if that was who she was – was killed. The case then took on a very different complexion. Because it was obvious that whoever had killed her had wanted to prevent her giving away what it was she knew – the identity of the *real* traitor. In murdering her, the killer exonerated her . . .'

'And left the real Clara exposed to danger,' said Rowlands.

'Just so. Which is why we have been searching high and low for her,' said the MI6 officer. 'Thankfully, Patrick here is going to help us.'

Rowlands was silent for a moment, digesting this information. 'What about Lafont?' he said. 'The bookseller. I'm sure he knows something.'

'I agree,' said Miss Barnes. 'We will certainly be paying him another visit. In fact, if you are agreeable, we will go there now. The shop opens at ten, so we will be in good time.'

In Rue des Écoles they found the same group of idlers on the pavement outside Lafont et Fils; the same earnest young people discoursing eagerly on a range of abstruse topics inside it. But of Pierre Lafont himself there was no sign. In the office at the back of the shop, they found a young man Rowlands supposed to be the 'fils' alluded to in the shop's sign, idly turning the pages of a newspaper. 'Yes?' he said in a bored tone, as they entered.

'We're here to speak to Mr Lafont,' said Iris Barnes, without preamble.

'Dad's not here.'

'I can see that. Where is he?'

'No idea. He went out.'

Something about the youth's manner irritated Rowlands. 'Stand up, can't you, when you're speaking to a lady?'

The other sniggered at this. 'I'm a communist. We don't hold with all that bourgeois rubbish . . . If you want to leave a message for Dad, I can give it to him when he returns,' he added hastily, perhaps seeing from Rowlands's scowl how little his remark had been appreciated.

'Never mind,' said Miss Barnes to the other two men. 'This lout doesn't know anything. We'll come back later.'

But as they turned to go, the bookshop owner's son abandoned his pose of indifference and scrambled to his feet. 'Wait. I want to know what this is about. Is Dad in some kind of trouble?'

'That's for us to know and you to find out,' replied Hackett in his idiomatic French. 'Until we've had a chance to talk to him, we've no way of telling how involved he might or might not have been . . .'

'Involved? What are you talking about? Involved in what?' Young Lafont sounded thoroughly frightened now.

'You'd better ask him,' said Miss Barnes. 'And you can tell him that British Intelligence wants to speak to him about the part he played in the Resistance between 1942 and 1944. That's the number to call,' she added, handing him her card. Rowlands wondered which of her various aliases was printed there.

'The help my father gave to the *Résistance* is something of which he can be proud,' said the young man defiantly. 'He has nothing to answer for.'

'Then he has nothing to fear,' said Iris Barnes pleasantly.

'It would appear that our bird has flown,' said the MI6 officer, as the three of them stood once more on the pavement outside Lafont et Fils. 'Although it's not certain that he's gone for good. I'll get someone to watch the bookshop, in case he returns.'

'I should get back to the hotel,' said Rowlands. 'I left a message for Walter saying I wouldn't be long.'

'I can drop you off,' said Miss Barnes. She must have signalled to the driver of the Citroën, because a moment later, the car drew up alongside. 'What about you, Patrick? Is there somewhere I can take you?'

'No, ye're fine,' was the reply. 'I'm meeting a feller at the Jardin des Plantes. It's not far from here. I'll let ye know if I hear anything about our missing girl . . . or about Lafont. Seems to me he could tell us a good deal about what we want to know – if we can find him. Nice to see ye again, Mr Rowlands. Say hello to that young countryman of mine, when ye next meet him, won't ye?'

Rowlands said that he would, and the two men shook hands before Hackett went on his way. 'Interesting man,' remarked Rowlands, when the Irishman was out of earshot.

'Oh, he is. A brave one, too. The French are giving him a medal for his wartime service, but he doesn't care to talk about any of that. You heard him. "Boy Scout stuff." But it was a lot more than that, I can tell you. He only escaped by the skin of his teeth being picked up by the Gestapo. Very fine writer, too, I believe.'

Rowlands said that he had gathered as much.

'Well, let's get you back to the hotel,' said Miss Barnes. 'I'm afraid I'll have to get back straight after that. I've a meeting at twelve, at the top of the Eiffel Tower, with one of our French Resistance allies – code name "Max". They do love a dramatic rendezvous, these chaps . . . Anyway, I'm hoping he can cast some light on the infiltration of our networks by enemy agents. We haven't always seen eye to eye with the French on these matters, so it'll make a nice change to have some cooperation.'

As the car sped along the Boulevard Saint-Germain, on its way to the Pont de la Concorde and the right bank of the Seine, Rowlands thought about what Hackett had said about the collapse of the Palace network. 'If Amélie wasn't the traitor, then who do you think it was?' he asked Iris Barnes. 'Could it have been Lafont?'

'I've told you, he had an alibi for the time it happened. Although he might have been working with a collaborator. We still don't have any hard evidence.'

'Do you think it could have been Lafont who fired that shot in the cemetery?' Rowlands persisted. 'I mean, *somebody* did . . . and it was somebody who knew we were going to be there at that exact time . . .'

'Don't think I haven't considered the implications of that,' she replied grimly. 'The trouble is, as you'll have realised by now, information gets passed on very quickly here. The Resistance networks may have broken down, but they've been replaced by other networks – networks of informers, and of those passing on secrets for gain. One might think,' she added sardonically, 'that the war was over. I can assure you, it's still going on.'

It was something he'd heard her say before, in another context. He didn't think it needed a reply.

Chapter Twenty

A few minutes later, they arrived outside the Hôtel Juliette. 'Give my regards to Mr Metzner, won't you?' said Iris Barnes. 'I hope he's healing up nicely.' She touched Rowlands's hand – a brief, friendly contact, to show she was still on his side. 'I'll let you know if I've any news of Clara.'

The car moved off, and Rowlands entered the hotel. It was a little after eleven – which was later than he'd said he'd be, but not by much. Even though they'd made no actual progress in tracking down Metzner's sister, he felt that he now had a clearer picture of the world she'd been caught up in – a dangerous world of subterfuge and lies.

He retrieved his key from the desk, climbed the stairs to the third floor and tapped on the door of the room next to his, where Walter – to judge from the silence within – must still be fast asleep. He knocked again: louder, this time. 'Walter? It's me, Frederick Rowlands.'

There was no reply. Trying the handle, he found the

door unlocked. It was immediately apparent that there was nobody in the room. The only signs of recent occupation were a few cigarette butts in a tin ashtray on the bedside cabinet, and a grip, containing a soiled shirt, under the bed.

Retracing his steps to the hotel lobby, Rowlands interrogated the concierge as to what he knew of Metzner's movements – which turned out not to be much. It transpired that the latter had gone out not half an hour before, leaving word that he would be back later. 'He did not say when he would return, m'sieur,' said the concierge. 'A note had been left for him at the desk and—'

'A note?' said Rowlands sharply.

'*Oui, m'sieur.* A woman left it.'

'Did she give a name?'

'*Non, m'sieur.* She left the note for Monsieur Metzner and went away again.'

'Describe her, will you?' Although Rowlands knew that – however precise the description – his chances of identifying the unknown woman from physical characteristics alone were remote.

Nor was the description precise. 'She was just a woman, m'sieur.'

'Old or young?'

'I think she was young, m'sieur. But I did not look closely at her.'

Of course you didn't, groaned Rowlands to himself. Just his luck to have stumbled across the only unobservant concierge in Paris. An idea occurred to him. 'Was she an American?'

The other thought about it. 'Perhaps, m'sieur. I cannot

be sure. I only heard her say a few words.'

'And what were those words?'

Again, the man took thought.

'She said, "You have a man called Walter Metzner staying here. I want you to give this to him." Then she handed me the note.'

'Did you see what it said?'

'*Non, m'sieur,*' said the concierge; adding, in a tone of affronted dignity, 'I do not read notes left for guests.'

Of course you don't, thought Rowlands, trying not to let his exasperation show. 'Did he – Mr Metzner – say anything when he had read the note?' he asked, hoping against hope that there might be a clue of some sort as to where Walter had gone.

'*Oui, m'sieur.* He said, "Tell my friend that I'm going to see her for myself."'

'He said that, did he?'

'*Oui, m'sieur.* He also asked me for a map – we keep them for guests. He studied it for a long time. Then he left.'

On the pavement outside the Hôtel Juliette, Rowlands smoked a cigarette and considered the message Walter had left. *I'm going to see her for myself . . .* The more he thought about it, the more baffling it seemed. It must refer to a meeting, surely – but with whom? If the woman who had brought the note had been Clara herself, then why hadn't she asked to see her brother in person? If it had *not* been Clara, but somebody else entirely, then who was it?

There was of course another possible interpretation of the message. At the Cabaret Au Lapin Agile, the night before, Walter had been deep in conversation with

Mildred Gelber. The topic had been the Seamstress portrait that – the American journalist had claimed – so uncannily resembled him. *I'm going to see her for myself . . .* Yes, that could be what it meant . . .

His mind made up, Rowlands collected his stick from the lobby where he had left it, and having asked for directions from the concierge, made his way along the now-familiar route to the metro station at Abbesses. He descended the steps beneath Guimard's ornate canopy (he remembered this, and the others like it, from his first, long-ago, visit to Paris), reaching the Line 12 platform as the train was about to pull out.

From here, it was a ten-minute journey to Concorde, where – having asked directions once more – he was escorted onto the Line 1 train by an officiously helpful member of station staff. Six minutes later, he emerged at the Hôtel de Ville metro station, and (having asked a passer-by to point him in the right direction) made his way towards the quayside and the two islands in the Seine that lay beyond. As he turned in the direction of the smaller of the two, he was disagreeably reminded of the time, almost two months before, when he and Iris Barnes had visited the Hôtel-Dieu hospital on the Île de la Cite, in order to identify the body of Claire Hubert.

Strolling along beside the river, with the sunshine warm on his face and the noise of the city reduced to a distant murmur, it was easy to forget the horror of that day, and the deaths that had preceded and followed it. But he could not forget – nor did he want to. He owed it to those women – Amélie, Claire and Sylvie – to find their killer, and to give them justice at last.

Reaching the Pont Marie, he crossed onto the Île Saint-Louis. Here, the memories were of a different, if no less troubling, kind. Harrington's party. It had been at that eminently civilised gathering of artists, writers and art collectors that he'd been struck by the hollowness of it all. Paris had seemed to him that evening no more than a beautiful stage set, peopled by phantoms. He thought, *They were all lying about something . . .* And the key to it was the portrait.

Reaching the house, he rang the bell and waited. At length, the street door opened, and a man – the concierge, presumably – asked his business.

'I wish to see Monsieur Harrington,' he said, in his careful French.

'I will see if he is at home, m'sieur.'

After a brief exchange on the internal telephone, he told Rowlands that he could go up. 'The lift is there, m'sieur.' Rowlands said that he preferred to eschew *'l'ascenseur'* in favour of the stairs.

'As you wish, m'sieur.'

Arriving at the third floor, he was admitted by the manservant, and found Harrington waiting for him in the big, airy drawing room. The four tall windows Rowlands remembered from the night of the party stood open, letting in a warm breeze. 'Mr Rowlands. Nice to see you again. Come in, come in. Sit down. Can I get you something? Coffee? A drink?'

Rowlands declined both of these, but took a seat on a sofa that stood at right angles to the one on which Harrington was sitting. 'Now, what can I do for you?' It seemed to Rowlands that there was a certain coolness underlying the American's affable manner – a feeling intensified when he added, 'I have to tell you that I don't have a lot of time to spare. I'm going to London for a week or two, with my friends, the Hathaways. We leave in a couple of hours, so . . .'

'What I have to ask won't take long. Has Walter Metzner been here?'

'Walter . . . Oh, you mean the little Jewish guy? No.' Harrington gave a bark of laughter. 'Why, have you lost him?'

'I'm afraid so.'

'Sorry if I'm being slow on the uptake, but I don't see why he should have come *here*. I mean, he and I only met for the first time last night, at the club. I didn't exchange more than two words with him.'

'I had an idea he might have come here because of the portrait. *The Little Seamstress*. Miss Gelber told him she had detected a strong resemblance between him and the subject of the portrait, so I thought Walter might have wanted to see for himself.'

Again, Harrington laughed. 'Oh, that was just some nonsense of Mildred's. She's a lovely girl, Mildred, but she does let her imagination run away with her sometimes. Typical journalist. Always looking for a story. And she was putting it away last night like nobody's business . . . Anyway, why does it matter to this friend of yours, this Walter guy, if my portrait looks a bit like him?'

'It's because the subject of the portrait – Amélie Mendl – was a friend of his sister's. The two girls seem to have looked a lot like each other – even to have been mistaken for one another . . .' It sounded thin, even to him; but something warned him not to say any more. 'Walter's been trying to find his sister, so this seemed like a clue, of sorts,' he added lamely.

'OK, OK, I get it. But I can tell you, Rowlands, your young friend is on a hiding to nothing. For a start, he looks nothing like my portrait. You'll have to take my word for it, of course, since you're not in a position to verify it for yourself,' he laughed. 'Amélie Mendl was a very beautiful girl. If anything, Diego's portrait didn't do her justice.'

'You knew her,' said Rowlands softly. Something had suddenly become clear to him.

'Sure I knew her.' For the first time, Harrington lost his breezy self-confidence. 'Matter of fact, it was at Diego's studio I met her. She wasn't calling herself Amélie, then. It was some other name . . .'

'Adèle Morisot.'

'That's the one. Like I said, she was a looker. We hit it off and . . .'

'You had an affair with her,' said Rowlands. 'It was *you*, not Diego Ruiz, that Julien Corbeau called a "traitor" on the night of your party.'

'Julien was talking out of his ass. So what if I *did* sleep with her? She knew she could get more from me than from some deadbeat artist . . . or "experimental" filmmaker, whatever that is . . .'

'And what did she get from you?'

'Money,' said Harrington coldly. 'She needed it for the "cause", she said. The Resistance cause, she meant. She wanted me to turn this apartment over to the comrades, too . . . but I refused to play ball. Catch me getting on the wrong side of our German friends, by allowing this place to become a safe house for the *Résistance*!' He gave the final word an exaggeratedly Gallic pronunciation.

'So that's why he called you a traitor,' said Rowlands. 'Because you betrayed the cause as he saw it – not because he was jealous of you for taking Amélie away . . .'

'No, that wouldn't have bothered old Julien,' the American entrepreneur agreed. 'He swings the other way, if you know what I mean?' He was silent for a moment, as if brooding on his injuries. 'If anyone had the right to be jealous, it was me,' he went on. 'I mean, I took her in, when she was getting by on tips from that waitress job of hers. I paid for everything. Bought her gifts. Expensive gifts, too. Then I found out she was just stringing me along. She'd been seeing another guy the whole time we were together. One of her Resistance buddies. I saw them together – holding hands, right out in the open, in one of those dives the Resistance people used to hang out . . . After that, it was over between us. I can stand a lot from a woman, but not being two-timed.'

Once more, Harrington fell silent; then he chuckled. 'I got one thing out of that business, at least,' he said. '*The Little Seamstress*. That picture'll be worth a lot in a few years' time, trust me. Diego's really making a name for himself these days. In another year or two, I can sell that piece for twice or three times what I paid for it.'

'I expect you're right,' said Rowlands. He felt nothing but contempt for the man. 'You do know Amélie Mendl's dead?'

'Yeah, I heard something about that,' replied the other in an indifferent tone. 'Kinda thing that happens in wartime. And now, Mr Rowlands, it seems to me I've given you enough of my time. Your friend isn't here, as must be obvious, even to you.'

Rowlands got to his feet. 'I was just leaving.'

'I won't say it's been a pleasure . . . Hey! Sounds like my friends have arrived . . .'

Because there came the sound of voices from the entrance hall. A moment later, Edgar Hathaway and his wife came in, both sounding in ebullient mood.

'All packed, Boyd?' demanded the writer. 'I don't see your bags in the hall.'

'Oh, Jackson'll send those on later,' replied Harrington, adding curtly, 'You're early.' It seemed to Rowlands that he hadn't quite recovered his equilibrium. He was glad he'd been the one to upset it.

'And here's my *compañero*,' cried Hathaway, throwing himself down on the sofa Rowlands had just vacated. 'How's it going, buddy? We had fun last night, didn't we?'

'We did,' said Rowlands. 'Hello, Miss Gelber.'

'Mildred, please! Good to see you, Frederick. Boy, did I have a headache after last night! Those cherry-in-wine things were pretty lethal. You, on the other hand, look as cool as a cucumber.' She, too, sat down, on an adjacent sofa. 'Walter not with you today?'

'That's just what's brought him here,' said Harrington. 'You spun him – young Metzner – some yarn about my portrait supposedly looking like him, and Rowlands here thought he must have come to check it out. Only as you can see, he didn't. Come here, I mean . . .' He seemed to realise that his irritation was showing, and made an effort to restore a mood of bonhomie. 'Either of you good people care for a drink?' It was noticeable that he didn't renew the offer of a drink to Rowlands.

'Not me,' said Mildred Gelber. 'I'm never going to drink again.'

'Don't listen to her,' said Hathaway. 'I'll have one if you're having one.' Then to Rowlands, who was still on his feet, 'You're not leaving, are you, *compañero*? We only just got here.'

'Mr Rowlands has to be somewhere,' said Harrington. 'And we've a train to catch.'

'So you're telling me that young Walter has disappeared?' said Mildred Gelber, cutting across these pointed remarks, as if they were of no consequence. 'I liked him, you know.'

'You made that perfectly obvious,' said her husband sarcastically. 'Where's that drink, Boyd? Some of us are dying of thirst here.'

'He left the hotel this morning, while I was out,' said Rowlands, addressing Mildred. 'I thought from the message he left – something about "seeing for himself" – that he might have come to look at the Ruiz portrait. But I was mistaken.'

'Have you tried the film studio?' she said. 'Only he talked about that, too. I gather his sister – or the girl who looked like her – appeared in one of Julien Corbeau's recent flicks. I haven't seen it, but . . .'

'It's called *Eurydice*,' said Rowlands. 'And I think you may have something there, Miss . . . Mildred, I mean. The studios at Billancourt will be my next port of call.'

'I'll go with you,' she said; then, at a protest from her

husband, 'Our train's not till four, Eddie. We've plenty of time to find Frederick's missing friend. We'll pick up a taxi in the Rue de Rivoli.'

At the Paris Studios in Boulogne-Billancourt, they were filming an epic about the French Revolution. As Rowlands and his companion got out of the cab, a rabble of *sans-culottes* in Phrygian caps, *pantalon* and wooden clogs, some of whom were carrying bloodied heads on pikes, came out of the main gate, laughing at something one of them had said, and lighting up cigarettes. 'You'd have thought the average cinema-goer would have had enough of violence and bloodshed,' observed Mildred Gelber. 'Instead, it only increases ticket sales.'

Shouldering their way through the throng of revolutionaries, they reached the gatehouse, where Rowlands enquired if Monsieur Laval was on site. The studio guard consulted a list. 'He's in Studio 3. The *Bridges over the Seine* set. I'd get somebody to take you, but we're short-staffed . . . Hey! Pick that up!' he yelled at a *sans-culotte* who'd dropped a cigarette butt. 'Do you want the studio to go up in smoke?'

In Studio 3, they were shooting a scene in which a young man – played by the current romantic lead, Lucien Léotard ('Rather a dish,' whispered Mildred) – was pleading with a young woman, played by *ingénue* Bérénice Bernard ('All eyes, teeth and tits . . .') to give him another chance.

'*Je t'en supplie . . .*'

'*Laisse-moi tranquille!*'

They did several 'takes' before the director was satisfied. 'All right – cut! Take five . . .' Then, noticing the newcomers, 'What are you people doing here? This is a film set, not a public right of way . . .'

'It's all right, Alain. I'll deal with this,' said Maurice Laval, who had been watching the filming from the sidelines. 'I've seen you before,' he said to Rowlands. 'But I can't put my finger on when it was . . . Not an actor, are you?'

'No.' Rowlands reminded the producer of his name, and introduced Miss Gelber.

'Of course. The *Eurydice* screening, right? You were interested in that girl – the amateur Julien got to play the title role.'

'That's right. It was about that I wanted to ask you,' said Rowlands. 'Has anyone else been here today, wanting to see that film? A young chap, aged about twenty-five?'

'It's funny you should ask that,' said Laval. 'There *was* an enquiry about that film, earlier today, as it happens. Around midday, I should say. I wasn't on set at the time – had to sort out a dispute about overtime with the lighting technicians on the big picture – but my assistant, Claude, can tell you about it.' He whistled, and the ASM came over. 'Tell these people what happened lunchtime. The enquiry about the Corbeau picture,' he said.

'Well, it was funny, really,' began the young man; then Laval interrupted.

'They're starting. Alain's looking daggers at me. He's a stickler for punctuality, that one. You'd better take them outside, Claude. And don't be too long. Nice to see you again, Mr Rowlands. Sorry I can't spare more time to catch up, but we're running over-schedule as it is.'

Outside, in the studio backlot, which had been mocked

up to look like a Parisian street from 1789, Claude told them what he knew. He'd got a call from the gatehouse about a quarter to twelve, he said. VIPs on site – or that was the impression he got. He'd hurried over there, because you never knew . . . Hollywood moguls, politicians, celebrities of all kinds. They got the lot. As it turned out, there were three of them – two men and a woman. It was obvious that she was the one in charge . . .

'What makes you say that?' asked Rowlands.

'Well . . . she had papers. Official-looking documents.'

'What kind of documents?'

Claude couldn't say. 'But she said she – they – wanted to look at the Corbeau film, to check that it wasn't defamatory, or libellous, or something. At least,' he added apologetically, 'I think that's what she said.'

'What about the two men?' said Rowlands. 'Did they say anything?'

'Not that I recall. The older one – he was wearing an English tweed jacket, with velvet patches on the elbows, like a college professor – said something about needing to be somewhere else. They were wasting time, he said. The other – he was about my age, maybe a bit older – didn't say anything. He looked kind of nervous, I thought. He kept looking around as if he wasn't quite sure whether he wanted to be there or not . . . But then of course he had his arm in a sling, so maybe he was in pain . . .'

'Maybe,' said Rowlands grimly. 'So what happened then?'

'Well, I took them to the screening room, didn't I? Thought it was the quickest way of getting rid of them, to tell you the truth.'

'And then you played them the film?'

'Only the first reel of it. I had to leave before it was time to change the reel, so I don't know if they watched it to the end or not . . . Funny, though,' he added, as if he had just thought of it. 'I didn't actually see them leave.'

'Can you take us to the screening room?' said Rowlands.

The ASM seemed to hesitate. 'I have to get back,' he said.

It was then that Mildred Gelber intervened. 'I'm a journalist, Claude – I may call you Claude, mayn't I? I write for all the famous American papers. The *New York Times. Life*. I can promise you some excellent coverage of the films you're currently shooting at Paris Studios. Only I need to visit that screening room. It won't take a second.'

'I . . .' Suddenly the ASM seemed to make up his mind. 'It's just this way. Past the guillotine. Don't trip over the basket. The paint on the heads is still wet.'

In the screening room, which turn out to be the same one in which Rowlands and Iris Barnes had watched the first reel of *Eurydice*, Claude pointed out the seats where Walter and his two as-yet unidentified companions had sat. Mildred at once sat down in the middle seat, where Walter himself had sat, said Claude; after a moment's hesitation, Rowlands took the one next to that. Now that he was here, he wasn't sure what the point of coming here had been – other than to establish that Walter had also been at the studio two hours before. He certainly wasn't here now . . .

'I think we've got all we need,' he accordingly said to Claude, who was clearly itching to get back to Studio 3 and *The Bridges Over the Seine*.

'Aren't we going to watch the movie?' said Mildred Gelber. 'Seems a shame to come all this way and not see what all the fuss was about.' Then, when the ASM started to protest, 'I can't very well write a piece about the studio if I haven't seen any of the studio's product, can I?'

As it turned out, the first reel of *Eurydice* was still set up in the projector. It was a matter of moments to wind it back to the beginning. And so, for the second time, Rowlands listened to the evocative jazz score; for the second time, heard the banter of Orphée and his fellow artists in the Artists' Café; then the shouts of the rabble, breaking in on this cheerful scene. Once again, he found himself envisaging the beautiful Eurydice, as the scene reached its climax and she burst into the café, with her cry of '*Traître*'. . .

'All right, we're done here,' said Mildred Gelber. 'Thank you, Claude. That was very interesting.'

'Glad to be of service,' muttered the ASM.

He was already starting to rewind the reel when there came an exclamation from the American. 'What the . . . ?' Then, to Rowlands, 'Something's caught on my skirt. It's a Bonheur original, so I don't want to snag the fabric. Give me a hand, will you?'

He went to do so, and his fingers encountered a small, flat metal object, caught between the edge of the tip-up seat and the armrest. It was not much larger than a thumbnail, and was attached to a fine chain. It was this that had become caught on the journalist's skirt. He released her, and scooped up the object. Now it was his turn to utter an exclamation.

'What is it?' She peered through the darkness at the

thing he was holding. 'Some kind of jewellery, from the look of it. A locket. Does it mean something to you?'

'It means that Walter was definitely here,' said Rowlands. 'I think he left it for me to find.'

Chapter Twenty-One

In the cab back to the hotel – they'd drop him off first, said Mildred Gelber, before taking her on to the Gare du Nord – Rowlands thought about what he'd discovered, concerning Walter Metzner's movements since they'd parted that morning, and didn't like what it meant. Because he felt sure that Walter wouldn't have left the treasured locket – his only relic of his and Clara's mother – if he hadn't wanted to send an urgent message to the person he hoped would find it. Himself, that was. Walter must have guessed that Rowlands would follow him to the studios. Leaving the locket behind had been a plea for help.

'I have to say,' laughed Mildred Gelber, breaking into these dark thoughts, 'it's been a most enjoyable afternoon, Frederick. When that gun went off, I nearly jumped out of my skin . . .'

They'd been walking back to the gate, after leaving the screening room, when a shot rang out.

'*Policier*,' said Claude, the ASM, without breaking stride. 'They're filming it in Studio 2. Vincent Noiret is starring, as Inspector Le Brun. He's one of our big stars,' he added hopefully to Miss Gelber, who said she'd make a note of it. She'd seemed highly amused by the whole affair – the hunt for the Metzner siblings, and the preposterous setting to which it had brought her and Rowlands, was nothing but a jolly adventure as far as she was concerned. The gun going off when it did (it wasn't loaded with real bullets, only blanks, Claude assured her) was the crowning note of black comedy.

For Rowlands, already convinced that Walter must be in danger, the incident only served to deepen his worst fears. These were confirmed when, having thanked the American journalist for all she'd done to help – 'My pleasure. I like a good mystery. I hope you find your missing friend. Give him my love, won't you?' – he entered the hotel lobby once more.

It was a quarter to four – Mildred Gelber would only just make her train, he thought – and Walter had been missing for almost four hours. Rowlands was reminded of the time, a dozen years before, when he'd searched for the boy and his cousin, Rowlands's nephew, Billy, all over Berlin. *If I don't wring his neck when I find him . . .* he thought distractedly; then brushed the thought away.

'Has Mr Metzner returned?' he asked the concierge, already knowing what the answer would be.

'*Non, m'sieur.* He left, as I have told you, at around midday.'

'Then let me use the telephone,' said Rowlands.

As usual, it was answered by Mrs Collins.

'It's Frederick Rowlands. Is Miss Barnes there?'

'She is out, m'sieur.'

'When will she be back?'

'I don't know, m'sieur.'

'Tell her to ring me on this number . . . One moment. What *is* the number?' he demanded of the concierge, who recited it.

'It's 42-54-82 – have you got that?'

'Yes, m'sieur.' She said it back to him. 'It is the hotel number, is it not?'

'That's right. Tell Miss Barnes it's very urgent. A matter of life and death.'

'I will, m'sieur.' Then she rang off.

One of the worst feelings, thought Rowlands, was to feel helpless in the face of a crisis; to know that one was unable to act, when every instinct cried out for action. He realised, in the same instant, that he had had nothing to eat since that morning. Not that he felt like eating – but he needed something to sustain him until the telephone call came . . .

'Would you do me a favour?' he asked the concierge.

'If it is in my power to grant it, m'sieur.'

'Could you get me a cup of coffee from the café across the street?'

'Willingly, m'sieur – if you will take care of the desk.'

He was gone no more than a couple of minutes, during which time Rowlands paced up and down, and considered the situation. That Walter was in peril of his life, he was not in doubt. Where he had been taken, after leaving the Paris Studios, was something Rowlands had yet to work out – as was the identity of those who had taken him. A man and a woman . . . Could the man have been Lafont? He wished he had a clearer idea of what the bookseller looked like. As for the woman . . . it appeared she had had some 'official' standing, if the ASM, Claude, was to be believed.

Rowlands racked his brains as to who it might be. The only female member of officialdom he knew was Iris Barnes. It couldn't have been her, for all sorts of reasons – not least because she was leading the hunt to find Walter's sister. And there was the fact that she'd been meeting someone that afternoon, at the very moment Walter was taken. The Resistance leader, 'Max'. . . Rowlands supposed that was where she was now.

The concierge, whose name, it emerged, was Pineau, returned with the coffee. Rowlands drank it gratefully. Still the telephone remained silent. Rowlands thought, *It's no good. I must go there* . . . It was the Hôtel Cécil he meant. 'I have to go out for a while,' he told Pineau. 'If Mr Metzner returns while I'm out, tell him I'll be back soon. Don't let him leave.'

'I will do my best to detain him, m'sieur.'

'And if a lady telephones, asking for me, will you tell her I'm on my way there . . .'

'A lady. Certainly, m'sieur,' said Pineau, with the air of professional discretion perfected by those of his calling.

'Oh . . . and thank you for the coffee.' Rowlands fumbled in his pocket for the small change to pay the man back; but the other said, 'No need, m'sieur. I have an arrangement with the café. The coffee is gratis. I hope you find your friend, m'sieur.'

With the feeling that doing something, however futile,

was at least preferable to waiting about doing nothing, Rowlands set out along Rue des Abbesses. From around him came the bustle of late-afternoon shopping crowds; the rattle of passing vehicles; the odours of ripe cheeses and fresh bread from the cheesemongers and bakeries, of fruit and flowers from the vegetable stalls. He was oblivious to all of this. Only when he reached the Place des Abbesses, and was preparing to descend into the metro station, was his attention arrested.

'Mr Rowlands! Frederick! Wait!'

A car had pulled up a few feet away from where he stood, with his hand already on the rail of the steps leading down to the station. He turned towards the sound of the voice. 'Miss Barnes,' he said. 'I was just on my way to see you. Walter's disappeared.'

'Get in, Frederick,' said the MI6 officer, without responding to this. Rowlands did as he was ordered. He became aware from the slight sounds of another body shuffling sideways along the seat that they were not alone in the car. 'You know Mr Diop, I think?'

'Yes. I . . .'

'Mr Diop works for me,' said Iris Barnes. 'Or rather – since he would probably prefer to say that he works for himself – he is sometimes on call, when I have need of him.'

'As he was that day in the cemetery,' said Rowlands, as the Citroën pulled away. 'For which I have to thank you, Mr Diop.'

'Oh, do call me Jerome,' said the young man. 'We jazz musicians don't like to stand on ceremony. So where do you think Walter has gone?' he went on. 'The last I heard, he was safely tucked up in bed, nursing that shoulder of his.'

'I think he was taken away against his will – or perhaps lured away by false promises . . .' He described what he'd discovered about Walter's movements at the Paris Studios. 'The worrying thing is no one saw them leave – Walter and the two people he was with. Do you think the man might have been Lafont?' he asked Miss Barnes.

'It's possible,' she replied. 'Although I'm not sure who the woman might have been. An accomplice, presumably.'

'It sounded to me as if she was the one in charge. Where are we going, by the way?'

'To see someone who might have news of Clara's whereabouts,' replied Iris Barnes. 'And where Clara is, Walter must eventually follow.'

If he hasn't already been killed, thought Rowlands bleakly. 'I don't like it,' he said. 'That business at the studio. I've a feeling it was all just a ruse to get him there. Now they've got him – whoever they are – they'll be able to get at Clara.'

'Perhaps,' said Miss Barnes. 'Although they'll need to find her first. But what made you think of returning to the Paris Studios in the first place? I mean, it was hardly the most obvious interpretation you might have put on the message Walter left. "I'm going to see her for myself . . ." That suggests he was going to meet Clara, face to face – not that he was going to watch a film in which another girl resembling her appears.'

'It wasn't my first thought, either,' admitted Rowlands. 'It was Miss Gelber who gave me the idea of going to the studio.'

'And how did that come about – that you met Mildred, I mean?' said Iris Barnes drily. 'You're a dark horse, Fred. I've always said so.'

Rowlands explained about the visit to Harrington's flat. 'There's something else I ought to mention,' he concluded. 'Harrington and Amélie Mendl were having an affair. It came to an end when he discovered she was seeing another man – a member of the Resistance, apparently.'

'Interesting,' said Miss Barnes thoughtfully. 'Did Boyd mention a name?'

'No. Just that he'd found them together . . . But don't you see? It makes him a suspect for her death.'

'It certainly widens the field,' said the MI6 officer.

Le Select was quiet this early in the evening, with only a few people having drinks on the terrace, and most of the tables inside still unoccupied. Leaving Jerome Diop outside, to observe the comings and goings of the brasserie's clientele (acting as lookout was one of his functions, Rowlands gathered), Rowlands and Miss Barnes went in. In one of the booths towards the back of the place, they found a man the latter introduced simply as 'Max', eating *soupe à l'oignon*. This, then, was the character with whom Iris Barnes had met earlier that day at the top of the Eiffel Tower, thought Rowlands, intrigued to meet a man whose reputation as a Resistance fighter had preceded him.

When he saw them approach, he got to his feet. 'Rosaline.'

'Oh, finish your soup, do! Max, this is Frederick Rowlands, of whom I told you . . .'

'*Enchanté, m'sieur.*'

The two men shook hands. From this brief contact, Rowlands got an impression of a tough, wiry individual of about forty years old, a little below his own height.

'Max worked with resistance groups in Paris and elsewhere, throughout the war,' said 'Rosaline', as the three of them sat down. 'It was he who brought the various networks together, to form a coherent force, under the Free French banner.'

'Yes, it wasn't as easy as it sounds,' laughed the Resistance leader, spooning up the last of his soup. 'The expression "rats fighting in a sack" comes to mind.'

Rowlands nodded, not yet sure where this was leading.

'Now he keeps an eye on the way things are going, vis-à-vis our communist friends,' the MI6 officer went on. 'Some of the groups remain loyal to the Free French movement – others, regrettably, do not.'

'It is true,' said Max. 'Sometimes our "friends" do more harm than our supposed enemies.'

'I can see that,' said Rowlands. 'But . . .'

'You want to know what all this has to do with a search for Clara Metzner – also known as Amélie Mendl?' said the Resistance leader. 'I will tell you. But first you must have a drink with me. It isn't every day that I get to meet a hero of *La Guerre Mondiale*,' he added, using the term by which the French designated the Great War. '*Une fine*, I think.' He clicked his fingers to summon the waiter, and ordered brandies all round.

When these had been brought, and the toast – 'To friendship' – given, Max said, in a voice so quiet that Rowlands had to lean across the table to hear him, 'Your Clara has been seen, here in Paris. I do not know where she is exactly – but I can suggest some possibilities.'

'She's alive, then?' said Rowlands, also keeping his voice low.

'But yes. Your Clara is a resourceful young woman. She is a member of the *Résistance* – that is to say, she was accepted as such under the name of her friend, Amélie Mendl. But I believe you already know of the change of identities?'

'I do,' said Rowlands. 'Although I'm not sure exactly how the trick was pulled off . . .'

'Easily enough, in August '44,' said Max. 'Quite simply, it was chaos. When the Boche realised they had lost the war, they began covering their tracks. Prisoners from some concentration camps were marched to others, deeper into Germany. Evidence of atrocities was covered up – not always successfully . . . My guess is that that was when the two girls – who had met in Ravensbrück camp sometime during the previous year – decided to change places. Amélie became Clara, and Clara became Amélie. Amélie/Clara made it back to Paris, in one of the trainloads of returning deportees. Clara/Amélie must have taken the opportunity to escape, because it was soon after that that she joined up with her friend's resistance network in Paris.'

'And you think she's here now?'

'Certain of it. Although after recent events, she'll be lying low.'

'I have to find her,' said Rowlands. 'Walter's life depends on it.'

'Yes, I imagine that's the calculation our enemies have made, too,' said Iris Barnes. 'We'll find her, don't worry. There are many places she could be hiding in Paris –

and Max here knows them all . . . But before we start our search, we're going to have something to eat.' She summoned the waiter. 'What have you got that's good?'

'Well, there are snails, madame . . .'

'No. What else?'

'We have *escalopes de veau à la crème* . . .'

'We'll have those. And a bottle of Saint-Émilion . . . Why, look who's here! Max, you know Patrick, I suppose?'

'But of course I know Patrick! How are you, my friend?'

'Fit as a fiddle,' was Pat Hackett's reply. 'Good to see you, Max.'

The two men embraced.

'I'm glad to see you, too, Mr Rowlands,' said the Irish writer. 'I don't suppose ye've run into that young countryman of mine, since ye've been here? He was supposed to meet me at six, and it's a quarter past now. Ye can't rely on these young fellers for timekeeping . . .'

Before he had finished speaking, there came the sound of loud protestations from someone trying to enter their part of the bar, against the wishes of the manager who must have been told to keep people away. A youthful voice said, '*M-mais oui! Vous d-devez m-me laisser entrer!*'

'It's all right, Gaston,' said Hackett. 'He's a friend of mine.'

A moment later, they were joined by a very flustered and out-of-breath Sebastian Gogarty. 'M-mister Hackett! I'm s-so s-sorry! I c-couldn't get the taxi driver to understand. He insisted on t-taking me to La Coupole, instead of Le Select . . .'

'Well, you're here now,' said Hackett. 'So no harm done. Will ye have a drink, Mr Gogarty?'

'Thank you. I w-will. Why, Mr Rowlands! H-how nice to s-see you again! I th-thought you'd left P-Paris . . .'

'I might say the same to you,' smiled Rowlands. 'Last time we met, you were on the point of rejoining your unit.'

'Oh, I've been s-summoned back,' was the reply. 'G-giving evidence, you kn-know, at the trial of that c-concentration camp guard. The one who—'

'You've said quite enough,' interrupted Iris Barnes. 'The trial's not until next week, and we can't have you discussing the evidence beforehand.'

'I'm s-sorry,' muttered Gogarty. 'Wasn't th-thinking . . .'

'I must say, I am most gratified,' said Max, in his urbane drawl, 'to find yet another Irishman prepared to fight for our cause.'

'Oh, there are q-quite a f-few others I could name . . .' began Gogarty eagerly; then subsided, perhaps at a look from Miss Barnes.

'Another plate, for my young friend here,' said Hackett to the waiter. Then, when they were once more left to themselves, 'Now then, Max. Where is it that you have in mind to take us?'

Chapter Twenty-Two

'You understand,' said Max, 'there were many "safe houses" – as you call them – in Paris during the war . . . We will go first – since it is the nearest – to the one under Montparnasse railway station. We sheltered many of our people there, during the bad times. Some of them were English, too. Downed aircrew on their way to the Shelburne Escape Line. You may have heard of that, Mr Gogarty . . .'

'I . . . I . . . b-believe I have . . .'

'Then you will know what a difficult procedure it was to get the RAF men out. They needed identity cards, clothing, passes for the trains – all of which had to be forged . . . It is possible,' he concluded, as the car which had brought them from Le Select drew up in the Rue Denfert-Rochereau, 'that one of our people may have news of your Miss Clara.'

They passed under the archway that led into the station, and crossed the concourse where trains could be heard arriving and departing, with all the commotion of grinding brakes, slamming doors and shrieking whistles that generally accompanied these operations. On the far side of this, screened by a booking office, was an inconspicuous door which opened onto a steep flight of steps, perhaps a hundred in all. Reaching the bottom of these, they found themselves in a basement of some kind. The air was stale and cold. No sound reached them from above, although they could not be far from the concourse, with all its noise and bustle, thought Rowlands.

Max flicked a switch, and at once there came the hum of electricity. 'We have an electric generator now,' he said. 'Before, it was bicycle-operated.'

With the Resistance leader leading the way, the five of them began walking along the first of what turned out to be a network of tunnels. At once a sentry stepped out from a niche in the wall. '*Qui va là?*'

'You know me,' said Max. 'And these are my friends.'

The man apologised. 'In this bad light, I did not see you clearly, m'sieur.'

'It matters not. You were merely doing your job. Now I have a question for you . . . Has a woman named Clara been here?'

The sentry barely paused before replying. 'No, m'sieur.'

'You are sure? She might be using another name . . .'

'There has been no woman here, m'sieur.'

'Very well. There are other places she might be,' said Max to the others. 'In fact, several of the railway stations in Paris have a similar arrangement to this one. The bunker under Gare l'Est, for example, was constructed during La Première Guerre Mondiale, to be secure against attack by gas. It has airtight steel doors. You will doubtless recall, m'sieur,' he added to Rowlands, 'the horror those of us who had been through that war had of poison gas.'

Rowlands said that he did.

'Of course,' went on the Resistance leader, 'the second war has been very different. Aerial bombardment is what we fear *now* . . . Come, we will go this way.'

As they passed further along the corridor, they could hear the sound of voices engaged in what sounded like a heated argument:

'*Absolument pas! Nous ne pouvons pas laisser cela arriver . . .*'

'*Mais nous n'avons pas le choix . . .*'

The argument broke off; then resumed, in precisely the same words:

'*Absolument pas! Nous ne pouvons pas laisser cela arriver . . .*'

Rowlands realised that he must be listening to a tape recording – an impression confirmed when they entered the room. Here, a solitary operative was listening in to what was being said – or had been said – elsewhere, winding and rewinding the tapes on a recording device. Max stopped for a word with him, before returning to their party. 'As you will have gathered, we still have our enemies,' he said drily. 'The war may be over, but there are many battles to fight.'

'Has he seen her?' asked Iris Barnes impatiently.

'He has not. But he will telephone the Hôtel Cécil if she turns up in the next few hours.'

At the far end of the tunnel they reached an iron fire escape, which led them, by way of a manhole cover, out onto the Boulevard Montparnasse. 'I thought this preferable to going back through the railway station,' said their guide. 'It is not too far from here to the Avenue de Suffren. There is an apartment there where I believe our friend may have spent a night or two – if my information is accurate.'

He and Rowlands fell into step, with Miss Barnes and Hackett a few paces behind them, and young Gogarty bringing up the rear. 'I suppose,' said the Frenchman, when they had been walking for a short while, 'that you lost your sight during the conflict to which I alluded earlier?'

Rowlands said that this was so.

'I began my law studies during the last year of the war,' said Max. 'My regiment was mobilised in September 1918 – the last to be called up.'

'You must have been very young.'

'I was eighteen. We were due to be posted to the Front in November – but then the Armistice was signed, and so I never saw action on the battlefield. I saw those who had,' he added, pausing to light a cigarette. 'Our unit was given the job of burying the dead . . . Forgive me. Would you like one?'

'Thank you, I would.'

'Where was it that you fought?' asked Max, as they resumed their walk.

'The Somme, first of all. Then Ypres.'

'Ah.' The brief sound conveyed a wealth of meaning. 'I believe we – that is, I and my countrymen – owe you our thanks,' he said.

'We were all fighting for a common cause, against a common enemy,' said Rowlands.

'You are right, m'sieur.'

They had by now reached the house in the Avenue de Suffren. 'There is nothing remarkable about the place, you know,' said Max. 'Even though it lies in the shadow of our dear Tour Eiffel . . .' This, Rowlands recalled, had been the Resistance leader's preferred meeting place, earlier that day. 'The apartment we are going to visit was owned by two sisters, Genevieve and Marie Tournier. They sheltered many of our people there, during the worst years.'

'What happened to them?' Rowlands was afraid that he already knew the answer.

'They were betrayed – and died at Ravensbrück, in March '45.' *Only three months ago*, thought Rowlands, with a shiver.

Max pushed open the street door. 'The apartment is on the second floor. I will get the key from the concierge.'

He went to do so, leaving Rowlands waiting in the lobby. Just then, someone came hurtling down the stairs, almost colliding with the blind man. 'Ouf! A thousand apologies, m'sieur. I did not see you there . . .'

The voice was familiar.

'Mr Corbeau?'

'It is. Have we met? I don't recall . . .' He must have taken a closer look, for he exclaimed, 'I remember now! It was at the Flore.'

'It was,' said Iris Barnes, arriving at that moment. 'Where are you off to in such a hurry, Julien?'

'Oh . . . nowhere special. People to see, you know . . .'

'I enjoyed your film,' said Rowlands; then, when this elicited only silence, '*Eurydice*, I mean. I thought it was very good.'

'I . . . that is . . . I am glad you liked it,' stammered the other, then made a dash for the door. 'So very nice to see you again, M'sieur . . . er . . . Sorry I don't have time to chat. Must fly . . .' With which he was gone.

'Go after him,' said the MI6 officer to Sebastian Gogarty, who had entered on her heels. 'See where he goes – but don't let him see *you*.'

'W-where shall I find you?' cried the unfortunate young man. 'If there's anything to r-report, I mean . . .'

'Come to the office,' was the reply. 'You know where that is, don't you? The Hôtel Cécil. Or better still, telephone. You can leave a message with Mrs Collins . . . He won't find out anything about our filmmaking friend that we don't already know,' she said, when Gogarty had disappeared on this errand. 'But I had to give him something to do. He's been getting on my nerves, hanging about.'

Having returned from questioning the concierge – 'She says there *was* somebody in the apartment . . . a woman, she thinks . . . but she isn't there now . . .' – Max led the way up the stairs to the second floor, and unlocked the door.

The flat had the smell of a place long closed up: an odour of dust and damp, overlaid with the faint smell of cigarettes. There were, however, no stubs in the ashtrays, or discarded packs in the wastepaper basket that might have given further clues as to the identity of the smoker. 'Our people take care not to leave traces,' said Max, extinguishing his own 'gasper'. 'I doubt we will find anything to help us here.'

He lifted a corner of a rug in the sitting room, and levered up the floorboard under it. 'Here they would have hidden their radio set,' he said. 'False papers, too. All of which would have been taken away when they were arrested.'

The rest of the search did not take long. The kitchen disclosed no dirty cups or plates; the bathroom no damp toothbrush, which might have shown that someone had been there in the past few days. The two bedrooms seemed no less devoid of clues. Only as they were about to leave did Rowlands find something. A book, tucked between the mattress and the bed frame, in the smaller of the two rooms. He handed the book to Pat Hackett, who flicked through a few pages, and read aloud:

'"*Wer, wenn ich schriee, hörte mich denn aus der Engel Ordnungen?*" I wonder who's been reading Rilke in German?'

'Presumably a German speaker,' said Rowlands. There was something else, too, underneath where the book had been. A handkerchief. He drew it out, held it to his nose; sniffed. 'Gun oil,' he said. 'But no sign of a gun.'

There was one other place they ought to visit, said Max, when the four of them stood once more on the pavement outside the apartment building where the ill-fated sisters had lived. ''Ackett knows where it is. I myself must leave you now. I am expected tonight in Lyons. Our people there are in need of reassurance that the communists will not destroy all that we have worked for.' He shook Rowlands's hand. 'It has been an honour, m'sieur. Good to see you, too, *mon cher*,' he said to Hackett. 'And you, too, of course, *chèrie*. I hope you find your lost lady. She has given you all enough trouble, has she not?'

* * *

'The old name for this place was the Barrière d'Enfer,' said Pat Hackett, as the car drew up in the Place Denfert-Rochereau. 'You'll see why in a moment. There's a sign written up over the door: "*Arrête! C'est ici l'empire de la mort.*" They say the bones of around six million people are entombed here – whether that's true or not, I couldn't say, but there are certainly a lot of 'em . . . The underground tunnels run for miles . . . which is why they were so useful to us, as a bolthole, during the war.'

While he had been talking, the three of them had reached what turned out to be a rusting iron door, set into the wall, beneath a partially collapsed stone archway. Dusty swags of ivy brushed their heads as they ducked under it.

A moment later, Hackett, who was leading the way, stopped short, with an intake of breath. 'Who's there?'

A figure, silent as a shadow, stepped out from the shelter of the archway. 'It's me.' It was Jerome Diop. 'I saw them go in, about an hour ago. Three people – two men and a woman. From across the street, I couldn't be sure if one of the men was Walter. But then I found this . . .'

He handed something to Iris Barnes, who, after a cursory examination, passed it to Rowlands. 'Jakob Metzner's trench lighter,' he said. 'That means it *must* have been Walter.'

'Are they still down there?' said Miss Barnes.

'The men are. The woman came out, maybe half an hour later. You said not to interfere, so I did not,' said Diop. 'I did get a better look at her the second time, though . . .'

'And?'

'She was young – no more than thirty, I'd say. Brown

hair, worn in a *chignon du cou*. A grey or light-brown raincoat. No hat . . .'

'Which could describe any one of a thousand women,' said Iris Barnes. She sounded puzzled, as if something didn't quite make sense to her. 'All right. Since you know what she looks like you'd better keep watch while Mr Hackett and I go in. Frederick, you'd better stay with him.'

'I'm not doing anything of the kind,' said Rowlands. 'I'm the only one of you who's used to moving about in the dark . . . I gather it *will* be dark?'

'As the grave,' said Hackett. 'Although "Rosaline" and I both have torches.'

'Besides which,' added Rowlands, 'Walter trusts me.'

This seemed to decide the MI6 officer. 'Very well,' she said. 'Have you got your service revolver, Pat?'

'Never go anywhere without it.'

'Good. Then let's get on with it. You first, then me, then Frederick. If we're not out in thirty minutes, call the police,' she added by way of a parting shot to the young Senegalese.

Hackett was already opening the door, which made a groaning sound, as if the hinges hadn't been oiled for a long time. 'Take care,' he said. 'I should have mentioned that the steps are very steep. They're arranged in a spiral, broken up by short landings. There are one hundred and thirty steps in all, descending to a depth of sixty-six feet. The first flight consists of seventeen steps. Remember to count them. After that, I forget exactly how many there are – but it'll be around the same number – fifteen or twenty steps, each time; then a short landing on the turn of the spiral. Keep close to the wall on the left-hand side. There's no banister.'

Then he was gone.

'I think I should come, too,' said Diop.

'You'll be more use keeping a lookout in case the woman comes back,' said Miss Barnes. You'd better conceal yourself, as before. If she returns – our lady in the raincoat – you'd better sing out. But take care – she may be armed . . .'

Then she, too, followed Hackett through the iron door in the wall.

When it was Rowlands's turn, he steadied himself on the edge of the door frame, feeling the scrape of its rusty surface against his palm, before taking the first step – conscious, from the sudden increase in the volume of air beneath his feet, that he was stepping into a void. If he missed his footing on the slippery limestone steps, it would be a long way to fall.

Chapter Twenty-Three

He took a step; then another, counting as he went. Five steps, ten steps, fifteen . . . sixteen . . . seventeen. Then the turn to the left of the spiral. He began counting again. As he descended lower he became aware of a musty smell that was perhaps no more than a lack of freshness in the air, but which might also have emanated from the vault itself – composed as it was of human remains. With that thought, he put out his hand (as Hackett had advised) to steady himself on the wall to his left. It took all his effort not to recoil from what his questing fingers found.

Bones. Layer upon layer of them, cemented into the wall, so that they had become part of its surface, smoothed by time and by the hands of those, like himself, who had passed by. Skulls, too – or the rounded upper portion of these – stacked one on top of the next, ad infinitum. Twenty-four . . . twenty-five . . . twenty-six . . . Suppressing his initial revulsion (whomever it was the skulls had once belonged to, they had been dead a long time), he continued his perilous descent. Below, he could hear the footsteps of the others on the stone steps. He slowed his pace accordingly, not wanting to come up behind them too quickly.

Twenty-nine . . . thirty . . . thirty-one. Another turn to the left. His fingers skimmed the naked skulls, polished smooth by hands other than his own. He remembered reading, or being told, that the remains were of those who had died during the Revolution . . . or perhaps it was because of the plague . . . They had been exhumed from their original resting places in Paris cemeteries, after these had become too full . . . What was it that the inscription that Hackett had quoted said? *Stop! This is the empire of death* . . . Well, that promise had certainly been fulfilled – and not only during the centuries that had passed . . .

Fifty-five . . . fifty-six . . . fifty-seven . . . Another turn. The air was getting cooler. As for sounds . . . there was nothing but the cautious tapping of his own footsteps, and the faint sound of water dripping from somewhere. His legs were aching from the relentlessness of the climb. Or descent, rather. A kind of purgatory, he thought. *Descend lower* . . . Mr Eliot, as ever, providing *le mot juste*.

Eighty-three . . . eighty-four . . . eighty-five . . . The smell of which he had been conscious all along was stronger now. A chalky scent – that was the limestone, of course – overlaid by a smell of decay. He wondered if in this lifeless place there could be living things . . . As he had the thought, there came a sound from below, as of rats scurrying, and he almost missed his footing on the stairs. 'Careful!' came a whisper from somewhere up ahead – it was Iris Barnes, he supposed. He steadied himself once more on the wall of bones and resumed his cautious descent of the winding stair.

At last this reached its end, and Rowlands found himself on level ground. The floor was beaten earth, worn smooth over centuries by the passage of feet. Reaching out his hand, he discovered that the walls here were made up of the same materials of which the stairs had comprised. Skulls and bones. He no longer shuddered at the contact, but found it curiously friendly – as if these long-dead denizens of the city above were welcoming him to their realm.

'Ye made it, then?' said a voice in his ear. Pat Hackett. 'Let me give ye an idea of the lie of the land . . . We're in the first of a series of galleries – some wider and deeper than others. There are markers along the way – some of 'em left behind by our people. Stubs of candles, too – for those who didn't have electric torches. We'd conceal messages, in hollowed-out niches between the rows of skulls, for our people to find. There are several miles of tunnels running under this part of the city. Useful, when ye needed to take cover . . .'

'I can see that it must have been,' said Rowlands. 'Which way do you think they'll have gone?'

'Couldn't say. We'll have to go carefully. If they're somewhere up ahead, we'll doubtless hear them . . . But ye'd better stick close to me. If they've followed the route I think they'll have taken we need to go straight ahead. There's a stretch of tunnel – ye'll need to mind your head – then it opens out into a bigger chamber. It's one our people used as a meeting place. There are several routes out of it, so it was always possible to escape if one had to.'

They proceeded along the tunnel, Rowlands keeping his head bowed to avoid hitting the low ceiling. A few minutes passed, during which the only thing he was conscious of was the faint sound of the others' breathing, as they trudged slowly along, following the beam of Miss Barnes's torch. He himself had only his hearing to guide him, and the wall on his right to steady him, as he moved forward. Suddenly, he found himself brought up short, almost stumbling against the MI6 officer as she came to a halt. 'Look out!' she warned. 'There's something up ahead . . . I can't see what it is in this dark.'

Hackett said, 'Bring your lights bit nearer . . . there! It's a body. A man's. There's a lot of blood . . .'

'Can you see who it is?'

With a feeling of dread, Rowlands drew nearer to where he guessed the corpse was lying, taking care not to slip in the blood that had formed a sticky pool in the narrow passageway. He reached out a hand, touched the sleeve of a jacket, and felt the rough texture of tweed. At once he was overwhelmed with a feeling of enormous relief. Walter had been wearing his naval officer's uniform. 'I think it must be Lafont,' he whispered to Iris Barnes. 'He was seen wearing a jacket like this at the Paris Studio.'

'Whoever he is, he's dead,' she replied. 'Let's hope we don't find any more like him . . .'

It was what Rowlands himself feared. What if they had come too late? Leaving the body where it was, he and his companions pressed forward, emerging at last into what felt to Rowlands like a larger and more spacious chamber. They were now in the heart of the ossuary, said Hackett. 'There are a lot of rooms leading off this one, and rooms leading off those – but this is the best equipped. There are camp beds, and even a cooking stove, although most of what we had down here has been dismantled or taken away. The radio set is long gone . . . and the weapons.'

But Rowlands was only half listening to this nostalgic catalogue. He strained his ears for any faint sounds that would tell him that somebody was there. 'Walter,' he called softly. 'You can come out now.'

But there was no answer.

'Of course, there were other advantages to the catacombs,' Hackett went on. 'Plenty of hiding places in the walls themselves – places where the earth had fallen away, leaving spaces large enough to conceal a man . . .' He must have been searching along the walls as he spoke, because a moment later there came a clatter, as of a pile of bones falling. 'Get back!' cried a voice Rowlands recognised. 'Don't come any closer or I'll shoot.'

There was the sound of a brief struggle, followed by a cry of pain from Walter, as the Irish Resistance fighter 'disarmed' him. 'If you think ye can get away with *that* old trick,' said the former, 'ye've got another thing coming . . . He doesn't have a gun,' he added. 'Just a broken piece of human femur . . . Although why ye thought ye had to put up a fight, young feller, I can't imagine.'

'You might have been sent by *her*,' replied Walter sulkily. 'I wasn't sure I could trust you. *She* tricked me. Told me I was going to see Clara . . . when in fact it was just some film with that other girl . . . the one who looked like her . . . Then they brought me here.'

'You must have heard me call out,' said Rowlands.

'How was I to know it wasn't a ruse?' said the young man. 'You might have had a gun pointed at your head.'

'Well, as you see, I don't.'

'It's as well for you that *you* don't have a gun,' said Miss Barnes severely. 'Or you might have found yourself on a charge of murder.'

Because they were now passing back along the tunnel where the body of Pierre Lafont lay. 'Is he dead?' asked Walter.

'Very.'

'I wonder how it is you're not,' said Pat Hackett.

'I . . . I ran away. The shot was very loud. He screamed and . . . and fell down. I didn't wait to see what happened. I just ran and ran . . .'

'Just as well for you,' said Miss Barnes. Her voice echoed eerily in the still air.

'But not, as it happens, for you,' said another voice, from the stairs above their heads. 'Don't move, any of you. Mr Hackett, you'd better drop that gun, if you don't want madame's brains spattered all over that chic leather jacket . . . That's right. Now kick the gun away . . .'

'So it was *you*,' said Iris Barnes.

'Who else would it be?' said the voice. Rowlands realised that it was one he recognised – there was that same slight accent when the speaker was using English, as she was now. The latter's manner of speaking, however, was very different from the way it had been. Gone was the meek, shy Louise Collins. In her place was an altogether harder, colder individual.

'You killed Amélie Mendl,' said Miss Barnes. 'All the time we were searching for her killer, you sat there, in my office, hugging that knowledge to yourself.'

'What if I did?' was the reply. 'And it was I who arranged her death. But I did not kill her.'

'Lafont did the deed, I suppose?'

'He did.'

'Which is why you killed him.'

'He talked too much,' said Mrs Collins indifferently. 'As you do, madame. People who talk too much annoy me . . .'

'Is that why you killed Claire Hubert . . . and Sophie Dubois?' said the MI6 officer.

'They were foolish girls,' said the secretary. 'They should have learnt how to hold their tongues.'

'As you did, of course,' said Iris Barnes. 'I must say, Louise, you concealed your past existence as a member of the Palace network very well. I suppose your husband was also a member of the network? Unless that was another lie?'

'It was the truth!' snapped the other. 'Martin was a hero of the *Résistance*. Even though, as an Irishman, he could have remained neutral, he chose not to . . . a decision you yourself made, Mr Hackett.'

'That's so,' agreed Pat Hackett. 'I did not, however, choose to betray my comrades.'

'Martin did not betray the network!' replied Louise Collins hotly. 'It was I he betrayed – by taking up with that whore.'

'I suppose you're referring to Amélie?' said Iris Barnes. 'Was the fact that he had an affair with her the reason you decided to turn in your husband to the Gestapo?'

'He betrayed me,' said Louise Collins stubbornly. 'I had no choice but to turn him in.'

'And those others – Amélie Mendl included – whom you betrayed? Those women who died at Natzweiler-Struthof and elsewhere – had you no thought for them?'

'They were not my concern,' said the other coldly. 'If anyone was to blame for their deaths, it was the Mendl woman. If she had not stolen another's lawful husband, none of this would have happened . . .'

Mrs Collins was silent for a moment, as if reflecting on her grievances. 'Enough of this idle talk,' she went on. 'There is unfinished business to deal with. You, madame, will be the first to die. I have long held you responsible for everything that has happened in these past two months. It was you, after all, whose insistence on discovering the identity of the woman in Fresnes prison alerted me to the fact that the Mendl bitch was still alive . . . Mr Hackett, I am afraid you will be the next to die. I would have spared you once, as a fellow countryman of Martin's – but I now hate your country as much as I once loved it. The boy I would have spared...' She meant Walter, Rowlands guessed. 'He was just a means to an end, which was to bring you here, madame. As for the blind man . . .'

But she never got to say what fate she had in store for Rowlands, for at that moment, his sharp hearing picked up the sound of a step on the stairs.

'Give me the gun,' said a voice Rowlands thought he knew. It, too, had a slight accent – but the accent was German, not French. 'Or it will be the worst for you.'

'No!' cried Louise Collins. She sounded terrified.

'Get away from me! You . . . you're not real . . . You're dead . . . Get back! You're dead!'

There came a scream, followed, seconds later, by the dreadful sound of a body hitting the ground from a considerable height; then a profound silence.

It was Rowlands who spoke first. 'Clara? Is that you?'

'It is. I . . .' She sounded strangely calm. 'I did not mean her to fall, Mr Rowlands. She . . . she must have lost her footing. The steps are very slippery. Is she dead?'

'Dead as a doornail,' said Pat Hackett, after a cursory examination of the body that now lay sprawled at the foot of the stairs. 'Her neck's broken. Hardly surprising after falling twenty feet . . . But she would have done for us all, ye know.'

'Yes, it was a very timely intervention,' said Iris Barnes, as the newcomer, having descended the remaining flight of stairs, stood among them. 'How was it that you knew where to find us?'

'I was following *her*,' Clara Metzner replied. 'I saw her and that man bring Walter here. She went away again. I followed her to where it was she went. Then she came back here – and so did I.'

'I should have been alerted both times,' said Iris Barnes. 'Someone has slipped up . . .'

Just then, from somewhere above, there came the anxious voice of Jerome Diop. 'Madame Rosaline? Are you all right?'

'No thanks to you,' replied Miss Barnes severely. 'You were to fetch the police, remember?'

'I . . . I was about to do so when I saw her arrive . . . the woman in the raincoat.' He had descended the stairs by this time, and must have stumbled over the corpse, as he reached the bottom of them, for he shuddered. 'Is that her?'

'It is. You were about to explain your failure to sound the alarm.'

'I was going to. Then *she* appeared.' He meant Clara Metzner, Rowlands surmised. 'She told me not to make a sound, so I did not,' he said miserably. 'Did I do wrong?'

'As it happens, you did not,' said the MI6 officer curtly. 'In the circumstances, your inaction was correct. In future, however . . .'

But nobody paid any further attention to her, or to the man she was berating. Because at that moment, Metzner roused himself from the trance into which the events of the past few moments seemed to have cast him. 'Clara,' he said. 'Is it really you?'

'No one else, little brother,' she said.

'This is how it was,' said Clara Metzner. It was the next day; the six of them – himself, Barnes, Gogarty, Hackett, Walter and Clara herself – were in Iris Barnes's office, or rather the larger outer office, over which Louise Collins had once presided. Jerome Diop, fulfilling his usual function of keeping watch, hovered outside on the landing. There being a shortage of chairs, Rowlands leant against what had been the dead traitor's desk, on which her shrouded typewriter stood as a silent reminder of her baleful presence at the heart of the SOE headquarters.

'The SS were clearing out the camp. It started at the beginning of April, and continued throughout the month, until only the very sick and old were left . . .'

Her voice, whose cadences had been as Rowlands remembered them from the time of their first meeting in Berlin, now assumed a monotonous tone, as if the speaker were forcing herself to recall things she would have preferred not to recall. 'Amélie was sick. She had been growing weaker, day by day. I knew she would not survive without me. When it came to our turn to be the ones to leave – they were marching us to another camp, people said – I made her come with me. So we began walking – there were hundreds of us, all women. Somebody said we were going to Mecklenburg – that is north of Berlin. Many of the women were too ill to go very far. Some dropped down in their tracks. Others were shot trying to run away. After a day, or perhaps two, the Russians came. They took those of us who had survived to another camp, where we were given food and allowed to sleep. The next day, we were put on a train to Paris.'

She was silent for so long that Rowlands thought she must have said all she meant to say. There was no sound in the room except the buzzing of a trapped fly, endlessly crashing itself against the windowpane.

At last, Clara resumed her tale. 'When we got to Paris, Amélie said, "You must leave me now. It is too dangerous for you to be seen with me. I have enemies here – one in particular." She told me the name. Collins. It was the same last name as that of the man who had been her lover. It was then I knew why she needed to hide. And so we decided to change places.'

She laughed – a curious, mirthless sound. 'In the camp, we had told each other everything about our lives in the time before. What we liked to eat, where we lived, all about our families . . . It was a kind of game – to remember what had been. Amélie said I should seek out her comrades – those who had been with her in the Palace network. She said they would protect me – which they did,' added Clara. '*She* would go with the rest of the returning deportees to the holding pen at Fresnes prison. She would be safe there, she said. When she was well again, she would join me . . .'

Another silence. Still the fly continued its futile assault on the windowpane. Somebody – Rowlands guessed it was Gogarty – got up to let it out.

'When Amélie did not come,' Clara Metzner went on, 'I went to ask for her at the prison. I was told she was dead. I did not, at the time, know *how* it was she died . . . but I began to be afraid for myself. That was when I wrote to you, little brother. The rest you know.'

'Not all of it,' said Iris Barnes. 'There are still some questions I'd like answered. How was it that you came to identify Louise Collins? From what you said just now, you only had her name to go on . . .'

'I saw her,' was the reply. 'It was the day I had arranged to meet Walter in Père Lachaise. I *did* keep the appointment, you see,' she said to her brother. 'I had arrived a few minutes early. I wanted to be "on the spot" when you arrived. After twelve years, I was not sure I would recognise you, and so . . .'

'As a matter of interest, where *were* you?' asked Walter.

'A few feet away, concealed by the Wilde tomb. I was on the point of revealing myself, when I saw *her*. A nondescript little woman, I thought at first. She might have been visiting a grave. Then I saw she had a gun. You arrived at that moment, with Mr Rowlands. I heard your voices. That was when she fired the shot. Then she ran off.'

'You didn't stay to see if the shot had killed me or not,' said Walter.

'I didn't have to. Mr Diop here' – the latter having put his head around the door – 'made his timely appearance. A little late, if you don't mind my saying so, Mr Diop . . . So I knew from what followed that your wound wasn't serious. It seemed more important to see where Mrs Collins was going.'

'And did you?'

'No. I lost her. But I was sure she'd try again.' The calmness with which Clara Metzner spoke was proof, thought Rowlands, of how much this young woman had changed, from the quiet, shy girl of the Berlin days to this formidable character. If truth were told, he found her a little frightening.

'I kept watch on the hotel,' she now continued. 'A much more salubrious establishment, that one, than the one where I'd left the message for you the day before. It wasn't until the next day that I saw her. *You* had gone out, by then, Mr Rowlands – but my lazy little brother had stayed in bed . . . or so I surmised. It was sometime later that I saw the woman – Mrs Collins – arrive. She was with the man I later learnt was called Lafont. They seemed to be arguing about something. Then Walter came out of the hotel. The three of them talked for a bit, then they all got into the car – a Peugeot – that Lafont was driving. Fortunately, I'd thought to hire a taxi, or I would have lost them. We caught up with them on the way to Boulogne-Billancourt.'

'So you followed me all the way to the Paris Studios?' said Walter, sounding amazed.

'I did. But by then you'd disappeared inside the studio gates. I wasn't sure if I should try and talk my way in after you, or wait until you came out again . . .'

'I must say, I wish we'd had a few more like you in the networks, Miss Metzner,' said Pat Hackett, with some admiration. 'We might have won the war a bit sooner than we did.'

'I've learnt how to look after myself,' said Clara Metzner coolly. 'Anyway, I hung around for a while . . . strange places, film studios. One never knows what's real and what's not. I swear, while I was cooling my heels outside the gates, I saw Marie Antoinette sharing a cigarette with Maximilien Robespierre . . . It reminded me of when Joachim worked at Babelsberg, all those years ago . . .' She broke off, as if the memory of that earlier life, and of the elder brother she would probably never see again, was too much to bear.

After a moment, she went on, 'I was starting to think I'd made a mistake, and that we'd followed the wrong car, when I saw you come out, Walter, with the other two. You were looking distinctly the worse for wear. Staggering about all over the place, as if you were drunk . . .'

'They'd put something in my coffee,' protested Walter. 'Sleeping pills. They must have done it while we were watching that film – the one with Amélie Mendl . . . only she called herself by some other name . . . By the way, I don't think she looked a bit like you. She was much prettier, for a start.'

'Thank you for those kind words, little brother. Well,

drunk or drugged, you were bundled into the car and driven off. I'd got the taxi to wait, so we were soon on your track again.'

'Your taxi fares must have been mounting up,' said Hackett drily.

'Oh, the cab driver was one of ours,' was the reply. 'He didn't want paying. Anyway, we followed the Peugeot to the Place Denfert-Rochereau. That's where the entrance to the catacombs is located, as you know. Walter got out of the car . . . Lafont had to help you walk,' she said to her brother. 'The Collins woman followed. All three of you went inside. I waited a long time – perhaps half an hour. Then she – Louise Collins – came out alone.'

'I saw her come out, that time, too,' put in Diop, who had managed to find himself a leaning post against a filing cabinet. 'I didn't know who she was, though,' he added apologetically. 'Or I'd have sounded the alarm.'

'I assumed she must have left Lafont to guard Walter. Either that, or she'd killed them both,' said Clara, in the same detached tone she had used to describe her experiences at Ravensbrück. Perhaps, thought Rowlands, these had left her incapable of feeling ordinary emotions. As if the horrors that she had seen had had a deadening effect.

'I heard them shouting at each other – Mrs Collins and Lafont,' interrupted Walter. 'It woke me up – I'd been out cold, after that stuff they gave me . . . I heard him say, "I won't do it! You ask too much, Louise. First the girl, and then . . ." But he didn't say any more, because it was then she shot him. It was very loud. That's when I ran off, into the tunnels. I knew she'd kill me, too, if she could.'

'You did the right thing, little brother. She would certainly have killed you . . . When she came out, I decided to follow her, to see where she went. There wasn't much I could do without a weapon . . .' Clara broke off, as if aware she'd said too much.

'But you knew where you could get one,' said Pat Hackett.

'Yes. I thought I'd drop in on my old lodgings – they weren't far from there, in the 7th arrondissement. I'd left a gun there. But first I had to see where Louise Collins went. And if she had any other accomplices . . .'

'You followed her here,' said Iris Barnes. 'It must have been late afternoon. I'd just come from a meeting with one of my . . . associates.' That would have been 'Max', thought Rowlands. 'I remember seeing a woman hanging about outside.'

'That was me.'

'I suppose it must have been. I didn't give it much thought at the time. Louise was already in her office, typing away. I remember thinking it rather odd that she hadn't hung up her mackintosh. She was usually so meticulous about tidiness. Anyway, it was then that you telephoned, Frederick, to say that you'd lost Walter . . . so I had other things to think about at that moment. Not least that there'd been some news of *you*, Miss Metzner. My associate . . . the one I'd met earlier . . . said he'd been informed that a woman answering your description had made contact during the past few days with one of our networks in Paris. So it was just a matter of time before we found you.'

'As indeed you did,' said Clara Metzner. 'I wish now

315

that I'd thrown myself on your mercy then, but I didn't know . . . that is . . .'

'You had no idea whether you could trust me,' said Iris Barnes. 'Given that the woman who'd kidnapped your brother, and in all probability murdered your friend, appeared to be working for me.'

'Just so,' said the other. 'You will understand,' she added, 'I lived in Berlin during the worst times, when one could not always trust the authorities.'

'I remember those times, too,' said Miss Barnes. 'Go on with what you were saying . . .'

'There is not much more to tell. I waited until I saw you leave this building, Miss Barnes. I had found a quiet spot in that little café across the street to watch the people come and go, so I was less conspicuous.'

'I certainly didn't see you,' laughed Miss Barnes.

'About half an hour after you had left, I saw the Collins woman leave. This was at about six o'clock. She was on foot, and so I thought I had time to get to where I believed her to be going – I mean the catacombs – before she got there. Which I did. The rest you know, I think . . .'

'There is one thing that puzzles me,' said Rowlands. 'If you were waiting outside the building all that time, when did you pick up the gun? Even in a car, it would have taken you at least fifteen minutes to get from here to the apartment in the Avenue de Suffren.'

'How did you know . . .' she began, then laughed. 'Of course! You people know everything. The answer to your question is that I asked somebody to collect the gun for me. There was a telephone in the café, you understand?'

'I see.' Rowlands thought of the man who'd hurtled

down the stairs, as he and Hackett had arrived at the safe house. Corbeau. Evidently another member of the Paris network. 'Did he bring the gun to you here, then?' he asked.

'As it happens, he was too late. Mrs Collins had just left the Hôtel Cécil, and I was anxious to lose no more time in getting after her.'

'The f-fact is . . .' Sebastian Gogarty had been following the conversation with barely suppressed impatience. 'I took it off him . . . the g-gun . . . I told him – Julien Corbeau – that I'd turn him in, if he d-didn't surrender it at once . . .'

'That was brave of you, Mr Gogarty,' said Iris Barnes, with only the slightest hint of mockery.

'He d-didn't put up m-much of a f-fight,' said Gogarty. 'Actually, he was quite a n-nice feller. Asked me to have a drink with him. We ended up at the S-select . . . had a g-good old jaw. D-did you know he m-makes films? Quite g-good ones too, from what I've heard.'

'So you weren't armed, after all, Miss Metzner, when you followed Louise Collins into the catacombs,' said Hackett, cutting across this agreeable reminiscence.

'No. I thought I'd be able to talk her round,' replied Clara Metzner. 'But as it turned out, I didn't have the chance.'

London, July 1945

Chapter Twenty-Four

It was a glorious day for a wedding. The sun shone, the clouds which had loomed ominously in the skies that morning had blown away, and it looked set to be a perfect summer's afternoon. Against all the odds, the repairs to the house in Grove Crescent, which had seemed as if they would never be finished, had been completed in time for the Rowlands family to move back into their old home, a matter of days before the date the young couple had fixed for their wedding.

Contemplating this fact, as he waited at the front door of Number 44 for the guests to arrive, Rowlands felt a warm glow of satisfaction. They'd done it. After four years of what had admittedly been a fairly pleasant 'exile' in Brighton, they were back together as a family . . . Although, he thought ruefully, it wouldn't be the same without Margaret. And then there was Anne . . . Only the other day, when he'd met her at the station, at the start of this specially extended leave, she'd said airily, 'Do you know, I've been thinking that when I'm finally demobbed, I might go back to Paris. Take up painting again . . .' No, on reflection, family life as they had known it had gone forever.

He distracted himself from these painful reflections by the thought of his garden – soon to be the backdrop for wedding photographs. As he'd taken a turn around it earlier that day, he had breathed in the scent of his favourite climbing roses: Madame Alfred Carrière, Albertine and Souvenir du Docteur Jamain . . . Yes, his roses would do him proud . . . but did they need more chairs? he wondered. As for bottles of champagne – would there be enough to go round?

With over thirty guests to accommodate, they'd had to set out trestle tables in the garden, by way of extending the dining table (which could only seat twelve). But with the French windows open, and the tables placed end to end, they could manage to seat the rest. It seemed to Rowlands a pleasingly bohemian arrangement – the sort of thing they did rather well in provincial France, he recalled. Thank goodness it had turned out fine!

Now, as guests who'd walked from All Saints' Church in the centre of Kingston began arriving, Rowlands readied himself to perform his duties as host. He'd be assisted by Edith, of course, as he always was – although it wouldn't have been fair to expect her to do more than play the gracious hostess when she was in her finery. Fortunately, they had Mrs Britcher, borrowed from St Dunstan's for the occasion, to help with preparing and serving the food, and two of the young people – Rowlands's youngest daughter, Joan, resplendent in her pale blue bridesmaid's dress, and Victor, his sister's younger son – to serve the drinks.

Edith, in any case, had other things on her mind – not least making sure that all the details of her daughter's special day were as they should be. There'd been the wedding breakfast to order – as it was summer, they'd decided on cucumber soup, lobster salad, chicken à la mayonnaise, cold ham, tongue in aspic, potato salad and game pies. There'd be strawberries and cream to follow – and then the cake. This had been made with the past month's sugar, butter and egg rations, contributed by every member of the household. Dried fruit (also hard to come by) had been hoarded for the same purpose. One of their neighbours, who was good at fancy icing, had decorated the finished cake. 'No cardboard cakes for *this* family,' said Edith.

The bride's dress had presented another challenge. Parachute silk was the obvious choice for any bride in the post-war era. The pieces of silk for the dress had been cut out and ready to sew when the parcel from Paris arrived. 'Chantilly lace,' said Edith, unfolding length after length of the heavy, creamy stuff. 'Sent from Bonheur Modes.' She'd picked up the card that had been slipped into the box. Read it aloud. '"I hope Margaret will accept this as an early wedding gift. Best wishes, Celia Swift."' She'd thought for a moment. 'A lace overskirt,' she'd said. 'And sleeves, of course. It'll look lovely. What a kind thought.'

Rowlands had never admired his wife more than at that moment.

She'd so been looking forward to this day, he knew – and not just because of the cake, and the dress, and her own new silk chiffon frock. 'It'll be just like old times, won't it, Fred?' she'd said to him that morning, as they'd got ready to go to the church. 'Giving a party . . . and all our girls being together.'

He'd agreed that it was like old times – although in fact it was nothing like. Those times were gone forever. This was a new world.

The proof of this, if any were needed, had been two days ago, when the country had cast its votes in a general election for the first time in ten years. Already, they were saying it would be a landslide for Attlee – although the results wouldn't be announced for another three weeks, to allow time for the postal votes of those serving overseas to be counted. He'd voted the way he always did – not without a pang for the old man who'd led them to victory. It seemed disloyal to be thinking of party politics when for the past six years they'd all been in it together . . . But people were sick of war, and of the old guard who had failed to prevent it. They wanted change – and who could blame them?

'Got those glasses of champagne ready?' he said to his two helpers, because he could hear the first guests coming up the path. These turned out to be his old friend Ian Fraser, and his wife. Fraser, now a Conservative MP (and how would *he* be feeling at the prospect of a Labour government, wondered Rowlands), was also head of St Dunstan's, the institute for the war-blinded, of which both men had been inmates. It had been he, only a few years older than Rowlands, who had shown the newly blinded young man that life was still possible – and that self-pity was not an option. The two men shook hands warmly.

'Lovely wedding,' said his old comrade. 'I don't know when I've been to a nicer one.'

'Margaret looked perfectly charming in that dress,' said Lady Fraser. 'And what wonderful lace! It's all the rage for brides these days, I'm told . . .'

Rowlands smiled. Everyone said that Margaret had made a beautiful bride. Although in his opinion, it wasn't the dress, or the expensive lace, that had made her so. 'Do go on into the drawing room, Lady Fraser,' he said. 'There are chairs . . .'

'I'm happy to stand after sitting down all that time in church. We always arrive far too early. Your garden's looking splendid, Frederick. I must take a look at your roses before the hordes arrive . . .'

Because they were coming thick and fast. Here at last was Edith, accompanied by her brother, Ralph, and his wife, Diana. 'Such a lovely, old-fashioned idea, *walking* to the reception,' she was trilling. 'If I'd known, I'd have worn more sensible shoes!'

'If *I'd* known, I could have lent the happy couple the Rolls,' said her husband.

'Oh, they're coming in Frank's car,' replied Rowlands, trying without success to suppress the irritation his brother-in-law's condescension always induced.

'Some old banger, no doubt,' guffawed Ralph Edwards.

It was, in fact, a 1935 Lagonda – but Rowlands didn't say so. He'd long ago decided not to cross swords with Ralph – if only because it upset Edith.

'Do you think we've enough food?' murmured the latter, as she went past him into the house. 'With all those naval friends of Frank's turning up at the last minute, and then those extra girls, I'm worried that we'll run out . . .'

'It'll be fine,' he reassured her. The 'extra girls' she'd referred to had only been two in number – friends of Margaret's from work. What kind of work, she was careful not to say – although Rowlands of course had a fair idea, since one of his cases, a few years back, had involved the secret world into which his eldest daughter's skills as a cryptographer had taken her. He'd met both the young women who'd been invited today, as it happened. Marjorie Milward was one – a nice lass from County Durham, if he remembered correctly; and the other, Mavis Lacey, was now an Oxford don. Dr Lacey, he should say. He allowed himself a brief tinge of regret at the thought of Margaret's abandoned (or only postponed?) academic career. The Mistress of St Gertrude's College, where – until conscripted by Bletchley Park – his daughter had been a junior research fellow, had sent a silver cake stand as a wedding gift.

'I shouldn't think either of those girls eat enough to keep a mouse alive,' he said, since Edith was still fretting about provisions.

Fortunately a distraction appeared in the form of Rowlands's sister, Dorothy – with whom his wife had never really got on, although there had been a truce of late – and Dorothy's husband, Jack Ashenhurst, another old friend from the St Dunstan's days.

'Dottie.' He kissed her. 'So glad you could all come.' Cornwall being a long way away, and the boys (he still thought of them as boys, although they were all young men now, he knew) having to come from the various military bases where they were stationed.

'Oh, we wouldn't have missed it for the world, would we, Jack?' she said, helping herself to a glass of champagne from the tray her son was holding. 'Seeing your Margaret tie the knot. I rather like the look of *him*,' she added, meaning Rowland's new son-in-law, Frank Dawson. His sister was nothing if not forthright in her opinions. 'Nice, down-to-earth young chap. I'd be surprised if he hadn't voted the right way . . .'

'Dottie!' Trust her to bring politics into it. Even though she'd softened her socialist views somewhat in recent years, she still had a shameless disregard for the social niceties. 'I thought we'd agreed . . .'

'All right, all right. I promise not to frighten the horses,' she said mischievously. 'Come on, Jack. We're lowering the tone.'

But Ashenhurst wasn't to be dragged away without a word to his old friend. 'Good to see your little girl settled,' he said. Like Rowlands himself – and most other St Dunstan's men – he found nothing odd about using phrases to do with sight. 'Some jolly nice hymns, too, I thought. "Praise My Soul the King of Heaven". One of my favourites.'

'Mine, too,' said Rowlands. There was a line from the hymn that summed up pretty well the way they were all feeling at this particular moment in history, with the end of a long and bloody war:

Ransomed, healed, restored, forgiven . . .

Would this be a chance to start again, for the younger generation, at least? One could only hope so.

More guests arrived. The Ashenhurst boys, Billy – the flying 'Ace', now a squadron leader – and his adopted brother, Danny, who'd also had a 'good war' as the saying went. He had a word with both of them, thanking them for coming. 'Think I'd miss our Maggie's wedding?' said Billy. 'Not a chance. Why, she was the one who used to read me bedtime stories when I was a nipper.'

'Stories, eh? What kind of stories?' chortled Danny.

'Never you mind, old bean.'

It seemed to Rowlands that both young men had partaken of a certain amount of alcoholic refreshment on their way to the wedding. With them was the Edwardses' son, Peter, now twenty-one and up at Oxford. Well, it would do *him* no harm to kick over the traces for once, thought Rowlands, who had always thought his wife's nephew rather an ineffectual sort. Disdaining champagne, the three lads made straight for the kitchen, where there was a firkin of beer. Assorted naval officers, including Frank's best man, whose name was Evans – a fellow officer on Frank's ship – went with them. Rowlands guessed they'd be carrying on the party later in the local pub . . .

The only one of Jack and Dorothy's boys not to attend the wedding was Walter. But then he and the sister with whom he had just been reunited were now in Berlin, to which they had returned soon after Rowlands himself had left Paris. 'We both feel that we must go,' the young German had said, with the earnestness that had always been characteristic of him. 'The city is in ruins – thanks to the efforts of our RAF – and there is much to be done to make it habitable again. I, with my medical training, can perhaps be of use.'

Rowlands said he thought it was a splendid idea.

Privately, he wondered whether returning to the city Walter had last seen as a child – a city, by all accounts, terribly changed – would be a salutary experience for a young man who had only recently learnt of the death of his mother in a concentration camp. But he knew nothing he could have said would have deterred the Metzner siblings from their plan. 'We have to see it for ourselves,' said Clara. 'To see it, and to know the truth of what was done to our people.'

Another of those who had been there on that last day – the day before he'd returned from Paris – was also absent on this occasion. But then Iris Barnes, or 'Rosaline', to give her *nom de guerre*, had never played much part in what Rowlands thought of as his 'real' life . . . Now, as he stood there, welcoming his guests, he recalled their conversation. They'd been alone in her office at the Hôtel Cécil. She'd poured them both a whisky. Both had remained silent for a while as they sipped their drinks and mulled over the events of the past few weeks that had brought them together.

'You know,' said Iris Barnes at last, 'I didn't see it. It was right under my nose, and I didn't see it. I must be losing my grip.'

'Treachery is like that,' he said. 'It's always the person one suspects least. Someone too close to one to see . . .' Or too inconspicuous to notice, he thought, but didn't say. 'I didn't see it myself, for a long time. Except . . .'

'Except what?'

'She was always *there*,' he said. 'Louise Collins. With hindsight, it couldn't have been anyone else.'

'Wonderful thing, hindsight.' They drank to hindsight.

'What will you do now?' she asked, after a few minutes had passed.

'Me? I'll go home. I'd like to enjoy the peace – since we've paid so high a price for it.'

'There is that, I suppose,' she said.

'And you?'

Iris Barnes laughed. 'Oh, I've things to be getting on with. No rest for the wicked, is there?'

'You're looking verra glum, old friend,' said a voice. It was Alasdair Douglas – Superintendent Douglas, he was now, although with retirement (he hoped) in sight. 'Surely ye canna be sad, on a wedding day?'

Rowlands smiled. 'I've got a sad sort of face,' he said. 'Let me introduce you to a few people . . .'

Because here were some other dear friends, come to celebrate his daughter's happiness. Jack Ashenhurst's sister, Cecily, and her husband, Bill Finch – who'd both been caught up in that Cornish affair, ten years back, Rowlands recalled, not without a shudder. This was no time for thinking about murder . . . As he introduced them – 'Superintendent Douglas, this is Dr and Mrs Finch,' – he wondered if the policeman would remember when they'd met before. If he did, he had the tact not to say so. 'Good to meet ye,' he said. 'Fine day for it.'

Tact was not the strong suit of Roberta ('Bobbie') Wilmott – one half of another couple Rowlands had known for years. They were St Dunstan's people, too – members of the bridge-playing set. He liked John, but Bobbie could be a bit much at times. 'I always said the law would catch up with you one day, Fred!' she shrieked, having overheard what he'd just said. 'What's he done,

Superintendent? Committed a murder?'

'Och, nothing o' the kind,' said Douglas, who disapproved of people making light of murder. 'Only forgotten to offer me a beer so I can toast the happy couple. I can't drink that fizzy stuff,' he added in an undertone to his friend. 'Gives me heartburn.'

'Victor, fetch Superintendent Douglas a glass of beer,' said Rowlands. He touched the face of his Braille watch. Where *were* they? Everyone else was here . . . Even Maud Rickards, his wife's old friend, with whom she had been a VAD in the last show, had managed to get leave to come – although she was 'inundated' with work just now, dealing with all the returning servicewomen taking advantage of the Further Education and Training Scheme, enabling them to waive requirements for university entrance. 'St Gertrude's is bursting at the seams, and still they come . . .' he heard her declare, speaking of the Cambridge women's college where she was bursar and where his own daughter had studied.

But where *was* his daughter? Perhaps Frank – unfamiliar with Kingston roads – had taken a wrong turning . . . As he had the thought, there came the sound of the Lagonda pulling up at the kerb. A moment later, he heard the voices of the newly-weds, and those of Helen, his mother-in-law, and Anne, his middle daughter, who'd travelled back in the car with them.

He felt his heart lift. 'Meg,' he said. 'Frank. Here you are at last.'

'Oh, Daddy, wasn't it a nice service?' cried Margaret, kissing him. 'I couldn't believe how quickly it all went, though. It was like a wonderful dream, wasn't it, Frank?'

Frank Dawson agreed that it was.

'The vicar said he might pop in later for a cup of tea,' went on Margaret. 'He's got a christening at two, so he couldn't come earlier . . .'

'I'm sure we can find a cup of tea for the vicar,' he said. 'Go and find your mother. She'll be wanting to get on with lunch.'

He shook his son-in-law's hand. 'Look after my girl, won't you?' he said.

'You can trust me for that, sir.'

'Come on, Granny!' This was Anne, sounding more like her old self than she had for a while. 'Let's see if they've left us any champagne. And let me help you with that veil, Mrs Dawson,' she added to her sister. 'As your matron of honour, I'm in charge of all that, you know.'

Rowlands felt a pang of sadness for his gallant daughter, knowing that – had fate proved kinder – she would have been looking forward to celebrating her wedding to the young Polish Resistance fighter she'd met at RAF Mildenhall while serving with the WAAFs. But Jan Wawrzkowicz was dead. All Anne had left was her memories – and the ring he'd given her before he'd set off on his last mission. As her father followed her into the house, he rested his hand briefly on her shoulder, in a mute gesture of consolation.

Meanwhile the young couple had been greeted with shouts of congratulation from those assembled in the dining room, whose French windows now stood open to the garden. The wedding breakfast could begin. As Rowlands took his seat next to his wife at the long table, leaving Margaret and her new husband to take their seats at the head of it, he felt, for the first time in months, that he had come home. All his dark thoughts could be banished – at least for the present. All that mattered was just this: these beloved people, in this place, at this time. Going over the words of the speech he was about to make, he thought, *Let it be a better world for them, and for their children.* Almost the whole of his own life had been spent in wartime. Let theirs be a lasting time of peace.

CHRISTINA KONING has worked as a journalist, reviewing fiction for *The Times*, and has taught Creative Writing at the University of Oxford and Birkbeck, University of London. From 2013 to 2015, she was Royal Literary Fund Fellow at Newnham College, Cambridge. She won the Encore Prize in 1999 and was longlisted for the Orange Prize in the same year.

@christina.koning
christinakoning.com